MW00635046

Taylor - Whea

1865-1965

1865	English Nobleman John Francis Taylor marries Mary Elizabeth Van Zandt
1867	John Francis Taylor's young wife dies
1868	Infant son adopted by sister – the Paul Wheaton
1869	family. Son takes the name of John Francis Wheaton
1870	John F. Taylor becomes known
1871	as simply the Tent Maker
1874	Tent Maker evangelizes Europe in summer
1875	Merchant marine in winter
1880	Commissioned by King & Queen as sail
1881	maker and crew member for church planting in the Philippines colonization voyage
1883	Sets sail for Pacific
1884	Tent Maker arrives on island – (first visit)
1886	Island successfully evangelized
1888	Arrives England – knighted for success of trip
1890	John Paul "Papa" Wheaton born to John F. Wheaton
1892	John Francis Wheaton emigrates to U.S with young family
1894	Tent Maker receives title of Ambassador to the Philippines as Sir John Francis Taylor
1895	Set sail for Philippines as Ambassador
1896	Diverted to New Guinea for six month stay
1897	Arrives at island for second visit in great ceremony and friendship. Marries Kalana
1898	Paiyan born
1910	Sir John dies from shipwreck
1912	After John's death islanders begin slow but
1913	steady slip away from the One True God
1914	falling back into idol worship, demonic
1915	activities and human sacrifice
1920	John Wheaton Jr. born—Papa Wheaton's first
1921	born son

Continued on back inside cover

I

*~ **His Story** ~*
As told by Grace Chloe Wheaton

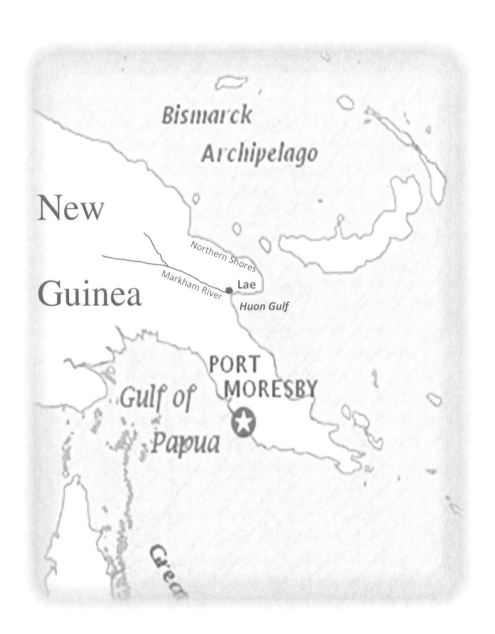

~ *His Story* ~
As told by Grace Chloe Wheaton

~ His Story ~
As told by Grace Chloe Wheaton

The
Journals
of Sir John Francis Taylor

His Story as told by Grace Chloe Wheaton

End Time Heroes
Living First Century Faith

A Novel by

David E. McFadden

V

www.DeeperLifeSeries.com

~ His Story ~
As told by Grace Chloe Wheaton

The Journals
of Sir John Francis Taylor

His Story as Told by Grace Chloe Wheaton

By David E. McFadden

About My Father's Business
A D e e p e r L i f e S e r i e s

www.DeeperLifeSeries.com

Printed in the U.S.A.

*Interior Formatting by David E. McFadden
(Interior renderings from public domain)
Cover Design by Wendy K. Walters | Palm Tree Productions |
www.palmtreeproductions.net*

ISBN: 978-0-9847653-4-8

For More Information or to Contact the Author:
www.DeeperLifeSeries.com

What Others Are Saying

'The Journals' is highly innovative, intriguing and inspirational. David presents the challenge of 'choose this day whom you will serve' with certainty and clarity. The biblical truths expressed are both enlightening and enriching. —Gene Carter

---

How is one's heart transformed—or the hearts of an entire people group? With a dose of mystery and drama, David carefully and skillfully weaves a story illustrating how lives are miraculously changed by the hand of God. *'The Journals' is a very entertaining novel.* —Veronica Guerrero

---

This fast paced novel will keep you riveted to the pages as the story unfolds. Not only is there a message for everyone who reads it, you will fall in love with the characters. I would recommend *'The Journals'* to Christian readers and non-Christian readers alike. —Mike Morris

---

David McFadden creates a refreshing story of faith and courage in *"The Journals."* An inspirational plot unfolds as believers promote and document the establishment of Christianity in a tribal island setting. *This book is a must read.* —Tony Gentry

---

I am pleased to say that once I started reading *'The Journals,'* I couldn't put it down. —Larry Angel

---

'The Journals' provides spiritual enlightenment and practical life applications. This is a good book for the 'entertainment' reader as well as for those who normally do not read fiction. This premiere edition will keep everyone interested and waiting for volume two. —Barbara Clawson

To the Holy Spirit…

For allowing me the joy and

privilege of taking His dictation.

Acknowledgements

To my friends and family, thank you. You have encouraged me in my efforts to glorify God through my writing. Especially to my wife for her understanding when the storyline and characters became a little too real.

Thanks to my reviewers: Cathy McFadden, Terre Henderson, Michael Thomason, Tony Gentry, Barbara Clawson, Kathy Drennen, Mike Morris, Larry Angel, Gene Carter and Veronica Guerrero.

Foreword

This is Grace's story, so I'm going to let her tell it. She did all the research and conducted the interviews. She meticulously combed through dairies, journals, countless newspaper articles and public records. Her efforts spanned five generations of relatives and ancestors. For over six years, Grace put her life on hold so these stories could be told.

The collection of stories, narrated by Grace Wheaton, tells of a Godly heritage that has been passed down from generation to generation like a baton in a great relay race—an eternal race. The characters in these stories, are her family lineage—men and women of great faith.

In this book, Volume One, Grace sets the stage for the presentation of a one-hundred year period from 1865 to 1965— five generations. The upcoming book, Volume Two, will begin in 1865 with the story of her great, great, great grandfather, a nobleman, who resided in the English countryside of Great Britain.

Each subsequent volume will bring you along on an exciting and adventurous journey of faith and family. You will laugh and you will cry. You will experience God's faithfulness and sense the joy that comes from serving a wonderful loving God. Biblical principles come to life before your eyes as you read the accounts of God's faithfulness portrayed by Grace and her ancestral heritage. Be enriched as you read these stories and glorify God.

In His Mighty Name,
David E. McFadden

Introduction

My name is Grace Chloe Wheaton and I have an amazing story to tell. *No, a story I must tell.*

I begin this story with my own personal struggle of personal faith. My dilemma was centered in the realization that I was living my parent's faith and not my own. Somehow I missed the fact that a person cannot be 'born a Christian' or someday just wakeup and 'you are one.' This phenomenon often happens in 'religious' households—Christianity by osmosis.

The story quickly shifts and becomes centered around my Great Uncle Paiyan (Pī yǎn; rhymes with Tai Pan) who challenged me to write the complete story of our family heritage. I didn't really know what his request would entail until I went with him to the mission field.

This first chronicle culminates with the discovery and preservation of my great, great, great grandfather's journals. His name was Sir John Francis Taylor, perhaps the foremost evangelist of his era.

One last comment before you begin reading the epic accounts of my heritage. In my freshman year of college, I had the most wonderful of all history professors. Dr. William Jarrett explained that history is in reality *His Story*. I will never forget Dr. Jarrett's lecture that day. This all important understanding of history is why I subtitled this book, and all the following volumes, as *His Story*.

In His Service,
Grace Chloe Wheaton

Chapter One

The Race for God

May 1987—Puget Sound is the most perfect place on the planet. It has everything—the mountains, the ocean, mild winters, mild summers, it's all here. Grace's mom and dad settled in the breathtaking vistas of Seattle after he retired from military service as an Air Force pilot. Grace Chloe Wheaton was born shortly after John and Elizabeth came here as fulltime missionaries. Seattle was the perfect home base for reaching the Pacific region with the Gospel.

This wonderful story unfolds with the now twenty-four year old Grace warming up for a twenty-six mile marathon race. This was her last race before entering full time service at St. Matthew's Episcopal Church as a priest. The race was set on a winding roadway cut through the mountainous coastline on the beautiful Puget Sound near Seattle.

Grace was experiencing a personal inner conflict. Her struggle was producing emotions that were surfacing and cracking the facade of daddy's perfect little girl. These were new feelings for Grace. As far as she knew she was happy with her life and the choices she has made. Yet, it was quite obvious that she had pushed herself to this point from internal pressures to perform and please others. What she didn't understand was that God was dealing with her. He was going to bring fullness and peace to Grace but it would be for His purposes.

Grace was at an emotional breaking point. Everything ahead of her was new and uncharted with little peace going forward. Yes, there is always uncertainty with the unfamiliar but there was more to her fears. Her inner turmoil made her future that much more uncertain. Something seemed desperately wrong and she wanted to escape what was set before her.

Grace began her marathon with these emotions and fears foremost on her mind. Instead of focusing on the race, she allowed her thoughts to capture her. Her resolve to run a difficult race was weakened. At this point, the crush of the race combined with her uncertainties could easily bring Grace to a crumbling heap of emotions. In the last few moments before the race began, Grace was on the verge of tears. In her strained weakness, and under her breath, Grace cried out to the Lord.

"Lord, I want to serve you but I want to know you... I'm so empty... Help me Lord."

Weeks before the race Grace got the idea to wear her priest's collar. She thought it would bring awareness to her parish and possibly be an inspiration to others of faith. Little did she know, in her naivety, that the collar would be a lightning rod for the wrong kind of attention. Just ten minutes into the race a theologically challenged heckler screamed out, "The Pope's a dope."

In an exhausted emotional state, Grace slowed her running to a fast walk... to a frustrated walk... and then to a defeated slump. It wasn't the heckler or what he said that mattered. It was just a breaking point for Grace as she sighed, "I can't do this."

An apparent concerned runner also stopped running mimicking Grace's descending cadence. "Can't do what?" Without looking up from her downward staring, hands on her knees stance, she said, "This whole thing is wrong"—still breathing hard.

"What are you going to do about it?" asked the person behind her. Grace responded from the depths of discouragement. "I don't know... I just don't know"—her voice trailing off.

It occurred to Grace that she didn't know anyone well enough in the race to be asking her these questions. She rose up and turned to see who had befriended her. To her amazement no one was there. She quickly looked ahead to see if the person had just simply continued running and she failed to see him leave.

Puzzled by the questioning voice, Grace left the roadway and made her way back toward the starting line. She needed to pick up her athletic bag from the trailer mounted rented locker. It was too soon for the shuttle bus to be running to the remote parking lot, so she walked over to the mostly vacant portable bleachers. Grace needed to sit and contemplate what had just happened. It was all a blur—something new for a methodical and sensible Grace. Did she really hear a voice?

Grace was still sitting in the bleachers staring down in deep thought when she felt the presence of a visitor—an intruder into her private space and thoughts. Initially, the only thing she saw was a khaki pant leg and a wingtip shoe. "Grace, what are you going to do about it?" The voice was unmistakably the same.

This time she was going to find out who was asking these personal questions. As Grace looked up, the only thing she could see was a silhouette against the bright morning sun— the mystery seemed staged. Grace held her hand to block the direct sun. She needed to see who had challenged her in her moment of lost heart. "Grace... it's Me."

Dumbfounded Grace slowly stood up. The visitor reached out to Grace with both hands palms up. "You said you wanted to know me. I'm here, let's talk."

Grace's mind was spinning. She knew the countless stories by memory; accounts of miraculous encounters with God—immediate answered prayer—a personal loving God—experiencing His presence. But now... today... for me? Grace slowly sat back down in awe and reverence pondering the possibility that God would meet her in this hour of great need.

In the most assuring and peaceful tone, the Lord spoke to Grace. *"Grace, you are experiencing a promise that I have made to those who seek me with a whole heart. Your family is carried along, generation by generation, by the promise that I have made to bless those who bless Me. Even though you do not know me, I have known you and loved you from the beginning of time. You have been set aside by the faithfulness of your ancestors, for blessing. I have called you to serve Me. You have been faithful to do what you knew to do. And even though you did not know Me, you loved Me."*

These were words that Grace somehow already understood even before she heard them. These words had been etched on her heart for years even before she heard them from the Lord Himself; it was a divine revelation. "Lord, it is so good that you are here."

"Grace, believe on Me and you will be Saved."

"Yes Lord, I believe on You and I want to know You more. Teach me to draw close to You and live in Your love for others."

> *"...Teach me to draw close to You and live in Your love for others."*

Grace was still sitting in a bowed and prayerful position when the first of the runners began to approach the 'now' finish line. Over the last two hours, Grace's private space had slowly filled with spectators. Now the cheers and screams were erupting; carrying the runners in their last leg of the race. Grace had been with the Lord for hours yet it seemed like only a few minutes.

Feeling drained yet filled, Grace needed time to contemplate what just happened. She mentally went over the events of the day; her end-of-the-rope hopelessness going into the race; her desperate whispered prayer; the letting go and giving up; the encounter; the laser beam accurate probing questions and finally receiving Jesus—the answer to the longing that had preoccupied her for the last year.

Even though Grace was emotionally spent, she felt

more alive than she had felt in a long time. This was a new beginning for Grace. Her future seemed brighter and clearer. Before today she had been unable to make sense of how her future might look. Now she could sort things out.

Just as Grace began walking toward the bus boarding area, Father Isaac came running from the direction of the judge's station. The somewhat pudgy pastor was breathing hard from his short jog trying to catch up with Grace. "Grace, sorry I'm late… did I miss anything? How did you do?"

Grace turned to greet her pastor; one of her biggest fans. "Father Isaac, the greatest thing has just happened. I came here to race for God but instead I met Him."

Baffled by such a comment, Father Isaac questioned, "What do you mean you met Him?"

Grace was not expecting Father Isaac's bewildered response. After a brief pause she replied, "I have been worried about a lot of things lately. God met me and assured me of His blessing on my life."

Father Isaac began blinking, a habit that he had when he was under pressure or processing information. "O.K., O.K. this is good but don't get carried away with the God talking part, that's not something that you want to tell others… you understand?"

Grace was too excited to be deterred. "But there's

7

more. It's just like I've heard all my life. God personally met with me and assured me of His love and how to know Him. Father Isaac, I'm not the same person I was a few hours ago. I feel different; something inside of me has changed."

Father Isaac raised both hands with palms out as if trying to stop traffic. "Grace my dear; these are things any young priest can get confused about. Let's keep this to ourselves. You have a bright future ahead of you and we don't want to start out on the wrong foot with the Bishop, now do we?"

"I don't quite understand," Grace exclaimed, "I want to know the God I tell others about."

Father Isaac, in an attempt to gain control of the situation began to pacify Grace. "Yes, but I think you may have things all mixed up. I tell you Grace, I can see this is very important to you so let's talk with Bishop Ivey first thing Monday morning. I think he can make sense of these things for you."

Grace was beginning to feel a little demoralized. Even so, she had no choice but to acquiesce to Father Isaac's suggestion. Father Isaac patted Grace on the back reassuring her as they turned to walk toward the shuttle bus. Upon reaching the shuttle, Father Isaac returned the athletic bag he carried for Grace as they walked. Seeing her off, he reminded

Grace of their Monday appointment. "Meet me at the church on Monday at nine a.m. I'll arrange everything."

Uncertainty began to flood Grace's mind and emotions once again. The encounter with God now seemed surreal. Mulling over Father Isaac's reaction and sentiments, she was feeling drained of energy as she rode the bus. Grace thought about her dad and wished he could be here for her, but he wasn't due home for another month. Thinking about her predicament, Grace began to make a mental list of people she could talk to. The list was very short. "Maybe Father Isaac was right; I should keep this to myself."

Chapter Two

All Things Work Together

Grace decided to drive the long way home. Take the high road as she called it—to give her more time to think. She stopped by '*April's Dine-In*' and ordered the Saturday special; something she does anytime she gets by this way. As Grace waited for her spinach quiche, she gazed out the window in deep thought. The elevated views of the coastline were breathtaking. It was then she remembered her friend Amy. "Yes, Amy... of course, Amy!"

Now she knew why she was prompted to take the high

road—it was the way to Amy's apartment. If she was home, Amy would be the perfect person to talk to. Grace quickly finished her lunch and headed north. She then turned on Bay View Highway—a prewar elevated causeway offering more spectacular views of the Puget Sound Bay. With mounting enthusiasm Grace mused out loud, "Surely, Amy would be home, after all it is Saturday."

Driving toward Amy's apartment, Grace was reassuring herself about her decision to drop in unexpected. Her thoughts were filled with joy and anticipation as she explored the possibilities of her visit. Grace also realized that she needed to lean on Amy's solid assurance and overcoming faith.

Amy had been Grace's roommate at the seminary. After a few months, Amy suddenly dropped out for reasons unknown. During their time together as roommates, Grace and Amy had grown to be very close and had since remained in regular contact, mostly by phone. It was a godly relationship in which each was encouraged in positive ways.

Grace had grown up knowing only unpretentious and transparent relationships. These qualities drew Amy to Grace's down-to-earth demeanor. Amy had been deprived of honest straight forward relationships so she hungered for what Grace had.

Amy had suffered at the hands of many who had tried

and succeeded in using her and manipulating her. She carried emotional as well as physical scars of cruelty from others. It was in these overwhelming circumstances that Amy met God. She perfectly displayed the miracle of a transformed life full of peace.

Initially, Amy's shame and guilt left her feeling worthless and dirty. She could not see how she could ever be of any value to her God who rescued her. As a broken vessel, Amy was not able to envision how God could possibly use her. Then one night, in utter despair, she cried out to God. Desperate and alone, Amy picked up her Bible and pleaded with God for an answer. That's when she read Romans 8:28.

Amy read these words: *"God causes everything to work together for the good of those who love God and are called according to His purpose for them."* She paused to reflect upon the verse when her heart and mind heard God's voice speak to her. *"My beloved Amy you are my redeemed. I can use all these things for My purposes. Be still and know that I am your God and that I love you with an everlasting love. My Amy, it is in your weakness that I will be glorified."*

Amy felt a cleansing sensation come over her. She experienced the shame and guilt lift, leaving her feeling clean and transformed. She felt whole. Since that night, when God touched Amy, she has learned to walk in a confident and concrete faith. She grew to understand that the tragic events of her past have uniquely prepared her to help people who have also suffered from the hands of others.

Grace had only been to Amy's apartment twice before today. Her last visit was during the previous holiday season. She wasn't exactly sure how to find her way through the maze of buildings that all looked alike. Except for the large numbers that read 1076A and 1076B and so on, every building was a mirror image of the last. Finally, Grace looked ahead and saw a building whose surroundings looked familiar. She stepped onto the narrow sidewalk leading to a large greenbelt area that she recognized.

Carefully checking each numbered door, for a clue that might jog her memory, she spotted... the fish! Grace recognized the Christian fish symbol on Amy's door. "I found it." She exclaimed out loud in her famous singsong way. Grace was so excited that she momentarily forgot all of the ups and downs of the day. Approaching Amy's door, Grace heard sounds that could only be described as muffled sobbing. The sounds quickly subsided when Grace began knocking. Patiently waiting, Grace silently studied her surroundings. It was now one p.m. as she knocked on Amy's downstairs apartment door for a second time. Grace smiled at the nearby children as they played on the neatly kept grassy area near Amy's stoop.

Grace was still distracted by the playing children when Amy opened the door. She immediately jumped at the sight of Grace and reached for a girl-buddy hug. "Grace, I am so happy to see you. It's been ages since I've seen you in person. Come in, you're just the person I could talk to right now. My life has been turned upside down today—I need your help and advice." Grace didn't know what to say except to empathize and console her dear friend.

Grace came wanting help and advice from Amy but now it seems as if she was going to be taking on more troubles and worries. It was at this moment that she heard a still small voice repeat a very familiar phrase that she had, just hours before, spoken to God in childlike faith: *"...Teach me to draw close to You and live in Your love for others."* Grace was struck with how fast God can answer heartfelt requests and petitions. "Here is my chance to live in Your love for others." Grace whispered under her breath.

"What did you say?" Amy asked as she closed the door behind them.

"Oh, nothing... I've had an unusual day myself. Please Amy, tell me what happened today?"

As Grace made herself comfortable on the loveseat, she could feel a stirring of heaviness trying to push its way into the serenity of Amy's quiet apartment. There was a menacing imbalance in the air. The otherwise peaceful ambiance seemed at a tipping point similar to the feeling when the weather makes a dramatic change—the calm before the storm. Had the emotional highs and lows of the day taken the edge off Grace's senses? Or, had the day's experiences prepared her for a looming ethereal showdown?

The eerie awareness was mutual, causing an awkward silence before Amy spoke. "Grace, my father has found me. He called this morning demanding that I see him." Grace wasn't sure what to say because the tone of Amy's voice wasn't that of desperation but she did appear anxious.

"What are you going to do?" asked Grace.

In a calm tone, Amy expressed only a need to work through some 'family issues.' "I know that this whole thing with my dad is in God's hands." Pausing, Amy chose her words carefully. "Grace, there is a real battle being waged for my dad's soul. I have a feeling that this will be the time that God will finally reach him. I'm not sure how but I have this knowing in my spirit. That is why I'm glad you're here. I believe that God brought you here to agree with me in prayer."

Grace agreed with the spiritual battle assessment. "Amy, I can sense darkness pushing as if your dad is being weighed in the balance."

Grace's concerns seemed small and diminished

compared to Amy's pending yet unknown trials with her dad. Then, Grace felt a new sensation in her spirit. It was different

> *God himself placed a burden upon Grace's spirit to give her His perspective.*

from anything she had felt before now. God was allowing Grace to personally experience Amy's passionate concerns. She could sense that the tugging on her heart was a God given burden. It was more than just empathy or compassion which is human response. God himself placed a burden upon Grace's spirit *to give her His perspective.*

"How can I help?" Grace asked, reaching out to hold Amy's hand.

Amy responded tearfully. "Would you please pray for me and my dad?"

Grace had read scripted congregational prayers from the pulpit. But she had never prayed personal prayers out loud in the presence of another person. Grace knew that Amy was asking her to do just that. Amy had prayed for Grace on several occasions and Amy's prayers were amazing petitions that were heartfelt, accurate and fruitful. Grace could now see that the previous path she had chosen to please God was indeed lifeless. Her only prayers had been rote prepackaged prayers that seemed doomed as they fell to the floor as lifeless idioms.

Grace came hoping to lean on Amy's faith but it was Amy who needed to lean on her. Grace was starting to realize that leaning on the faith of others is what she had done all of her life. This realization empowered Grace to open her mouth and to speak boldly. So boldly that she surprised herself.

"Heavenly Father, You have made Yourself known to me today. Thank You for loving me and caring for me when I was lost and afraid. Lord, thank You for answering my prayer so quickly. I pray for Amy and her father and above all else I ask You to bring restoration to Amy's relationship with her dad, Vernon. Lord, I ask You to heal Vernon's mind and his emotions and to cause him to come into relationship with You. Lord, in Jesus' name I push back the darkness that is trying to steal Vernon's soul away from Your outstretched arms. I pray that Amy's meeting with her dad will bring You glory and honor. In Jesus' name. Amen."

Inwardly, Grace was awestruck yet humbled by the power she felt in her prayer—it was full of life. Experiencing the conviction of a Spirit led prayer was something new for her. It reminded her of when her dad would pray. A great blessing flooded over Grace as she realized the burden she carried for Amy was gone.

Sensing the atmosphere shift within the room, Amy felt the oppressing fog of anxiety lift, revealing the Light. "Grace thank you for your wisdom and for praying such a powerful prayer. I am so grateful for your strong faith in the Lord. You're a good friend to have, thank you. Tell me what happened to you today; it sounds good?"

By now, Grace was even more excited to tell her story to Amy. Starting at the beginning, she explained how God met her in a most unusual way. "The most amazing thing happened at the race today… "

Grace went over the events of the day, her concerns with Father Isaac and the upcoming meeting with Bishop Ivey. Grace and Amy prayed that God would reveal to Father Isaac and Bishop Ivey the truth of God's desire to have a personal relationship with each person. They also prayed that the meeting would be peaceful, productive and that the Truth would be discovered and revealed.

Chapter Three

The Meeting

Grace's perception of her race day encounter with God had re-centered since the last time she talked to Father Isaac. His disparaging response to her wonderful experience had dampened her joy, but fortunately, her visit with Amy lifted any doubts intended to discourage Grace. Amy's encouragement and their mutual prayers had given Grace a new level of reassurance and confidence. What a difference a day can make when you have experienced God's touch.

Grace felt a little reminiscent as she prepared to leave for her meeting with Father Isaac and Bishop Ivey. Reflecting over the past two years of study, Grace realized she would soon be moving from her dorm room. The page was turning to a new chapter in her life.

Grace often walked to her church, St. Matthew's Episcopal. The bay area landmark was easy to recognize; known for its exquisite architecture as well as a flawlessly manicured landscape. Puget Sound mornings are often dew soaked this time of the year with this morning being especially wet and a little cool. However, with the bright sun and the wind at her back she felt quite comfortable as she walked the eight blocks to her meeting. It was a walk she had made countless times over the last few years.

Father Isaac seemed nervous as he waited to greet Grace under the massive portico that extended out over the cobblestone entry. As Grace approached, Father Isaac eagerly corralled her into the foyer. He wanted to speak privately to her even though no one else was around.

With a look of concern, Father Isaac nervously implored, "Grace, Bishop Ivey is running late. We have a few minutes to discuss what we're going to say to him. If he asks, I'm expecting you to recant your story about a personal conversation with God. We can then quickly go on to some other concern for his consideration; accommodations, transportation, you know the things we have discussed before."

Feeling God's strength to confront Father Isaac's

irrational fears, Amy asked resolutely, "Father Isaac, I am a bit surprised at your behavior; you seem threatened or fearful. Are you afraid of a personal God?"

Father Isaac was being backed into a corner and he could sense it. He instinctively knew he was the one who would end up on the defensive in this meeting today. He wanted to avoid it at all cost. His miscue in arranging the meeting had him on edge and he fired back at Grace too strongly. "How dare you speak to me that way? What gives you the right to question my faith?—you're the lesser here."

The overstepped response did not faze Grace. She realized she was experiencing the spirit behind the man. Grace was having her spiritual eyes opened. God was allowing her to see yet another glimpse into the spiritual dimension. Father Isaac could not see the truth because it was being hidden behind a veil of religiosity.

To Grace's amazement a deep compassion rose up in her. Once again, God placed a burden on her heart; this time for Father Isaac. This was all so new yet profound. Grace was experiencing God's goodness as He used her to bring about His purposes.

Bishop Ivey entered through the side door employee entrance and had been looking for Father Isaac and Grace. He approached the huddled pair from the direction of the rotunda that was just inside (from) the foyer. The rotunda was a massive architectural focal point embellished with intricate handwork. The exquisite workmanship consisted of mosaic tiles, masterfully crafted woodwork and plasterwork that dated well into the last century. Father Isaac had his back to Bishop Ivey as he approached their hushed conversation. Hoping to alert Father Isaac, Grace made exaggerated eye contact with him.

In a businesslike tone, Bishop Ivey spoke first. "Grace Wheaton I presume?"

Grace's reply was short yet respectful. "It's my pleasure Bishop Ivey."

Bishop Ivey was a leader of a local ecumenical movement desperately wanting to see the Episcopal Church reunite with the Roman Catholic Church. Within his more liberal diocese, Bishop Ivey had managed to shape a minor consensus of opinion about reunification. However, with his controversial obsession with the Pope, he ruined any chance of support from Cardinal John Whittington.

Father Isaac felt he had not accomplished his mission to subdue Grace and her narrative about meeting with God. With a nervous and insecure acknowledgement, Father Isaac addressed his superior, "Bishop Ivey, welcome. Come, come; I already have coffee brewing in the library."

In all the years of coming to and studying within the many buildings on the church campus, Grace had never been inside the massive library. This was not a church library in the traditional sense but a private enclave for the senior clergy. Awe inspiring would be an understatement to describe this imposing chamber wrought with intricate woodwork that must have taken years to complete. Considering the era of construction, it was hard to imagine the time consuming process required to put this one room together.

Grace, Father Isaac and Bishop Ivey each chose a large overstuffed wingback chair. The luxurious leather chairs encircled an oversized rug emblazoned with a tapestry depicting the passion of Christ.

Bishop Ivey wasted no time getting to the matter at hand. "Grace?"

"Yes, Bishop Ivey."

"I understand you have heard from God himself. He spoke to you?"

Grace was completely fearless for once in her life. What could be said for or against her was of no concern. However, she did have this burden that God had placed on her heart for Father Isaac. She was now interested to see how God was going to release that burden. With that thought in mind Grace responded, "Actually that is not completely true." At that point Father Isaac perked up and looked straight at Grace. "You see, Bishop Ivey there is more, much more, to the story."

With godly compassion and respect, Grace explained the events of the last seventy-two hours. Bishop Ivey raised his eyebrows several times and nervously shifted in his chair as Grace testified of God's personal presence. She talked about the reality of His healing power and His abundant provision for those who will seek Him with a whole heart. Grace was also able to explain her reason for coming to St. Matthew's and why she wanted to be a priest.

Bishop Ivey pressed Grace, "This is all quite interesting Grace but you are aware of the church's stance on God speaking to individuals today; is this correct?"

Calmly and succinctly Grace answered, "I never realized the significance of such a stance until Saturday, but yes I do."

Relentlessly, Bishop Ivey pushed to make a stern assertion. "Do you know what this means if you do not renounce this so called encounter with God and forget it ever happened?"

Grace had never been as collected as she graciously replied to Bishop Ivey. "No sir I don't."

"Grace, as you may know, Father Isaac and I were taking a chance when we agreed to allow you to become a

> *In her spirit she also knew that God's way was the best way to resolve this debate.*

candidate for priesthood. As a woman, your internship is new for the Episcopal Church; you understand? Now you have opened Pandora's Box right here in our own parish and we will be disgraced unless you forget this whole thing."

Grace was determined to see this conflict to its end and not allow the root cause to be covered up and hidden. In her spirit she also knew that God's way was the best way to resolve this debate. If she relied on God, Satan's plans to steal God's destiny from the three souls sitting in this room, would be defeated. Determining to honor God in what she said and did, would orchestrate an outcome that would bring Him glory. God could, at the same time, bring about the changes He desires in Father Isaac and Bishop Ivey. Grace did not realize that she had spoken aloud while she was thinking, "I have to choose between God and man."

Bishop Ivey was getting edgy and wanted to bring the meeting to a close. He was waiting for Grace's response, when he heard her indistinctly say something under her breath. Impatiently he curtly asked, "What did you say?"

In a very humbled state Grace replied, "Excuse me sir, I

was just thinking. What must I do to honor you and honor God at the same time?"

This question left Bishop Ivey baffled. He couldn't answer except to say what had already been on his mind. "Only the Pope can hear from God. That's the way it has always been and that's the way it will always be. Now, young lady, you must come in line with this or I will have to rescind our agreement with you and you will have to leave our parish."

Grace was unmoved by such a heartless statement. "Bishop Ivey, before I give you my reply may I ask Father Isaac a question?"

Grace's question sparked a curious tone from Bishop Ivey. "Yes, I believe that would be in order if you think this question might help us come to an agreement."

Grace felt God's hand on her as she looked straight into Father Isaac's eyes. God wanted to do a work in his life and she knew it. "Father Isaac, two weeks ago you delivered a very unusual sermon to the church. I mean that it was much different than I have ever heard since I have been here. Do you remember it?"

Father Isaac was nervous and fidgety; blinking his eyes as he sometimes does. There was much more on the line here that begged an answer. "Of course I do. I warned you earlier about questioning my faith and I won't have it; you understand?"

This straight talk and the emotional rebuke had Bishop Ivey's attention. "Father Isaac, what could possibly have you so upset? I didn't hear anything that would trivialize your faith, so tell me what is going on. What did you speak on that Sunday that would bring such a response?"

Chapter Four
None Should Perish

The tension had reached its peak. It was a very long uneasy minute before Father Isaac could speak. "God desires that none should perish. I've known that verse from as far back as I can remember. I was taught that every man, woman and child regardless of faith or no faith would eventually be with God, because this scripture says that God desires that none should perish. If God desires something then He is certainly able to bring it about. A loving God would never send anyone to hell; it just can't be. Bishop Ivey, this is your stance as leader of this diocese. Is this right?"

Bishop Ivey was nodding in cadence with Father Isaac's spoken but labored words. "Universal salvation, yes of course; every knee shall bow, every tongue shall confess that Jesus Christ is Lord. Yes, every person will eventually be saved."

Father Isaac continued, "I'm a torn man, Bishop Ivey. Three weeks ago, in my study, I was preparing for my sermon. I came across a verse of scripture that I have never been able to make fit with our belief in universal salvation. Then I heard what I thought was an audible voice telling me to turn to another scripture and then another and then another. I was up nearly all night, looking up verse after verse. Then it occurred to me that the few scriptures we have used to conclude universal salvation were nothing more than a twisted attempt to make a case for our hardened hearts."

Bishop Ivey was turning red in the face and in a controlled voice as possible blurted out, "You of all people. Where do you get this information?"

Father Isaac knew that Bishop Ivey's question was meant to be rhetorical but he took the opportunity to answer anyway. "In Matthew 7:13, and following, we are told that the gate to God's Zoë life (abundant life in Christ) is narrow and there are few who find it and broad is the way that leads to destruction. Bishop Ivey, I discovered that true Salvation is not all inclusive. According to scripture, there will be destruction for most. Most will refuse Jesus as Lord and Savior. Many will take the name Christian but few will truly know Jesus and will be rejected. Once I recognized this truth, many other scriptures confirmed that true Salvation is for those who will receive it here in this life and to live wholly for the Lord. Bishop Ivey, the scriptures we have used to make the point of universal salvation have been a dishonest attempt to make our point. Lastly, it is only a loving God who would sacrifice His only Son so that we might have eternal life with Him. Not a single person needs to miss heaven if only they will believe. This is what it means when the scripture tells us that God desires that none should perish." The power and anointing, on Father Isaac's words, was undeniable.

Bishop Ivey was contemplating in silence with a stern look on his face. It was apparent that his very soul was in the balance. *We know that the truth of God's word is full of living power. It is sharper than the sharpest knife, cutting deep into our innermost thoughts and desires. It exposes us for who we really are.* In one side of the balance were the realities of believing Father Isaac as well as Grace's line of reasoning. The other side of the balance meant turning his back on a lifetime of believing and teaching error. It meant facing immeasurable ridicule from the thousands who had bought into his line of reasoning. Because of a hardened heart, Father Isaac's side of the scale seemed empty by comparison. The grace, love and abundance that Grace had testified of earlier were veiled to him by a religious spirit brought about by extreme pride.

Instead of addressing Father Isaac, Bishop Ivey turned to Grace and asked with a stoic deadpan expression, "What was your earlier statement concerning a choice between God and man?"

"Bishop Ivey, this is a decision every person has to make. Will it be our way or His way; my will or His will? Is your hope in God or in the devices of man? This was the very choice that I had to make Saturday morning. As a result of bending my knee and yielding my heart to God, He has honored me and lifted me up from the very moment I said 'yes' to Him. My life has been changed for His glory."

Grace reverently paused as she noticed Bishop Ivey's emotional facial inflections. "My earlier question was, 'What must I do to honor you and honor God at the same time?' You see, God has impressed on me that, at this moment, I cannot honor Him unless I honor you."

Bishop Ivey found these statements so profound and Christ-like that he could not speak to them. He had read these concepts before in scripture but now they had life with meaning. "How can you speak this way? My heart feels like it has been pricked."

Grace, with the utmost candor and reverence, spoke with God's anointing on every word. "Bishop Ivey, what you are experiencing is the work of the Holy Spirit touching you

29

and giving you an opportunity to receive the truth of God's Word. You can, at this moment receive God's provision for Salvation. You can know Him personally. This is a moment in time that God has orchestrated for you to know Him. It may not come again."

Bishop Ivey crumpled in his chair and began to sob. "It is too much to ask. I can't do this, it's too much."

Grace realized that these were the very words that she had uttered just a few days earlier. The agony of letting go of your own will can be heart rending. "Bishop Ivey, I know how you feel but you can trust God with your life, He is a good God who loves you."

Bishop Ivey suddenly stopped sobbing and stood erect and straightened his vestments. He had an odd proud countenance that was sobering to look at. Emotionless, he made what seemed like a canned statement. "I have been a pillar in this church and community for decades. I love my church and the Pope more than my own life, so there will be no more of this talk, no more."

In another particularly odd and mechanical gesture, Bishop Ivey turned his body at an angle away from Grace and Father Isaac. It seemed as if he wanted to be shielded or hidden from a frontal exposure as he continued to speak. "Father Isaac, I want a full report on the disposition of this matter by Friday.

I also want to know the full extent of the sermon you delivered two weeks ago. If you do not tell me, word for word, I will find out and there will be consequences. Do you understand?"

Chapter Five
Out of the Darkness

The dramatic confrontation, in the church library, played out as if the whole scene was being choreographed on *the ultimate* theatrical stage. The interactions were so intense, any on-looking virtual audience would have been sitting on the edge of their seats. All eyes now shifted to Father Isaac. What would be his response to this poignant display of rejection—turning ones back on the greatest love ever offered on earth or in heaven.

If it were not for the love of God, Father Isaac's heart would have failed him. Seeing the realty of his own fate set before him in such graphic terms opened his eyes to the sheer godlessness of Bishop Ivey's wrong decision. Bishop Ivey had chosen the love of man and a life without God.

Father Isaac, at that very moment, knew he would choose differently. He would choose a life with God no matter the consequences. With these thoughts in mind Father Isaac professed, "It's done, my fate is sealed. I only have one life to

> *"It's done, my fate is sealed. I only have one life to live and I will live it for God..."*

live and I will live it for God. I have to trust my life to the One who is able to save me; no one else."

Grace saw an opportunity to bring consolation and reassurance to the moment. Thoughtfully she said, "Father Isaac, do you remember Amy Wylie who was with us for a short time a few years ago?"

Father Isaac was still a little wide eyed and flush from the intense emotions of the just finished meeting with Bishop Ivey. The question did not resonate until his racing mind settled down. "Amy Wylie? Yes of course... petite blonde headed, very smart and if I remember correctly a little on the quiet side. She left because her father threatened the Bishop in his office, I remember it very well. Quite a commotion he caused, that Mr. Wylie."

Grace had not fully known the circumstances behind Amy leaving but she suspected something along those lines. "Father Isaac, I feel I should share something very important. Saturday afternoon, Amy and I prayed for the outcome of this meeting today—that the truth would be revealed. We also prayed that you would receive God's grace in Salvation. Father Isaac, do you realize that is exactly what happened here today? The truth was revealed to Bishop Ivey in no uncertain terms and you chose God's will for your life and said 'no' to the religiosity of man."

Father Isaac sheepishly responded, "Grace, I'm not sure what I've done today but I could not see myself walking the same path that Bishop Ivey just chose. He looked like a dead man walking and yet when I look at you I see the life of God coming from you. What you said and how you said it, as well as your actions, shows me that God is real in your life. You demonstrated His love in the face of a harsh rebuke. Grace, I want what you have. I want to know God the way you do."

Grace continued to lead Father Isaac toward the place in time that God had arranged to know Him. "Father Isaac, you know this passage out of Romans as well as anyone: *"if you confess with your mouth that Jesus is Lord and believe in your heart that God raised him from the dead, you will be saved. For it is by believing in your heart that you are made right with God, and it is by confessing with your mouth that you are saved."* Father Isaac, it is a matter of taking this promise, from God, for yourself. Make your confessions personal—really mean it from your heart and then tell others what God has done for you."

Father Isaac knew that this was his time to finally get it right with God and not pretend any longer. He knew the cost for a 'yes' to God would be high but that didn't matter to him. He had been living a lie too long and now was the time to give it all to God. With a heart that was ready to receive, Father Isaac asked, "Grace, will you pray with me?"

As if speaking to a young innocent child, Grace tenderly lead Father Isaac to a point of prayer. "Father Isaac, you start by telling God what's on your heart and I will pray after you finish."

Father Isaac prayed, "God, I am so sorry for trying to do this without You; what a fool I've been. Please forgive me. I want to live for You and You alone from this point forward. I ask You to lead me and guide me moment by moment, day by day. Please draw me closer to You and teach me how to love others with the same love that You have."

Grace was moved to hear such a repentant prayer that was truly from a heart broken for the Lord. "Heavenly Father, thank You for Father Isaac's contrite spirit and humbled heart. Holy Spirit, I ask You to seal the work that was done here today and according to John 14: 15-17 where Jesus spoke: "*If you love me, obey my commandments. And I will ask the Father, and he will give you another Counselor, who will never leave you. He is the Holy Spirit, who leads into all truth.*" Thank You Lord for such a wonderful promise that we can have for today. Amen."

Chapter Six

The Report

The next few days were like a little bit of heaven on earth for Father Isaac. The heavy weight of living to please others was lifted. The Lord led him to a scripture in Proverbs that revealed where he had lived spiritually for the last twenty-three years *'Fearing people is a dangerous trap, but to trust the Lord means safety.'* Everyday seemed to be a new opportunity to grow in knowing God more and deeper. One thing was for sure, all of the years of knowing *about* God would prove to be a blessing as he embarked on his new journey of *knowing* God.

Father Isaac had spent many hours contemplating how to put together his report for Bishop Ivey. He had requested a full report on Father Isaac's plan to bring Grace Wheaton in line with church doctrine. If Grace ultimately decided to remain noncompliant, Father Isaac was not sure how to proceed especially since he was now at odds with a doctrinal position of his own bishop. At that moment Father Isaac could not imagine how this difficult situation was going to be resolved. However, he now had the faith to know that it was in God's hands and there was a larger purpose in all of this.

Bishop Ivey had insisted on a word-for-word accounting of Father Isaac's controversial sermon. Father Isaac went to the large beige file cabinet to retrieve the sermon notes that he had prepared three weeks ago. The sermon notes were always meticulously filed by his secretary according to date. When he could not find the file he was concerned because the file was crucial for his report. He then performed a second, slow and methodical, file-by-file search. Frustrated, he decided to page his secretary. "Andrea, can you come in here please?—I need help with a file."

Andrea was a large woman in her mid-fifties who would not fit the stereotype of a church secretary. She had short spiked hair with bleached ends and wore high heeled boots when she could. To complete the look, she almost always dressed in a black body suit that was covered by an A-line dress in some variation of bright colors. With a congenial tone Andrea inquired, "Yes sir, how may I help you?"

Father Isaac had the utmost respect for Andrea. She was the best admin that he had ever worked with. Even with her unusual outfits, she was an outstanding communicator and by far the most efficient and well organized person he had ever met. She would know the exact location of the file. "Andrea, I'm looking for the file that contained my research and preparations for the sermon of April fourteenth. It contained the sermon notes that I need to copy. Do you know where that file is?"

In a matter-of-fact way Andrea answered, "I have not

seen the file. Was the file cabinet locked?—you know how you forget."

Thinking through his normal routine for leaving the office, Father Isaac reluctantly answered, "It wasn't locked but you know we lock the office door every night and set the alarm." Father Isaac felt as if he needed to defend himself with an often repeated refrain.

Feeling unable to be of any help, Andrea stated, "Well sir, I don't have an explanation then. I have not needed the file and no one has asked for it." Andrea saw an opportunity to interject some of her trademark wit, "I can't imagine someone taking a file of sermon notes except a member of your fan club, maybe a roadie." Andrea liked a well-placed joke if it was appropriate. She thought that her comment was definitely cute but Father Isaac was in a serious mood.

> *"Who would want the file? This is so odd." Father Isaac mumbled to himself. ..."*

"Who would want the file? This is so odd," Father Isaac mumbled to himself. He would just have to fill out the report without the talking points that were in his sermon notes. As for Grace, he would need to meet with her, once more, to clearly convey her thoughts and intentions. This needed to take place today since it was already Wednesday.

Grace had been contemplating her life without St. Matthew's for the last few days. There was no use pretending that things would upright themselves and be as they should. Even with Father Isaac's dramatic conversion, Grace knew that she needed to make other plans for her future. Was full time ministry still something she wanted to pursue? Grace majored in world history and minored in anthropology; that ought to be good for something, she thought. Never thinking for a minute that she would be having this mental discussion, she hadn't considered choosing an alternate career path. Grace's deep musings were interrupted by a rare ring of her door bell.

Grace was headed to the door when the phone rang. Quickly, she decided to answer the door and let the answering machine pick up the call. Two young men, dressed in black suits and thin neckties were standing at her door. Their eagerness was admirable.

Grace was always amazed at the young men from the Jehovah's Witness Church. Their consistent uniformity and 'scrubbed clean' ruddy complexions created a stereotype in her mind. The truth is that the Jehovah's Witness' send their best and brightest to evangelize for their faith. It is easy to respect their faithfulness in witnessing.

Unlike many, Grace had never been defensive or annoyed when a 'Witness' came to her door. However, she was intrigued that they would come to the dorms of an Episcopalian Seminary to evangelize. Now that Grace has found personal faith, she was especially empathetic toward these young men who were so zealous to please God.

Grace already knew the prepared introduction about sitting down to look over a few scriptures; sort of a mini bible study. She chose to meet with them outside to take the pressure off the prepackaged pitch and avoid the one sided presentation. Stepping out onto her front walkway, Grace was the first to speak as she greeted the young men. "Hi, my name is Grace Wheaton. May I get you a glass of cold water?"

Robert, the older of the two boys politely answered, "Oh, no thank you ma'am. We are in the neighborhood conducting bible studies. Would you be interested in knowing what the bible says about the things that are happening in our world today? If you have a few minutes we would like to sit down with you and share from God's word. Would that be O.K.?"

Grace felt compassion for the boys but for some reason God did not give her the burden which she had felt with Amy and Father Isaac. "And what are your names?" Grace respectfully asked.

Feeling more at ease, Robert gave more than his usual short answer. "I'm Robert and this is James. We travel together on a mission for two years so we can introduce people to God's word.

Grace graciously engaged her visitors. "Robert, James, I am blessed that you are so eager to serve God and willing to tell others of His great love. Before you leave may I pray with you?"

Robert, who seemed to be the spokesperson, stepped back to create more space between him and Grace. "That's O.K. ma'am we'll be on our way."

James wasn't so sure. "I think it would be O.K. if Ms. Wheaton prays for us, Robert."

In a big brother sort of rebuke, Robert insisted, "We're not supposed to, James; let's go. Good day ma'am."

Something within James didn't want to miss Grace's prayer. He appreciated her kindness and generosity that seemed genuine and tangible. James leaned in and earnestly appealed to Grace. "Ma'am, I'd like you to pray for me."

Grace calmly and graciously asked Robert if he would like to join them but Robert refused and took another half-step back. In a big sister way Grace asked, "James, would it be O.K. if I lay my hand on your shoulder?"

Timidly, James replied, "We're especially forbidden to allow that; sorry Ms. Wheaton."

Grace then reached for James' hand and he didn't

refuse. As she held his hand in prayer, she spoke God's blessing over James' life as well as Robert's. "Heavenly Father, thank You for Robert and James. They are good young men who seek to serve You; what a blessing they are. Lord, I ask You to reveal Yourself to them as You came to me only a few days ago. Lord, I ask You to draw them close to You and show them Your overflowing love that You have reserved for each of them. Lord, even as I speak, touch their lives with Your tender mercies and flood them with Your love. Holy Spirit, I give You permission to invade their lives with the Truth of Your Word and open their eyes to the fullness of Your Gospel. I ask this in Jesus' name. Amen."

When Grace looked up, Robert had stepped in closer only to retrace his steps just as Grace saw him. She smiled at Robert with such reverence that he became completely disarmed. Grace noticed that James had been silently weeping during the prayer. She knew that God was going to do a work in this young man's life. She also realized that today she was only a seed planter. Someone else would bring in the harvest of James' and Robert's souls. As the boys rode off on their bikes, Grace whispered under her breath, "What a wonderful God we serve."

As Grace made her way back to her dorm room, she recalled a statement that she had heard once which seemed to fit the moment: '*It is the love of God that brings man to repentance.*' Grace felt blessed to be a part of God's plan to draw those two boys to Himself. She was smiling as she reentered her dorm room and went straight to the answering machine to see who had called earlier.

"Grace, it's Father Isaac. Please call me when you get in."

When Grace returned Father Isaac's phone call, Andrea answered the phone and chatted with Grace until Father Isaac picked up. "Grace, can we meet today? I am preparing my report for Bishop Ivey and I would like to discuss how to frame this in the best possible way. Can you come?"

Grace was willing to meet with Father Isaac but she was hungry and needed to eat. "Do I have time to grab a quick lunch?"

"Certainly, come when you can," replied Father Isaac.

Chapter Seven

Upended

It had already been a glorious day. Grace's future seemed to be opening up before her in an unfolding revelation of God's goodness. She thought to herself: How can it get any better than this?

Instead of walking, Grace chose to drive her little red Toyota Tercel to Café Express—a delightful delicatessen located just off the boulevard ten blocks past the church. About halfway to the restaurant, Grace checked her rearview mirror for traffic. As she looked up, she saw what appeared to be a crumpled bicycle, in her peripheral vision, on the opposite side of the boulevard. Grace became anxious as she contemplated the possibility that Robert and James were still in the neighborhood.

Grace quickly eased over into the left lane so she could make a U-turn at the next opening in the median. As happens in these tense moments, everything seemed to be happening in slow motion. Making her way back, she saw the bent wheel of an upended bicycle.

Curious onlookers had started to gather so Grace had to carefully navigate around several bystanders as she pulled over to the curb. She could now hear sirens coming from behind her as she approached the accident site. She could not see anyone who would have been a rider; only the mangled bicycle. When she got out of her car, she noticed that Robert and James were huddled under a nearby shade tree engaged in, what appeared to be, a heated exchange.

As Grace approached them, Robert wanted to avoid her and began walking away. James was in protest over Robert's actions and began to go after him. It was apparent Robert was injured as he was limping badly and holding his arm. James slowed his pace a little allowing Grace to catch up to his stride.

Out of breath, spent with emotion and trauma, James grasped Grace's arm to signal a stop. Before catching up to the injured Robert, James wanted to enlighten Grace to their plight. "We're *not allowed* to get hurt on the mission field and Robert is blaming you and me for this. He thinks that by allowing you to pray for us we are being punished so that we'll be found-out by the elders."

As the ambulance approached, several bystanders pointed in the direction of James and Robert who were still on the extra wide median. The ambulance slowly made its way along the curb to catch up with Robert just as he gave in and stopped his retreat. He was in pain and near shock, no longer able to stand. As the EMT's approached to give first aid, Robert proceeded to lie down on the grass.

James implored them to not render aid because they were forbidden unless it was a life or death circumstance. The ambulance technician knew that Robert needed medical attention so he instructed James, "Sorry son, we cannot by law, leave this scene and not render aid as we see it at this time."

As Robert lay on the ground, he was trying to refuse the EMT's help but could not gather his words together enough to make sense. The always professional paramedics began preparing Robert for the ride to the hospital. Since they did not know the extent of Robert's injuries, he was painstakingly fitted with a neck brace and carefully strapped to a special trauma board.

With all the extra effort, Robert appeared to have passed out by the time he was loaded into the ambulance. As it began to drive away, you could see the paramedics working on

Robert through the large rear windows of the ambulance. He was being fitted with I.V. tubing as well as wiring to monitor his vital signs. It was at this point that James howled, "We can't take blood transfusions."

Grace could see the terror in James expression so she acted quickly to assuage his fears. "James, I'll take you to the hospital and we can let them know your concerns—I'm sure they'll understand." Grace needed to snap James out of a daze. "*Let's go!* We need to get to the hospital." James jumped in the car expressing fearful dread.

Even in his frightened state, he was also deeply grateful that there had been someone present to help and offer a calming force to this day gone awry. Tearfully, James offered, "Ms. Wheaton, thank you for helping us. I don't know what we would have done if you hadn't shown up."

Before Grace pulled into traffic she leaned over to James to get his full attention. "James, everything is going to be just fine. You have my word on it."

"God knows everything that happens to us and trust me, He is with us right now…"

"How can you know that?" James asked in the childlike tone of a six-year-old who was scared of what lay ahead.

Grace pulled into traffic as

she continued to speak to James. "God knows everything that happens to us and trust me; He is with us right now. He knows your concerns and your fears. Just take a moment and ask Him to help you face your fears; to be with you and give you strength."

After several minutes of focused attention on the traffic, Grace glanced over to look at James who was still in a prayerful posture. His lips were moving and his face was sincere as he petitioned God.

Grace found a close in parking space in the otherwise crowded emergency room parking lot. In the strain of the moment, she leapt from the car forgetting her purse. She made an acrobatic reach for her purse, grabbing it by the straps. Her purse snatching gymnastics were reminiscent of a relay runner half-stepping for a second grab of the all-important baton. By now, James had made it to the lightning quick automatic doors of the emergency room entrance; disappearing out of sight. Even though Grace was an accomplished runner her adrenaline was not pumping like James.'

Grace caught up with James at the E.R. information desk just as he was being given an identification wristband. Ignoring Grace as she approached him, James turned to enter the triage area. With a stern but protective tone, Grace told James to stop. "James, you need me. Come here and wait while

I get a wristband." James instinctively knew what she meant. In his panic he was no good to anybody and would probably make things worse.

Grace and James located Robert in ER 4C; a typical emergency room alcove with curtains partially drawn. James was relieved to see that Robert had not been given a blood transfusion, which helped him calm down. The ER nurse approached the cubicle and indicated that the doctor would see Robert next.

Grace studied James as he stared at his friend who was still semiconscious. She couldn't help but notice how James looked so young and innocent in this scary and uncertain moment. Grace spoke with comforting assurance, "James, everything's going to be just fine."

He replied in a clear but emotionally spent tone, "I know that now... I prayed to God for the first time today... I mean I *really* prayed."

Grace could see that James' distress level had subsided and he was in a more rational state. Seeing an opportunity to make an important phone call, Grace asked James if he would be alright for a few minutes. James was feeling much better as he smiled and nodded in a reassuring gesture.

Grace needed to call Father Isaac to let him know what had happened and why she hadn't come when she agreed.

Using the phone at the hospital information desk, she called the number to Father Isaac's office. "Andrea, is Father Isaac still there?"

In her usual sweetly efficient tone Andrea replied, "Yes, but he is worried about you. I'll let him know you're on the line."

Father Isaac was relieved to hear that it was Grace on the phone. "Is everything O.K.?"

Grace felt too rushed to fully explain everything that had happened so she asked to postpone their meeting. "Father Isaac I'm sorry that I stood-you-up but something happened that prevented me from coming. Can we get together tomorrow morning at nine a.m.? I can explain what happened then."

Father Isaac could sense the urgency in Grace's voice so he kept it brief. "See you in the morning, Grace."

"Thanks Father Isaac... be praying for me." Grace disliked being so brief but under the circumstances she felt it was necessary.

As Grace headed back to Robert's cubicle, she rounded the corner just as the doctor stepped out from behind the privacy curtain. "Oh Doctor, I'm Grace Wheaton and I know these boys. What can you tell me about Robert's condition?"

The doctor informed Grace in a matter-of-fact tone, "I'm sorry Ms. Wheaton but the boys just left." With a gasp,

Grace turned on her heel to run after them. Before she could take a step, the doctor grabbed her arm. "Ms. Wheaton, the boys are fine; I examined Robert. There were no head injuries and his rib cage is intact. His arm is awfully scraped up but it's not broken. He was more afraid of me than of his injuries, so I released him without any paperwork—*I let him go as if he had never been here; do you understand?*"

The doctor held Grace's arm while she processed what he said. He looked-her-in-the-eyes and then gave her a slight nod. The doctor turned to go to his next patient when Grace returned the favor and grabbed his arm. He turned to face Grace only to be greeted with a sternly inquisitive facial expression that begged, why? The doctor knew exactly what those boys were facing. "I was once a Jehovah's Witness on a mission. I know what this means to them. They'll be O.K... Now let them be."

Chapter Eight

The Traditions of Men

The storm slipped in overnight when no one was expecting it. The sheets of rain were coming down in waves; sometimes horizontal as the wind swept over the two story dorm buildings. The flatter areas of the lawn were at least ankle deep as the water failed to move quickly enough to keep from backing up and standing. Grace couldn't remember the last time it had rained so hard. Timidly peering out the front window, still wearing her robe, she wrapped herself in an anxious self-hug.

Grace was contemplating making the trip to the church but wasn't sure she wanted to risk going out during the storm.

She decided to call the church to let Father Isaac know she didn't feel safe coming in during this downpour. "Andrea, may I speak with Father Isaac?"

Andrea was distracted with the noise and commotion of the storm but managed to speak to Grace. "I'm sorry but Father Isaac hasn't made it in yet and he hasn't called. You had a nine o'clock didn't you?"

Grace replied, "Yes, but I'm afraid that I'm stuck at home with this heavy rain."

Andrea had come to work early avoiding the current windstorm and torrential rain. The church building was taking a beating especially on the west side where Andrea's office was located. She understood Grace's dilemma and assured her to stay put until the storm was over.

Just as Andrea was putting the phone in the cradle, she screamed. A tree limb came crashing through the leaded glass window located in the hallway between Father Isaac's office and hers. Grace heard the startling scream just as the phone line clicked on her end. She redialed several times but kept getting the 'busy circuits' signal. Not knowing what could have happened, Grace had no choice but to get to the church. Near panic, Grace dressed and then climbed into her rain slicker and boots.

An umbrella would be of no use in this type of storm so

she debated on whether to take the time to search for the rain slicker hat—like the saltbox girl wears. She found the large droopy hat on the first try and was out the door.

The rain had let up a little but was still a deluge by anyone's description. By the time she made it to her car the rain had subsided even more so she felt better. Even still, Grace needed to get to the church as fast as possible. She was really concerned about Andrea and needed to make sure she was O.K.

Just so Grace would know the storm wasn't over, the wind severely buffeted her car several more times in the eight blocks to the church. As Grace pulled under the massive portico she could see a large tree limb jutting through the church office window. The front entry doors were still locked so Grace had to wade through standing water to reach the side door where the staff parked and entered the building. It was only a light sprinkle by the time she approached the side door.

Grace reached Andrea's office to find her struggling with the oversized mop. "Andrea, are you all right?" Andrea had already retrieved the large yellow mop cart that the janitorial crew used to clean the floors. In all the fluster and chaos, Andrea forgot that the rain soaked alcove was carpeted and a mop wasn't going to be very useful.

Andrea quickly turned to see Grace in her bright yellow raingear and apologetically said, "Oh Grace, I'm so sorry about the scream. I immediately knew what you must have thought. I was never in any danger. I was just startled by the crash and the noise."

Relieved, Grace shifted into her efficient and in-charge mode. "Andrea, let's call Mr. Lopez and see if he can come in to vacuum the water and board up that window."

"Oh honey, I'm way ahead of you; he's on his way here now." Putting away the mop, Andrea gave up on her fruitless efforts and threw some towels on the floor.

Father Isaac was soaking wet by the time he reached the church building. He had been caught in the very worst of the downpour. He looked like the proverbial 'drowned rat' as he stepped into Andrea's front office. In a slightly sarcastic tone, Father Isaac greeted Andrea and Grace. "Good morning ladies, which one of you ordered the rain?" His humor really lessened the gloom of the moment—a welcomed diversion.

Father Isaac kept a full wardrobe in his office-suite. He was headed to his office when he asked, "Andrea, have you called anyone to assess the damage to the building?"

Neither of the two ladies had thought about the broader scope of things, besides surveying storm damage wasn't exactly within Andrea's job description. She politely replied, "Only Mr. Lopez to cleanup this mess."

Father Isaac had seen some missing roof tiles as he

walked in and suspected more damage. He especially wanted to avoid any further loss caused by roof leaks. "Look up our insurance agent and give him a call. Ask for his claim adjuster as well as an independent appraiser, ASAP." Father Isaac had been in a similar storm damage claim years earlier and learned that an independent appraiser was essential on a large property like St. Matthew's.

Before retreating to his office and closing the door, Father Isaac turned his attention to Grace and asked in an almost cheerful tone, "Grace, can you give me about twenty minutes to shower and change clothes? Oh, and could you put on a pot of coffee?—I'm chilled to the bone."

Grace couldn't believe how upbeat and... well... genuinely happy Father Isaac appeared, considering the circumstances. Grace was not a coffee drinker but had brewed plenty for her parents and for guests. "Yes sir. I'll be happy to make you some coffee."

After a quick twenty minutes, Father Isaac stepped back into his office dressed in a dark blue suit. He had changed into a normal business suit which was a bit unusual for a day spent at the church. Grace inquired, "Father Isaac, do you have business elsewhere today? You don't look the same without your vestments."

Father Isaac's posture and demeanor was inspiring to

behold. "Grace, I don't feel the same. I feel as if I've been set free. I'm sleeping better and this morning in my normal time of devotions I actually talked to the Lord as if He were my friend and confidant. It is a wonderful life we live in the Lord. I feel happier than I have felt in many years." At that moment Grace could see that his countenance confirmed what he was saying. Father Isaac was truly happy and deeply settled.

Grace wanted to delve deeper into the possible meaning for Father Isaac not wearing his vestments. "Well, I have to ask you… does the lack of proper dress mean anything else?"

Father Isaac seemed ready to talk about the supposed mystery. "It is interesting that you should pose that question. I have been asking myself that very thing. Let me tell you what I read this morning that has a lot to do with my mood. I think it will help you understand. In Matthew 15:9, I saw this whole situation, that you and I face, opened up right before my eyes.

> *"I have been trying to live the traditions of man and in the process denied the power of God in His Word."*

Here is what it says: *"And in vain they worship Me, teaching as doctrines the commandments of men."* Then I followed the reference to Mark 7:13 which reads, *"…making the word of God of no effect through your tradition which you have handed down. And many such things you do."*

Father Isaac was excited as he shared the feelings of freedom he had experienced from the truth of God's Word. "Grace, this is where I have been living for all of these years. I have been trying to live the traditions of man and in the process denied the power of God in His Word. These verses describe our predicament."

Father Isaac's 'take' on the 'traditions of men' was something Grace hadn't considered for herself. She enjoyed the formality, the liturgy and ceremonial traditions of the church. That is one reason she chose St. Matthew's as her church and for her study. However, she could now see the effect it might have on the clergy who had to perform and live with the tenets and covenants of such formalities. She could also see how being freed from the restrictive manmade traditions could be liberating. Grace asked Father Isaac her first thought. "What do you think this will mean to your standing with Bishop Ivey and the leadership within the diocese?"

Father Isaac was not considering anything beyond his current sense of freedom and contentment. He thought for a few minutes before he responded. "Our diocese is one of the most liberal in the country so I don't think there is a problem with stepping outside a particular norm. However, it may mean that I will have to compromise and be more vocal on other issues that I don't agree with."

As he spoke, Father Isaac was realizing that his answer was more along the lines of thinking out loud. He was considering among other things, what it would mean to discontinue the meaningless tradition of wearing his vestments.

Father Isaac continued, "There will undoubtedly be tradeoffs that I will have to make if I stay with St. Matthew's. Liberal issues that I have avoided will now be forced upon me as a consolation." These vocal deductions were now becoming the new reality as he looked at Grace and voiced his latest musings. "Grace, I'm not sure it's worth it; the compromises I'll have to live with every day."

Grace was beginning to see that Father Isaac's pending crisis was much bigger than the two of them realized. Even so, Grace could envision an upside to His staying as the officiating priest of St. Matthew's. Without hesitation she put a positive spin on the otherwise difficult situation. "Father Isaac, if you stay, St. Matthew's could *truly* become your mission field. Think of the facts. The people here know you, trust you and you are well loved. If you were to leave, it would take years to achieve the same level of influence that you have here. Consider what God could accomplish with you here at St. Matthew's. God brought you to Himself for a purpose. I believe He has you here and wants to use you here at St.

Matthew's."

Father Isaac hesitated momentarily in thought. "Grace, I believe you are absolutely right on. How could I have been so blind to the obvious?" Father Isaac was now on a new track with his thinking and was trying to consider all the possibilities as well as the potential problems he would face. "Grace, you're right… I will stay… I must stay. But… I will not compromise on any point. I will be true to the Lord and not to any man who wants to diminish the truth of God's Word. I'll stay as long as I can under those conditions. I will be God's man-of-the-hour for this church until He sovereignly moves me. I trust myself into His hands."

Grace was witnessing the courage of a man who had been truly changed by the Lord. She didn't mention it but Father Isaac's nervous habit of blinking under stress, was gone. Grace was genuinely inspired by Father Isaac and wanted to express her gratitude for his mettle. "Father Isaac, your courage and determination are commendable. I'm glad I know you and have you as my pastor."

Father Isaac humbly accepted Grace's esteem. "Thank you Grace, you have been a great encouragement to me as well."

Father Isaac continued with the matter at hand as he shared his thoughts with Grace on how to proceed with the report. "Grace, I'm going to file my report with Bishop Ivey and give him the whole truth and nothing but the truth. I believe God will honor the truth of His Word and, as you brought out, will bring a harvest here at St. Matthew's. As for you young lady, as your pastor, I release you into the harvest field that God has prepared for you. We both know that it is not here at St. Matthew's. However, you must promise to stay in close touch with me and continue to pray for me."

A week ago, a pronouncement of *'you must go'* might have been a hurtful if not an offensive statement. As it turns out, Grace was relieved that Father Isaac spoke with such heartfelt clarity. The truth is that Grace hadn't been sure how to broach the subject of her departure since she had decided, early in the morning, that she would be leaving St. Matthew's. Seeing the certainty of God's control and direction in her life, she was thrilled to be in the center of His will.

"Father Isaac, thank you for your understanding and goodwill towards me. Would it be alright if I go and gather my personal belongings? I have some things in the changing room as well as the study?"

Father Isaac was quick to reassure Grace that there was no hurry to her pending departure. "Grace, you don't have to leave this minute."

"Oh, its O.K., I wanted to leave as soon as we had

discussed the details of your report. Actually, you helped me through the difficult moment of telling you that I was planning to leave. Thank you for that."

Father Isaac, in a consolatory tone, agreed to Grace's request. "Well yes, gather your things and I will help you get them to your car."

For some reason, Grace wanted to walk out the door alone. In her mind's eye she just saw it that way. "That's O.K., I only have a few things that I can easily carry—not much at all. Besides, I'm not going anywhere soon. This really isn't a permanent goodbye; we're just turning the page."

Father Isaac felt a little awkward but relented. "If you're sure, then by all means."

Before leaving, Grace had one last request. "Father Isaac, I'll need to be moving out of the dorm by the fifteenth…"

Father Isaac interrupted Grace midsentence. "Grace, take as long as you need in the dorm. I have the authority to extend that privilege as long as is necessary."

Grateful, Grace replied, "Thank you Father Isaac. My plan is to get a short term job for the summer or at least until my dad gets back from his mission trip. When he gets back, I would like to spend some time with him and get his counsel. The extra time in the dorm would be very helpful, thank you.

Please tell Andrea that I will see her soon and I won't leave without saying goodbye."

With that, Father Isaac stood and gave Grace a pastoral hug and walked her to his office door. As he stood in the doorway, he watched as Grace walked down the hall toward the study. He thought of all of the incredible things that had transpired in the last week. "Amazing," he said under his breath.

Chapter Nine

Lord Help Us

Grace retrieved her books and files from the study as well as some liturgical garments from the changing room. As she stepped outside the front entry she couldn't help but notice that almost all signs of a storm were gone. Except for a few puddles of standing water, and of course the tree limb, it was hard to imagine that just a few hours earlier a storm raged with such destructive fury. Now, the day was bright and sunny. A fitting metaphor for her new beginning that was unfolding at that very moment.

Her car was still parked under the portico just as she had left it earlier that morning. As Grace began putting her things in the back seat, she noticed a young Hispanic couple coming toward her. The teenage girl was crying and in obvious pain as the young man held her—trying to comfort her as they approached Grace. The teenage boy was upset and asked Grace for help. "Lady, are you a nun? We need a nun."

With concern Grace replied, "No, there are no nuns here. How can I help you?"

Antonio quickly introduced himself and Maria with the hopeful expectancy of a scared youth. Estranged from their parents, Antonio and Maria were young lovers who had been living together, as much as possible, for almost a year. Last fall, Maria's strict and devout Catholic parents realized that her relationship with Antonio had gotten out of control. They tried to break up their relationship but that turned out to be impossible. When Maria became pregnant and began 'showing' in early March, her parents were incensed with anger and disappointment. Feeling no other choice, they kicked her out of the home.

Antonio and Maria were left to fend for themselves; wherever or however they could. Things hadn't been too bad as Maria's Uncle Philippe had allowed them to stay with him until they could afford an apartment. Antonio had proved to be a hard worker able to get regular construction day-jobs. Just as motivated, Maria planned on graduating early from high school under a special program for unwed mothers. She wanted to be at home to raise her baby.

During the worst part of the morning's storm, Maria started to experience severe abdominal pains. Barely seven months pregnant, she and Antonio were near panic. Antonio was delirious with fear and worry for Maria. "I don't care about the baby! Save Maria!" Grace ignored the fearful remark because she felt that under normal circumstances, he wouldn't have said it.

"Antonio, Maria, we need to contact your parents, let's go inside and call them."

Antonio quickly snapped back, "No, they hate us. They'll just yell at us some more. We can make it without their anger. Let's go Maria."

Reaching out to grasp Grace's hand, Maria painfully squeaked, "Antonio, please, we need this lady's help. I'm hurting and I want to save my baby." Turning to face Grace, Maria continued, "My parents are Renaldo and Julia Padilla. Call them please, hurry!"

Grace helped Antonio ease Maria into the front seat of the car. She then ran inside repeating the phone number in her mind so she wouldn't forget it. Grace began speaking even before she reached the open door to Andrea's office. "Andrea, I need to use the phone, quickly." Grace dialed the Padilla's number and fortunately a woman picked-up on the first ring.

In broken English, the young lady who answered indicated that the Padilla's would be out for the rest of the morning. Grace left a message for Maria's parents indicating that she was taking Maria to the emergency room at Seattle General Hospital, Southwest Branch.

Grace wanted to contact Antonio's parents too but he still refused to allow them to be involved. Grace did the only thing she knew to do and that was to drive the young expectant couple to the ER at Southwest General.

It was déjà vu for Grace as she entered the doors of the emergency room for the second time in two days. Once Grace helped them with the admission process, she asked to be excused so she could call Father Isaac. Maria's pain had subsided. With the welcomed relief, she nodded for Grace to go ahead.

It seemed as though the payphone was in the noisiest part of the emergency room waiting area. Grace had to cover her ear so that she could hear. "Andrea, this is Grace. Is Father Isaac still in?"

"Yes, please hold." Andrea knew this was not a time to chat so she put Grace on hold and buzzed Father Isaac. When he didn't pick up, she quickly dashed into his office to find out why. Father Isaac had left a note on his desk and then apparently left using his private door. The note read: *'Had to leave. Hope to be back this afternoon.'* In all the years Andrea had worked for Father Isaac this was the first time he had left without letting her know. This was completely out of character for him.

Returning to the phone Andrea exclaimed, "Grace, Father Isaac has left and I don't know where he's gone. I'm worried."

Grace quickly updated Andrea on the situation with Maria and Antonio. "Would you give Father Isaac the information as soon as you see him?"

"Grace, do you want me to come to the hospital after I lockup?"

"Andrea you are wonderful. I'm sure we'll be here for a while but page me before you come."

The ER nurse had just finished checking Maria's vital signs when Grace returned to the admission area. Since the initial triage procedure indicated that the baby was not in danger, Antonio and Maria were sent to the waiting room to be called. As the three made their way to waiting area, Grace asked, "Maria, do you mind if I stay with you for a while or at least until your parents arrive?"

Feeling much better, Maria graciously replied, "That would be so kind of you. You have already done so much and we appreciate everything."

Grace went to the vending area to find some snacks and upon returning, she saw Antonio and Maria quietly talking. As Grace watched from a distance, she couldn't help but notice their loving gestures and 'grownup' appearance. Grace was now realizing how well-mannered this young couple was. She suspected that they had been raised in good homes and knew right from wrong. Feeling they needed a little space and some time alone to sort through their situation, Grace stood back and waited. After a long pause in their conversation, Grace approached the seating area.

> *"...He's kind of the black sheep in our family and has been looking out for us—he understands about being rejected."*

Taking the seat next to Maria, Grace queried, "Maria, I couldn't help from hearing that you live very close to the church."

In a surprisingly upbeat tone, Maria replied, "Yes, we are staying with my Uncle Philippe. He's kind of the black sheep in our family and has been looking out for us—he understands about being rejected. Uncle Philippe is real nice to us but all of his friends are really rough so we want to leave as soon as we can."

Antonio chimed in wanting to make a point of his own. "We wanted to pay rent to Uncle Philippe but he wouldn't take our money so we've been saving to get our own place. By the way Grace, I'm sorry for what I said about not caring whether the baby lived. I want this baby as much as Maria; please forgive me."

Grace, in a much older sounding even motherly tone, replied, "I understand Antonio; you love Maria very much."

As if on cue, Maria let out a scream as she experienced a sharp pain in her abdomen. A startled Grace ran to the admissions desk to plead for immediate help. "Can we please see a doctor, now?" Before Grace reached the desk, the admissions staff-nurse was already on the phone requesting a gurney for Maria. "Thank you, Lord!" Grace exclaimed under her breath with heartfelt gratefulness.

Under the tense uncertain circumstances, Grace was remarkably calm. "Maria, they're coming with a gurney to take you back so that you can be examined. Just hang in there for us." Maria wailed again in pain. Without asking, Grace placed her hand over Maria's expanded belly. In a grateful and expectant gesture, Maria quickly placed both of her hands over Grace's hand. Grace began to pray, not in a quiet and peaceful cadence, but in a confidant exuberance intended to counter the tone of Maria's pain.

Spiritually, metaphorically speaking, Grace was giving birth as she prayed that God would bring life where the appearance of death was trying to take a foothold. This was not a time for timidity as Grace began to pray "Lord, help us... " As Grace continued to pray, the admissions nurse came over and put her hand on Maria's shoulder and joined in prayer. The whole waiting room seemed to be on alert as an older couple, sitting in the corner, began to pray silently for Maria.

The gurney arrived just as Grace finished asking God to be glorified; stating that His healing touch would be a testimony of His goodness and mercy. The male nurse was all business as he curtly directed Grace and Antonio, "Please move away ma'am. You need to give us room to work." The nurse was a little gruff but he didn't have time for niceties.

As Maria was being wheeled away, Nancy, the admissions nurse would only allow Antonio to go with Maria. Nancy had now become a kindred spirit with Grace and a 'friend' in only a few short moments. "Grace, I'll call you back as soon as the ER nurse will allow it."

Grace slumped into a waiting room chair, emotionally exhausted. Going over in her mind all of the nonstop action, she thought: this has been a day, *no, two days,* for the record books. Grace envisioned a moment of respite, a time to rest her eyes and try to calm down. But it was not to be. Renaldo and Julia Padilla came bolting through the emergency room doors.

Julia Padilla was a heavyset woman. There was no

hesitation in her momentum as she briskly walked toward the admission desk flailing her arms in a hysterical manner. Her oversized handbag would have been a lethal weapon if anyone had been in her way. "My baby! My baby! Where's my baby?" Mr. Padilla wasn't far behind.

By the time Grace made it to the admissions desk, to greet the Padilla's, Julia was being escorted back to see Maria. Renaldo was left standing as he was advised that it was best for his daughter if he waited in the waiting room.

"Mr. Padilla? Hi, I'm Grace Wheaton. I brought Antonio and Maria to the emergency room."

Renaldo's expression went from concern to that of anger. "That no good lowlife—is he here?"

Grace took that challenge head-on as she tried to redirect his misguided anger. "Mr. Padilla, Antonio is the father of your grandchild and he loves Maria very much."

"How could he? He's shacked up with my little girl no telling where and under what conditions."

Grace needed to bring the conversation under control for the sake of Maria. "Please hear me sir, for the welfare of your daughter and your grandchild. Can you please put your disappointment aside for now?"

Having heard the word grandchild for the second time, it finally came through to Renaldo. "I'm sorry; it's not like me to carry on like that. It has been very difficult since our Maria's been gone, she's so young and we miss her."

Grace was relieved to see this doting father calm down. "I'm sure everything will be fine with Maria and the baby. Maybe this is an opportunity for the family to come together and support her so the baby can come into this world under better circumstances."

Renaldo was won over but he still wanted to have a say in the matter. "You're right but that puny little kid is going to marry my Maria and keep his nose clean—none of this shacking-up stuff."

Chapter Ten

Broken Hearts

Earlier that Morning: Father Isaac stood at his office window in hopes of catching a glimpse of Grace as she was leaving. He was going to miss her. She had become like a daughter to him and now she was leaving. He picked up on her desire to leave unceremoniously so he reluctantly agreed.

As Father Isaac watched for Grace, he noticed a young couple walk up the sidewalk toward the church entrance. Once they approached the portico ensconced entrance, his line of sight did not allow him to see their interaction with Grace.

Father Isaac quickly made his way to the front vestibule

to see if what he suspected was true. From his close up vantage point, he definitely recognized Antonio in the back seat of Grace's car. Father Isaac's knew what he had to do—he had found Antonio Ramirez.

Somehow, Grace's trip, to use the phone in Andrea's front office, was timed perfectly to miss Father Isaac as he went to identify Antonio. He went around using the staff hallway, from his private door, as Grace came around from the public entrance to Andrea's office. Amusingly, the same scenario happened in reverse when he went back to his office to write the note for Andrea. It was as choreographed as any slapstick comedy ever produced by early Hollywood. The routine offered a bit of comic relief even though unnoticed by mere mortals.

Father Isaac had known the Ramirez family most of his adult life. He was there when Antonio was born and involved with him and his family on a many special occasions. Almost nine months ago Antonio 'ran away.' Julio and Cristina Ramirez were dear friends but they would not give any details of Antonio's disappearance. Father Isaac knew there was more to the story but was cutoff when he probed to find out how he could help. In a moment of anger, Julio even went further and insisted that Father Isaac forget about Antonio. Now, having seen Antonio, Father Isaac felt he needed to try to meet with the Ramirez's.

The mystery of Antonio's disappearance actually began when the Ramirez's moved to Tacoma, Washington, just south of Seattle, over a year ago. Julio needed to take a promotion with his company so the move to Tacoma was not optional. As with any high school senior, the pending move to Tacoma was upsetting. Antonio initially refused to leave the hometown where he grew up. The family pulled together and made plans for Antonio to stay with his uncle during the week so he could finish his senior year. The arrangement worked out well for everyone. Over the summer, after Antonio graduated, he slowly began to make his transition to Tacoma to live with his parents.

That's when Antonio met Maria and his world turned upside down. To say that he was smitten would be an understatement. He began to spend more time in his old neighborhood with friends, and less time in Tacoma with his parents. Every spare minute was devoted to Maria, at least as much as her parents would allow. Then one morning last October Maria's parents became suspicious when they found Antonio sleeping in his truck in front of their house. When confronted, he quickly drove off.

Maria's parents wrongly speculated that he must be homeless or an itinerant worker. Maria was called-on to explain the aberrant occurrence but she froze in fear of her sometimes harsh and over protective parents. "No daughter of ours was going to be seen with a migrant worker." Maria was forbidden to see Antonio at all. Maria also knew that if her parents found out that Antonio was defying his parents it would be all over. This was not how she was raised.

Maria was torn between her parents and Antonio's dying devotion to her. Despite bouts of strictness, she had a good upbringing with loving parents who doted over her. She was especially close to her mother and had always been honest and open with her. Maria decided to tell the whole truth no matter what the outcome would be. Her parents had taught her that transparency and honesty were very important in any relationship. Now was the time to find out if that was true.

The evening of Antonio's early morning escape, Maria asked if she could talk to both of her parents about a very important matter. "Mom, dad, I would like to explain what has being going on with Antonio and me. I want you to get to know him. It's not what you think… the migrant worker stuff. …"

Meanwhile, Antonio's parents were becoming increasingly upset as they began to lose track of him. By October, he began a cat and mouse affair with his parents who were trying to catch-up to him. Antonio was able to stay ahead of the phone calls that his parents were making to his friends.

Even his cousin Jaime was put on notice to report Antonio's whereabouts.

Then early one October morning, Antonio was caught in front of Maria's house, sleeping in his truck. He decided to go home and lay low for a while. He figured that Maria would be in trouble and he didn't want to make it any worse for her. Once he got home he would write to her with a plan on how they could be together. Unlike Maria, talking to his parents was out of the question. In his mind, talking was nothing more than a yelling match and it never went his way. Even so, he needed a place to stay so he was going to have to act better—even if it was only to get what he wanted.

As he was driving toward home, Antonio was mentally rehearsing how he would greet his parents when his Ford Ranger truck just quit running. This was the first time his truck had given him trouble—it had always run perfectly. He checked the gas gauge which still showed a quarter-of-a-tank.

Checking the gas gauge reminded him that his dad had not yet cut-him-off the Shell gas card given to him three years ago. Suddenly, the truck lurched forward and hummed as smoothly as ever. Then an unexpected thought just popped into his head. It was a memory verse, from a catechism class, he learned years ago. *"It is painful to be the parent of a fool; there is no joy for the father of a rebel."*

A fearful dread came over Antonio as he realized that, yes, he had been playing the fool. His parents were strict but they had always been generous with him and up until this summer they had complete trust in Him; allowing him wide leeway in the decisions he made. A heavy guilt was almost suffocating him as pulled into the driveway.

Antonio carefully parked his truck making sure he didn't take too much of the driveway; an often heard complaint from his dad. He retrieved the key from atop of the porch light and slipped in the side door under the carport. His dad would be home in a few hours and he needed to decide how he was going to step back into their lives. The sudden remembrance of the verse out of Proverbs had humbled him but he didn't know what to expect from his mom and dad.

Antonio heard the kitchen door, leading to the carport, open and shut. He knew that his dad had seen his truck so there would be no surprise. Antonio jumped from the couch and headed for the kitchen to make the most of the reunion after weeks of dodging his parents. His last thought was: *I wish mom was here.* Then the lights went out—Julio had had enough.

> *His last thought was: I wish mom was here. Then the lights went out—Julio had had enough.*

Julio Ramirez had been an undefeated Golden Gloves boxer in his late teens and was known in those days for his violent temper. Every fight was won because he worked himself into a rage before the fight. Then, while in his early twenties, Julio's mother died. The death of his mother was traumatic for Julio causing him to lose heart and enter into a lifeless existence. After her death, nothing ever made him angry or happy; he was just numb.

Antonio had never seen his dad's anger; only a somewhat lethargic man who seemed to be just coping. If a problem arose his dad's first response was to reach for his wallet to make it go away. This pseudo generosity was a mask for his pain.

Julio grabbed a wet wash cloth and tossed it onto the prone Antonio so that it flopped on his face. The emotionless Julio leaned back against the counter and crossed his arms to wait for Antonio to come to. With a painful moan, Antonio asked, "Dad… is that you?"

Antonio's vision was blurry with bright white spots in the center of his sight. Julio did not answer but just looked on as his son struggled on the floor. Not even knowing what happened, Antonio groped for his dad and finally was able to get up. He stumbled over to his dad and threw his arms around him. "Dad, I'm so sorry. I'll never do anything like this again. I love you so much." As Antonio uttered those words he collapsed in his dad's arms.

Chapter Eleven

A Friend in Need

Back to the day of the storm—Tacoma. Father Isaac's timing was perfect. He pulled up to the Ramirez's house minutes before they arrived home from Cristina's doctor appointment. Julio had taken the day off from work to be with his wife while she had a M.R.I. scan on her head and neck. Cristina had been suffering with ever increasing migraine headaches and her primary care physician thought it was time to do further testing.

Father Isaac had been prepared to wait in his car until Julio made it home from work but his midday arrival was much better. Julio parked the van and walked Cristiana toward the side door under the carport. He had her huddled under his arms as if protecting her from an unknown harm. That's when Julio noticed Father Isaac as he got out of his car and walked briskly towards them.

Father Isaac was in a business suit and somehow didn't look the same to anybody who knew him. For all practical purposes he looked like an insurance salesman so Julio hurried a little quicker to avoid having to brushoff the stranger.

"Julio, it's me, Father Isaac. May I talk with you?" Julio stopped but didn't respond immediately. The visual image in his mind had to catch up with the sound of a familiar voice.

"Father Isaac, longtime no see. What brings you to Tacoma?"

Father Isaac anxiously exclaimed, "It's important. Can we talk?"

Julio invited Father Isaac to come in and sit while he helped Cristina into bed. The medical center had to use a tranquilizer to get her to calm down in the close confines of the M.R.I. machine. She would be drowsy for a few more hours.

Julio had barely reentered the front room when Father Isaac began speaking. He felt the urgency to give his findings to Julio without the normal small talk. "I saw Antonio this morning." Julio broke down crying on the spot. He had taken the brunt of this long drawn out dilemma upon himself.

Julio had kept the heart wrenching events, of last October, to himself. He was the only one who knew what transpired that evening. When he knocked his son unconscious, Antonio apparently suffered amnesia from being hit so hard. And Cristina never questioned what might have caused the bruises.

Unknown to Julio, Antonio was jolted into remembering about three weeks later. Antonio saw his mom and dad arguing in the kitchen. Julio was leaning against the kitchen counter with his arms crossed. As Antonio looked on, everything came rushing back to him. All of the information that had been processed by his five senses, that had been repressed, began to flood back. As if in slow motion, he could see the images unfold beginning the split second before his dad's fist hit him. All the sensations were being revealed as if for the first time. He could hear the sound of his jaw popping and then the commotion as he hit the floor. He could feel the sensations of pain and then the wet rag hitting his face.

Antonio went flush with anger and stormed out of the

house and that was the last time His parents had seen him in nine months—that's when he 'ran away.'

However, in the terrible moment when Julio hit his son, something broken in Julio began to heal. He was no longer numb and emotionless. His lethargy had given way to emotional mood swings. Often easily brought to tears since that night he struck Antonio—the night he had shamed himself. He was definitely a changed man but was it for the better? Sometimes, he seemed like a pot ready to boil over.

Julio was expressionless as he slowly sat down on the sofa next to his unexpected but welcomed visitor. Speaking what was foremost on his mind, Julio lamented, "Father Isaac, Cristina's sick. The doctor thinks she has a tumor that's causing the migraines. We're going to be admitting her next week if the M.R.I. and other tests confirm the doctor's best guess." Pausing for a moment to find the words and push back the shame, he quietly asked, "Tell me about Antonio... is he O.K.?"

Moved with compassion for his dear friends, Father Isaac told Julio what he knew. "Antonio was at the church this morning just after the storm letup. He was with a young girl. I'm not sure but I think she might have been expecting—she looked pregnant. She was holding her abdomen and seemed to be in pain. One of our interns was trying to help them. I knew they were in good hands so I left immediately to come here and see if I could get you to come."

Julio was in a dilemma with Cristina being sick. He didn't feel he could leave her. "My friend, can you go and be with my son... tell him that I love him."

Both men stood up as Father Isaac prepared to leave. In a very distressed tone, Julio asked Father Isaac, "I know we don't go to your church but could you pray to Mary, for Cristina and me. We need God's help." All of the events of the past year were coming to the surface as Julio began to silently weep with his head bowed—a broken man succumbing to the pressures of life.

Just as Father Isaac was preparing to pray, a delicate and frail Cristina appeared in the doorway of the front room where the men stood. "J.R., ...what's going on honey?" whispered Cristina.

Julio, concerned about upsetting Cristina tried to assure her. "Oh sweetie... everything's fine... Father Isaac is just here to see about you."

Cristina knew Julio all too well. "I heard you talking about Antonio... what is it... is he alright?" The weak but fiery Cristina had grown weary of Julio avoiding the realities of life. "Damn it Julio, you'd better start telling me the truth! Where's Antonio!?" The pressure was too much. Julio sat hard on the sofa and put his head in his hands; he just wanted to escape the moment.

Father Isaac did not want to get caught in the crossfire but he felt he needed to do something. He asked Julio's permission to tell Cristina what he knew. Without looking up Julio nodded yes. Father Isaac carefully tried to reassure the sickly Cristina. "Cristina, Antonio's fine; I saw him this morning... he's O.K... he's fine."

With the intrigue growing, Cristina was getting stronger by the minute. "So what's all the hush-hush talking about?"

Father Isaac responded as if he was on the witness stand for his life. "The young lady he was with seemed to need medical attention and I believe they were on the way to the hospital."

All of the sudden, Cristina seemed to be at full strength. "Julio, I want to go right now. Get yourself together and let's see what's happened to Antonio."

Everything was shifted into high gear and happening quickly. "I'll call my secretary and see if she knows anything." As Julio and Cristina packed an overnight bag, Father Isaac made some phone calls to find out what he could. "They are still at Southwest General—do you know where that is?"

Cristina rolled her eyes and snapped back, "We just moved an hour away... we didn't leave the planet."

Father Isaac smiled and whispered under his breath "Yep, she's back"

Chapter Twelve

The Reluctant Reunion

Father Isaac proceeded ahead of the Ramirez's since Cristina so eloquently reminded him they knew their way around town. Just as Father Isaac entered the freeway he realized how messy this reunion, of sorts, could be. From what he knew, there was

> *Every pastor has heard the refrain many times: 'not my child.'*

good chance they didn't know Maria. Thinking back to the conversation, where he spoke of a girl in trouble, his mention of her was ignored.

During the summer after Antonio graduated, the Ramirez's had witnessed a change in Antonio and realized his erratic behavior must have something to do with a girl. Today, however selfish their thoughts, Julio and Cristina's concerns were not with the girl. As with any proud parent the bad behavior of their beloved child was the result of some other corrupt character. Every pastor has heard the refrain many times: 'not *my* child.'

It wasn't until Father Isaac arrived at the hospital that

he really began to worry. First, he found out that Antonio wasn't married to the young lady he knew nothing about. And since he didn't have any personal information, it took a while for the volunteer at the information desk to put the pieces together. …Maria Padilla had just been transferred to University Medical on the north side of Seattle.

Father Isaac had just gotten the information he needed when he spotted Grace crossing the main lobby in a hurried stride. "This doesn't look good." Father Isaac uttered as he began to pursue Grace. Having seen Father Isaac in her peripheral vision, Grace slowed her pace to allow him to catch up to her. Finally, getting close enough to callout without creating a scene, Father Isaac asked, "How's Maria… may I ride with you?"

Fortunately, Grace had parked in the 'clergy parking' near the front entrance close to the revolving doors. Father Isaac caught up to Grace as she was unlocking her driver's door. "It's serious. Get in."

In the fretful haste, Father Isaac had a lapse in judgment. The Ramirez's were close behind and yet he left Southwest General without helping them make the connection. Since Antonio and Maria were not married and the Ramirez's didn't know anything about Maria, they would have to go through the same ordeal that he had just gone through, except worse. Father Isaac could only hope that they would speak to the same volunteer that he did.

"Grace, bring me up to date. How did this all come about?"

In rapidly punctuated responses Grace explained, "Their names are Antonio Ramirez and Maria Padilla. They came by the church this morning needing help. Maria was experiencing pain so I brought them here. Before we left the church I called her parents and left a message. Maria's parents arrived very quickly and were not happy campers."

Trying to catch her breath Grace held up her hand to indicate that there was more. She was pulling in to heavy traffic so there was a delay in continuing the story. "Renaldo and Julia Padilla were at the hospital but are now ahead of us; they are following the ambulance. Which by the way, I'm not sure the best way to get there."

Father Isaac quickly recited directions. "Just exit Thirty-Fourth Street and turn right. I'll tell you from there. O.K., so what seems to be the problem with Maria?"

Grace continued her fast paced answer session. "This is Maria's first baby, she is petite and has been under undue stress; the baby is trying to come early. To date she has not had any prenatal care. The way I understand it, they have sort of been on-the-lam, avoiding their parents. The Padilla's insisted that Maria be moved to University Medical because of their prenatal care unit. The thought is the baby will be taken by C-section if it is deemed necessary. If not, they will try to delay the birth with mild sedation and complete bed rest. Believe it or not the risks are about the same. The baby is strong and healthy so the concern is with Maria."

It was a lot to take-in but Father Isaac had been down similar roads before. As a priest and pastor, he was called upon to be a source of strength during difficult times like these. Sadly enough things don't always go as hoped. He has presided over more than one infant burial. The most heartrending days of his life have been consoling families of lost babies.

Father Isaac knew he needed to let Grace know the other half of the story. "Antonio's parents are going to be there as well. They shouldn't be more than thirty minutes behind us."

"How did you know to contact them?" Grace inquired looking somewhat puzzled.

"It is a very long story but I'll give you the short version. I've known the Ramirez family for many years. When I saw Antonio walking with Maria this morning I went to see his parents. They have wanted to find him for months."

"Father Isaac, I just realized something. No, I think the Lord just revealed something to me. This whole thing is a plan to bring two otherwise dysfunctional families together. God wants this baby to start its life in a healthy loving family, how much the better." After pondering more about the series of events, Grace further expounded on her revelation. "You know, I'm not so sure that it didn't start with the storm. That seems to be what brought on Maria's severe pain that started this chain of events."

Father Isaac couldn't wait to chime in as he had his own thoughts. "You know what I like about this whole scenario? We get the privilege of being involved in God's plan to heal these families."

Grace exited the freeway and then took a right on Thirty-Fourth. Father Isaac gave turn-by-turn instructions right on cue. "Go up four blocks; take a left on Elm, then left into the parking garage at Elm and Thirty-Sixth." Father Isaac had been here more times than he wanted to remember.

Southwest General had called ahead and the ER staff was waiting for Maria when the ambulance arrived. She was taken directly to the prenatal care unit which was a state-of-the-art facility. Dr. Richard Hamas was the OB-GYN on duty but had been scheduled to leave at 2:00 p.m. When he heard of the incoming patient, he decided to be available to help in the assessment of Maria and baby Padilla's condition.

Maria's gurney made its way down the pristine pale blue corridor to examination room PN.EX. 3B. Julia Padilla was one half step behind Maria's medical entourage. She looked as if she was walking twice as fast as everyone else because of her short legs.

Once again Renaldo Padilla was instructed that he would have to be excused and wait in the family waiting room. Father Isaac and Grace stepped out of the elevator just as Mr. Padilla was making his way to the dimly lit waiting area.

Upon seeing Cristina's dad, Grace knew immediately what she needed to accomplish—she had less than thirty minutes to be successful. "Mr. Padilla, I would like you to meet Father Isaac, he is the Pastor and the officiating Priest of St. Matthew's Episcopal."

Exasperated, Renaldo Padilla interrupted Grace. "Miss Wheaton, I don't need a priest and if I did I have my own."

Grace knew that her work was cut out for her as long as Mr. Padilla had such a bad attitude. "Oh, no Mr. Padilla, Father Isaac is here as a friend in an unofficial role only."

Renaldo Padilla cocked his head and sarcastically quipped, "Oh, really? Sorry, but I have never met a priest that wanted to be anyone's friend unless there was money involved."

Father Isaac saw his opportunity to turn the tide with a little humor. "Oh, that's a zinger… I hadn't heard that one before… that's a good one."

Mr. Padilla hadn't meant for his comment to be anything but what it was, as insulting as possible without being struck by lightning. He took a long look at Father Isaac and broke into a grin. "Hey, I like this guy... are you sure you're a priest... where's your funny suit?" There was not anyone around, who had heard the conversation, that could keep from laughing but it was Father Isaac who laughed the loudest.

"Mr. Padilla, I need to talk to you about something important." Grace implored.

Mr. Padilla was still chuckling under his breath and continuing to size up Father Isaac as he said, "If it's about my baby girl go ahead. If not, it's going to have to wait."

Grace did not have Mr. Padilla's complete attention. He was not used to giving his full attention to anyone. Grace had never been easily intimidated so she spoke with such sternness that Mr. Padilla snapped his head around. He was not used to any woman talking to him that way. "What I have to say is definitely in Maria's best interest." When he saw the seriousness in Grace's eyes he backed off his tough guy routine.

Having Mr. Padilla's full attention, Grace continued. "Do you remember your promise to let everything go so that Maria could get the best of care and support?"

"Yeah, yeah I did and still do... no problem... is that

it?"

Grace held her breath momentarily to choose her words carefully. "Mr. Padilla, I know how you feel about Antonio; his parents will be here shortly."

Renaldo's angst was palpable. "Oh for Christ's sake, you got' ta be kidding me. What in the world do they have to do with this? It's my little girl in there."

With a steady reassuring voice Grace replied, "Whether you like it or not they're extended family now and for Maria's sake, everyone needs to get along."

Mr. Padilla was red faced making all kinds of noises trying to blow off steam. He muttered something like "…getting my hands on that Antonio… nobody makes me do something I don't want to do."

It took a full fifteen minutes of pacing and being left alone but Mr. Padilla became as docile and cooperative as a kitten. "O.K…. I'm good… I'm in this for Maria and the baby… let's get on with this."

Grace was thinking ahead for other possible landmines and the only unknown quantity was Mrs. Padilla. Just as Grace was planning a strategy, for defusing her objections, Antonio and Mrs. Padilla walked out arm-in-arm. She had found the son she had always wanted. The two were all smiles and beaming with excitement as Antonio spoke up. "Everything is going to be just fine. All of Maria's symptoms have dissipated… everything is normal."

Mrs. Padilla threw her arms around her husband and whispered, "Our baby girl is going to be alright. And look, we have a new son… isn't he adorable?"

Chapter Thirteen

The Love Bug Bites

Dr. Richard Hamas was as handsome as he was compassionate. He had decided early-on in his practice that he would go against the conventional wisdom within his industry. *He would become personally involved in his patient's welfare.* Many have gone this route and failed because it just doesn't work. Getting personally involved and *'caring'* is considered medical career suicide—always has been. First, you forfeit the *economies of scale*. Second, the strain on your personal life is suffocating and lastly, the average patient will selfishly suck the strength out of any doctor who tries to be compassionate and caring.

However, much to the surprise of his peers, Richard Hamas, has become highly successful at his young age. In less than ten years in practice, he is no longer taking patients—a milestone many doctors never achieve. Yes, there is less money but the measure of his sense of fulfillment and significance is off the charts—it is why he chose to be a doctor.

In a compassionate tone and with perfect delivery, Dr. Hamas addressed Maria's parents. "Mr. and Mrs. Padilla, I'm sure you know by now that Maria will be just fine. She was just experiencing undue stress and her body was just not up to it. We're going to keep her here for a few days and monitor her condition. If everything still looks fine in a few days we'll release her. I am insisting on complete bed rest for the remainder of her pregnancy and she needs to get on a prenatal care regimen immediately.

I would love to take her on as a patient but I'm not taking any new patients at this time. However, my partner Bill Trombley is an excellent doctor and he is open for new patients. Here is his card. Thank you, as a family, for being so supportive of your daughter. An involved and caring family will make a lot of difference in Maria's delivery."

Richard Hamas had crested in his business career and could finally consider the possibility settling down with a wife and having a family. He had stayed focused and did not stray off his determined path. Being true to his plans paid off handsomely but now he was ready to share his life with an equally determined woman.

Dr. Hamas had noticed Grace as he was talking to

Maria's parents—glancing over in her direction several times. If his presentation had not been committed to memory, from the numerous times that he had delivered it, the truth is, he would have been speechless.

For the first time in Grace's adult life, she was acting coy. She actually felt a blush come on her face—a very odd sensation for her.

A crisp, cold and mechanical voice beckoned over the loudspeaker, "Dr. Richard Hamas, you're needed in delivery."

Dr. Hamas quickly excused himself. "Folks it's been nice visiting with you today... I'm being paged. Bill Trombley will make rounds in the morning and you can get to know him... bye now."

> *"You got it real bad... you got it as bad as my baby girl Maria."*

Grace, let out a gasp as if she had been holding her breath. When she realized how apparent her demeanor was, her blush went to full red in embarrassment. Mrs. Padilla, turns out, is a real card. She waddled over to where Grace seemed permanently planted and immoveable. "You got it real bad... you got it as bad as my baby girl Maria." If it were possible, Grace would have blushed even more. These thoughts and feelings were completely foreign to her. She was thankful that Mrs. Padilla understood enough to keep her voice down. "Don't worry honey. If I got anything to do with it, he's all yours."

The timing couldn't have been more perfect. The call for Dr. Hamas brought relief to a charged emotional romp with Grace's emotions. Grace needed to come back down to earth and the change of pace, that unfolded next, allowed her to breathe again.

Chapter Fourteen

Comic Relief

Just as Grace had calmed, Julio and Cristina Ramirez walked through the noisy, automatic sliding doors to the emergency room admissions area. The Ramirez's were completely unaware of the intense emotions that had played out over the last several hours. When they spotted Father Isaac, he was still enjoying the teasing by Mrs. Padilla. The lighter tone brought relief to Julio and Cristina Ramirez who had been worried about their son with little information to feel good about.

The moment of truth had arrived for Antonio. With the unexpected arrival of his parents, he became restless and nervous. To be a man worthy of Maria's love, Antonio knew he was going to have to grow up and take the heat—a step necessary for any young male to step into manhood. The attention that his 'new mom' had been pouring over him was a tonic of self-assurance giving him strength to rise to the occasion.

He was not accustomed to the kind of loving attention that Julia Padilla was giving him. Antonio knew his mom loved him deeply but she was not the touchy-feely type. Cristina Ramirez didn't really know how to express the outwardly emotional love that the male ego enjoys and responds to. Antonio was also thinking how he had let his guard down with his dad. Could he bring himself to do it again?

Antonio squared his shoulders and symbolically stepped out from behind Mrs. Padilla's apron of protective love. "Mom, Dad this is Renaldo and Julia Padilla. They are the parents of my girlfriend and soon to be wife, Maria Padilla.

"Now hold on young man!" Renaldo squawked as he was trying to talk and clear his throat at the same time. Just as he got the last word out of his mouth, Julia stomped on his foot so hard you could hear bone crunching. Everyone stopped breathing at the same time waiting to see what would happen next… *nothing*. Renaldo relented with moistened eyes, "Go ahead son. What were you saying?"

In the moment of silence that ensued, Cristina Ramirez calmly asked, "How is Maria doing… is she alright?" As if the two mothers were the only ones in the room, their conversation continued, "She's sleeping right now. She's been lightly sedated so she can rest. She'll be here for a few days…"

Grace was exhausted and very hungry. She had missed breakfast because of the storm and skipped lunch because of the hospital juggernaut. Now it was approaching the dinner hour. With her head cocked and looking toward Father Isaac, Grace blurted out, in a testy tone not at all like her. "You owe me dinner; I'm sorry but I'm hungry and you're buying." Father Isaac was a little shocked. In the four years that Father Isaac had known Grace, she had always been what her name implies—ultimate grace.

Father Isaac, in a conciliatory tone, relented to Grace's sulky charge. "Well… O.K. then, let's eat… what are you hungry for?" Father Isaac was just as hungry so he was a little frayed around the edges himself.

Grace wanted to eat at her favorite diner, so she suggested, "'*April's Dine-In*', it's a little out of the way. Do you have enough time?"

Father Isaac nodded as he reminded Grace about his car. "Don't forget that my car is still at Southwest General."

Chapter Fifteen

Going Home

The early morning storm combined with an unfolding series of trying episodes made for a very long Thursday. The eventful day kept Father Isaac from his formal duties and in his absence he had left Andrea hanging. His unexplained behavior was a first for him as the immediate leader of St. Matthew's. Father Isaac had never been more than a few minutes out of reach from his daytime duties at the church.

Would this be his new way of doing things? Out into the fray, coming home a victorious warrior? As a spiritual leader, was this how life was to be lived? These questions were going to take some serious thought to find the right answers. As pastor and priest, he would have to find a balance, that is, if he was expecting to stay. *Balance* was the word he had been looking for. Balance was not compromise—he was not going to compromise, but yes, he could find a balance.

Things were evolving quickly for Father Isaac. When he came into work Friday morning, everything at the church seemed different to him. He didn't feel a sense of belonging— his home away from home. When he walked into his office, it was as if he had been gone for a long time. He was coming back only to find he was entering someone else's domain.

At that moment, in his peripheral vision, he saw a figure sitting in the large wingback chair near the bay window. "Good morning Father Isaac, you're early today."

"Bishop Ivey, I wasn't expecting you."

With a sly and curt reply, Bishop Ivey retorted, "Oh come now Father Isaac let's don't play this game. You knew I'd be here to receive your report."

Bishop Ivey's tone was nothing short of eerie. Father Isaac was sensing a dark presence hanging in the room. "Yes, but I thought it would be by appointment; maybe over lunch. Also, I needed about thirty minutes to put the finishing touches on it before I gave it to you."

Seething and with gritted teeth, Bishop Ivey went on, "Oh don't bother, I have what I need. I think you know that it's over for you here. Compromise indeed… who do you think you are? Don't you know who you're dealing with?"

Father Isaac was frozen and immobile not knowing what to do or say. He seemed to be powerless to move or speak. "Help me, Lord Jesus." Father Isaac spoke these words ever so softly. Those were the only words that would come out of his mouth. He was thinking of other things but those were the words that came out.

The unseen worlds were about to clash in a spectacular fashion. Bishop Ivey roared just like a real lion. Father Isaac felt the power of that roar as it reverberated through the room—it shook his body. (Was this an actual roar heard with natural ears or was this a supernatural occurrence manifesting itself in the natural realm? Father Isaac only knew what he experienced with his five senses, not its origin.)

The Lord spoke to Father Isaac's heart: *"My son I have not given you the spirit of fear; but of power, and of love, and of a sound mind."* Without hesitation, Father Isaac responded to the *Word of the Lord.* He began to spontaneously praise the Lord *like he had never known to do before.* It was from a heart of thanksgiving as he bowed down to praise the risen Savior and to call upon His name in adoration and worship. He began to sing a *new song* of love and devotion to the Lord of lords and King of kings.

In an ethereal response to the Lord's habitation, Bishop Ivey and the darkness fled. The room became serenely quiet and reverent as the glory of the Lord filled that place.

Father Isaac stood a changed man. He now knew beyond any doubt that his work was indeed done here. He walked over to his desk and took only one thing. It was the Holy Bible that his wife gave him twenty-three years ago when he graduated from the seminary. He was beginning to understand how the contents of this book would be his sustaining force for the rest of his life.

A passionate sense of longing for his wife began to rise up in Father Isaac. He had an intense desire to go and pay her a visit—he had a lot of catching up to do.

They say you always come back home. Father Isaac's life was at peace and it seemed right to be heading back to his roots. He had faced spiritual wickedness and death and he was still standing. *Now,* he had something to bring back to his family and friends who had sent him off to change the world.

The official purpose for Father Isaacs 'extended leave,' was that he was 'taking a sabbatical.' The more favorable explanation had been arranged by Cardinal John Whittington. Father Isaac had an exemplary record of achievement and enjoyed a high regard among his peers within the clergy.

Bishop Ivey failed to show up for a series of recent meetings, so an interim Bishop was assigned to investigate the whole affair. It quickly became apparent that Father Isaac was a victim of shameful conduct by Bishop Ivey. In consideration, Father Isaac was granted a generous one-year severance

> *In consideration, Father Isaac was granted a generous one-year severance package...*

package with a standing offer to regain his position anytime he wanted to return.

Father Isaac was leaving this beautiful community he had called home for more than twenty years. He was ready to leave town after weeks of attending to the myriad of details involved in pulling up roots. Before hitting the road, his last stop was to visit with Grace and say his last goodbyes.

Grace was doing some moving of her own. Her dad, John Wheaton Jr., was back from the mission field for an interim leave. This would allow Grace the chance to move back home until she could find a new direction for her life. Father Isaac pulled into her dorm parking lot just as she was in the last stages of packing her belongings.

Grace was summoned by melodic rapping to the loose fitting screen door of her dorm room. She was appropriately dressed in her grubby 'moving day' clothes as her greeted her good friend. "I was hoping you would stop by before you left. Aren't you running a little behind schedule?"

Father Isaac was feeling nostalgic and sentimental all at the same time. "Oh Gracie, it's so hard to leave such a wonderful place and the many good friends God has given me." After a short pause of reflection Father Isaac mused, "Grace, do you realize that we are both going home?"

Grace was in a more down to earth, pragmatic mood. "Well, there is a little difference. I'm moving fifteen miles and you're moving fifteen-hundred miles."

Father Isaac nodded as he continued his conversation with a sense of freedom and adventure. He was both relieved and hopeful about the new chapter in his life. "Grace, it's all good, everything going forward feels right."

Ending his visit, Father Isaac was carrying a box for Grace just as her dad drove into the parking lot. John Wheaton backed the rented moving van into the parking space next to Father Isaac's white Volvo. John Wheaton Jr., sometimes called John Jr. but never just 'Junior,' stepped down from the oversized cab of the box truck. John had hoped to see Father Isaac before he left; the timing was perfect. "Father Isaac, you look ten years younger. Things must be going your way."

Father Isaac felt ten years younger as the events of the last month had been a genuine renewal experience for him.

"John, I'm having the time of my life and I've never felt better. By the way, as of today, it's Frank Isaac. You really are seeing the new me."

John was seeing firsthand the dramatic changes that Grace had relayed to him about Frank. "Well Frank that's wonderful. Grace has told me of some miraculous things. If you have time maybe we can have an early lunch and you can fill me in on some of the details."

The lunch invitation reminded Frank that he was behind in his schedule and needed to get going. "John, I would love to but this was my last stop before hitting the road. I could spare a few minutes to help you with anything heavy."

Grace knew that Frank was well behind his announced schedule to be gone by an eight a.m. leave time. "Go… go Father… I mean Frank, we moved all of the big stuff yesterday; we'll be fine."

Frank felt a release to leave and gave John and Grace his famous priestly hug. "I'll write when I get settled, bless you guys!"

Chapter Sixteen

The Detour

Frank Isaac intended to simply enjoy his drive from Seattle to Cincinnati by making the trip as time consuming as possible. Not to procrastinate or delay this new chapter in his life, but to unwind the past so the first step taken on new soil would be firm and sure. He stopped on any whim and lingered as long as he felt the urge. There was no avenue of curiosity left unexplored.

Frank felt very comfortable in his 'new skin.' Along his extended passage toward home, he talked and mingled with total strangers as if they were old friends. He left a trail of best friends and not just acquaintances.

Some of the most treasured moments were eternally etched in the hearts of those who were drawn to Frank's Christ like persona. His kindred relationship with God was apparent causing many to hunger for what Frank possessed. As he shared the reality of God's goodness and mercy, there were many who received the Good News of Christ's redemption.

Frank's last destination, before stopping to call his parents, was one final act of closure. Mount Olivet Memorial Cemetery was across town from the older more prestigious neighborhood where he grew up. By the time he made his last turn off the highway his heart was aching—this visit was long overdue.

Frank's longing seemed to have surfaced weeks ago when he was confronted with the reality that his life was taking a dramatic turn. He needed some kind of reassurance that he was going to make it—he wasn't going to sink. Sure, he had assurance from his Heavenly Father, but he had had a covenant with his wife that is second only to his covenant with God. He began to long for his wife.

It was late in the afternoon when Frank, ever so slowly, turned into Mount Olivet Memorial Park and began to follow the narrow lane that laced the serenely quiet grave marked landscape. Even though it had been more than two years since he had been to visit Carey Lynn, he could have driven blindfolded to her gravesite.

Frank paused to reflect upon his relative short marriage that had been more than anyone could have dreamed—not one minute of regret. He decided to make this time with Carey Lynn a reflection of the new freedom and joy that he had discovered. Yes, this would be a celebration of new beginnings. A celebration of new life springing up in a place marked with death. Somehow, that inspiration seemed so fitting yet odd from a worldly perspective. But in God's Kingdom, life is always preceded by death. Frank momentarily pondered how Carey Lynn would feel about his newness of life. "Yeah, you're going to like what's happened, Sweetie." He said aloud as if she was standing there with him.

Frank's time with Carey Lynn extended to just before dusk. For over two hours, Frank talked and laughed—he even told a few jokes. He listened too. Frank contemplated how their future might have been.

At one point during a long stretch of silence, he distinctly heard the words New Guinea. He initially assumed the sounds were carried over the gently rolling grounds and thought nothing of it. This time it was unmistakable, sounding like an echo, he heard: "New Guinea."

He stood up and surveyed the surrounding area for

someone who could be talking. The serenity was uninterrupted by a single person. Frank was not fazed by this seemingly strange occurrence because he was still focused on his time with Carey Lynn. It felt good to stand and stretch his legs so he began to walk around and talk as if Carey Lynn was right by his side.

Frank stopped as if on cue and began to study a grave marker. He read the inscription and felt particularly moved for, by what seemed to be, no apparent reason. He then read aloud the poignant sentiment left by a beloved spouse. "His heart was in New Guinea because His Lord met him there."

Frank was overwhelmed, not because of the obvious connection to the words he heard earlier, but because God, in an instant, supernaturally captured his heart. What happened next was extraordinary. Frank saw his future flash before his eyes. It was as if God pulled back the curtain of eternity and gave Frank a brief glimpse of his destiny.

In a real sense, Frank felt the breath of God blow over him—He was that close. Frank had no choice but to fall prostrate and be perfectly still. This was not a time for response—*be still and know that I am God.*

It was now past dusk and Frank mulled over in his mind the significance of his experiences and what they meant. Surely, God had met him in this place. He had solace and an elevated sense of closure with his deceased wife. He now realized that this was a needed and final requirement so that no unfinished business would hold him back. He was also certain, that in some way, New Guinea was definitely in his future.

Chapter Seventeen
New Beginnings

Paiyan Wheaton Taylor is bigger than life. His arrival from the mission field was a rare event so John initially wanted to surprise Grace. However, he quickly changed his mind because the special occasion was too important plus there was much to discuss. "Grace, your Great Uncle Paiyan will be here next week. He has something special planned that includes you."

Grace had often thought of Uncle Paiyan over the last few months. As the miracles were coming rapid fire, she was reminded of the many stories (adventures to the younger Grace) that were centered on Uncle Paiyan.

Grace had only met her Uncle Paiyan twice before. When she was eight years old, Grace was almost fear struck when she first met him. Uncle Paiyan was of Polynesian descent so he was very large and stocky. Combined with dark red skin and a weathered complexion, he had the appearance of a warrior—there was fierceness about him.

On his second visit, an older Grace connected with her Uncle Paiyan differently. She had a greater understanding of who he was and her miraculous relationship with him as a family member. The truth is: if it wasn't for Paiyan, Grace would have never been born. (That is an incredible story yet to be told.)

Paiyan was coming to the States for several reasons. The main purpose was to help John Jr. form an advance team effort for a later major missionary push into New Guinea; an island nation just north of Australia. New Guinea would be considered one of the northwestern-most countries within the South Pacific region.

Paiyan envisioned an opportunity for Majesty International Missionary Group (M.I.M.G. or just M.I. for short) to establish an outreach on the island of New Guinea. As founders and senior pastors of M.I., John Jr. and Paiyan were in charge of forward planning. Their privileged duties also included preaching and teaching while on M.I.'s trips and conferences.

Paiyan's second reason for his trip to the States was specifically to see Grace. Paiyan was in his late eighties and he wanted Grace to help him accomplish a dream. Paiyan's heartfelt desire was to preserve the amazing story of how the Wheaton and Taylor family legacies were intertwined as well as how God intervened in own his life.

Grace, John and Paiyan's shared ancestry was rich with amazing and adventurous stories of lives consumed for God's kingdom. There were numerous stories that could be told of miracles of faith and healing. Paiyan's wanted the story of their joint heritage recorded. And yes, by divine providence, Paiyan was actually Grace's great uncle.

John continued, "I'll let Uncle Paiyan tell you about his plans and the surprise he has for you. In the meantime, I would like for you to be thinking and praying about the main reason he's coming back to the States." There was an earnestness wrapped in John's vocal inflections, giving Grace pause.

Allowing a few moments for the words to sink in, Grace responded, "O.K. dad what's on your mind?"

John took and deep breath because he knew how much there was to tell. "Grace, M.I.M.G. has been given an opportunity to go into New Guinea in a big way. God has thrown the doors wide open for us. Uncle Paiyan is coming so we can form an advance team that will go to New Guinea prior to the actual push. We will also need to begin raising the additional funds so we can be effective when we get there."

John's excitement was contagious. "Dad, this is wonderful news. This sounds really big. Tell me about your advanced planning; the team you want to put together."

John continued, "So far we have a medical advisor onboard—a prominent M.D. here in Seattle. As usual, Paiyan will be our liaison with the community and civic leaders as we establish key relationships in New Guinea. Our three most loyal and generous contributors are with us, on this project, one-hundred percent. They will step into a real time backup role. Any prayer support or financial emergencies that come up will be handled quickly. Their behind the scenes support is essential so we are not left in a crisis seven-thousand miles away.

We have two key positions we need to fill. The first is that of a liaison to work with the indigenous religious communities of New Guinea. Second, we need a person to gather information for relief efforts in the areas we'll be ministering. Fortunately, I have a person in mind for the relief efforts position—his name is Bruce Phillips out of Dallas, Texas. In any missionary outreach endeavor, these key positions are necessary to reach *'the whole man': spirit, soul and body."*

John finished his enumeration of the team members then continued with the need for prayer and financial support. "Just as important, as any preparation for the trip, we need to rally our base of support here in the States. In the upcoming months, we need to strengthen and expand our network of prayer warriors as well." Doing a quick mental inventory of all the topics covered he forgot to mention Paiyan's request. "Oh... I almost forgot. Your Uncle Paiyan wants you to pray about being his personal assistant on the trip—he requested that I ask you."

It seemed as if Grace had not heard the jest of the last sentence her dad spoke about Paiyan's request. She was just thinking ahead. "Dad, who's going to help you... who's going to be your assistant?"

John couldn't believe he had forgotten one of the most important bits of news. "Oh, Gracie! ('Gracie' was John's favorite term of endearment for Grace. For years it was 'Princess' but she outgrew it, so now it was just Gracie but only by loved ones.) Your brother Paul may be coming home to join us. He was the first person I needed to call when we got the news about New Guinea. It was essential that Paul put in for an extended leave as soon as we set our dates. It turns out that his commanding officer is in Washington D.C. on a temporary assignment. Until he returned to base, he was unwilling to sign-off on Paul's request—the timing is going to be close."

The request made by Uncle Paiyan, to be his assistant, had just begun to sink-in to Grace's thoughts. "Dad, do you think I have what it takes to be of any help to Uncle Paiyan?"

John's jaw almost dropped open. "We'll let's see... a seminary degree in theology, a major in world history as well as a minor in anthropology... and dare we forget a near 4.0 grade average... Oh! Oh! And your senior thesis was written on *'The Effects of the Gospel on the Indigenous Tribes and Peoples of the South Pacific.'* Grace, you could very well be the most qualified person that I know."

> *Every girl lives each day to soak up her daddy's approval and affection.*

Grace was admiring her dad's somewhat comical and animated delivery that displayed his immense pride and affirmation that he held for her. Grace took a few moments before responding as she felt tears welling up in her eyes. Every girl lives each day to soak up her daddy's approval and affection. "Well, daddy... I guess you have a point... we may as well put this education to good use."

Chapter Eighteen

Great Uncle Paiyan

Even at eighty-nine years of age, Uncle Paiyan was an imposing figure. His posture was near perfect and his shoulders were almost as wide as the average doorframe. And believe it or not, his hair was only slightly graying. Anyone's best guess would be that he was in his sixties. Paiyan was set to deplane in Seattle wearing his trademark smile as well as a loud Hawaiian shirt. He claimed that people were not as intimidated by him when he looked like a dumb and happy tourist.

John Jr. and Grace were waiting for Paiyan to emerge from the concourse when Dr. Richard Hamas approached from behind and tapped John on the shoulder. Grace was not aware that the eminent doctor, chosen for the advance team, was none other than Dr. Richard Hamas. John turned to greet Dr. Hamas; a recently made friend. "Richard, I am so glad you could make it… Paiyan should be out any minute. Doctor, I would like for you to meet my daughter, Grace."

Richard Hamas and Grace Wheaton were now formally introduced. With a controlled awkwardness they shook hands and spoke in unison, "Nice to meet you."

John continued with his introduction of Dr. Hamas. "Grace, Dr. Hamas will be our medical advisor who will be assessing the need for future medical missions to New Guinea.

M.I.M.G. hopes Dr. Hamas will join our efforts so we will have a greater impact as we minister the Gospel in New Guinea. Richard, Grace is going with us as Paiyan's personal assistant and stenographer."

Grace wasn't sure what John meant by 'stenographer.' It was the first she had heard anything about taking dictation. "Dad?"

Just as Grace voiced her one word question, Paiyan came bounding out of from the crowd. "Hey! My man, John! And my sweet little niece who is all grownup… give me a big ole hug."

Grace was overjoyed to see Paiyan in such good health—she had been a little worried. He looked like he was in the prime of his life. "Uncle Paiyan, you must be living right; you look great."

The jovial Paiyan quipped, "It's the rice and fresh fish, Gracie, and… *the grace of a merciful God.*"

After a round of introductions, Paiyan addressed Richard and warmly greeted him. "Doctor, you are an answer to my prayers, my brother. The need is very great in the islands. You will be a blessing to hurting and lost souls. People respond to the love of God expressed in the miracle of modern medicine. I am so glad you can join us."

Richard felt an immediate connection to Paiyan. He

was living up to his bigger than life reputation—full of life, a big heart and going all out for God's Kingdom. It was obvious that Paiyan had the anointing and favor of God on his life. Richard had an intense desire to *finish strong* and what an exemplary person to emulate. "Paiyan, the pleasure and honor is mine."

John chimed in and suggested having lunch at a quiet restaurant where the conversation could continue. Maggiano's was the perfect spot to find a quiet nook so details and plans could be discussed. "Richard, why don't you take Paiyan in your car; you guys can get to know each other. Do you know how to get to Maggiano's?—good... meet you there."

John had taken notice of Grace's apparent bashfulness when being introduced to Richard Hamas. As they were walking to the car, John asked Grace, "Do you know Richard?" Grace was caught little off guard but recovered quickly. She felt she really needed to find composure from this point forward, especially if she was going to be traveling around the world with Dr. Richard Hamas.

In a perfectly controlled response, that surprised even her, she stated, "I met the good doctor at University Medical Center when Maria Padilla was admitted by her parents, in late spring. We were never formally introduced, so I actually didn't know him until today."

John was impressed by Grace's attempt to cover up the obvious. She was blind to the fact that her response was a singsong string of words that did not possess one ounce of candor. The resulting smile on John's face expressed his heartfelt joy.

The lunch crowd was already gone so the atmosphere was perfect for their meeting. John understood that the team needed to become *as one-in-the-Spirit,* so the first order of business was to go to the Lord in prayer. He then wanted to bring everyone up to date on key points and assignments.

With a measure of controlled enthusiasm, John began the meeting. "O.K. everybody... for today, I have a short list of essentials so everyone will be on the same page going forward. A firm date is set—we're leaving in two weeks, August fifteenth. We'll be in route a full day plus a lost day due to the International Date Line.

We already have several appointments with strategic church leaders in the capitol city of Port Moresby. They have arranged a mini conference with three-hundred pastors, civic leaders and local dignitaries invited. Our main focus, for this advance trip, is to share the vision that God has given us. The official theme and emphasis for the conference will be: '*The Gospel of Christ is for the Whole Man, Spirit, Soul and Body— We are to be Made Complete in Christ.*'"

Paiyan was eager to fill in some details about the open door that God provided. Before he began to speak, he wanted to make sure he had Grace's full attention—this was mostly for her. "Grace, I want to explain why I have asked you to travel with me. As you know, I have always believed that my immediate family was the only one to escape the volcanic eruption that devastated our original island home. About a year ago, I heard that two other families had been able to evacuate as well. I was told that those two other families took with them the knowledge of Christ to New Guinea.

Six weeks ago, I took some personal time so I could go to New Guinea and checkout the rumors for myself. I was determined to find out the truth. After three weeks of searching, I found not two but five families had escaped death. All of these families now lead ministries, of some kind, on the island of New Guinea."

Grace was so engrossed with the story that she only wanted to hear more but she had to comment. "God works in marvelous and mysteries ways. He used a terrible and tragic event and turned it around to be a blessing for the peoples of New Guinea. Uncle Paiyan, did you know any of the people who escaped?" Paiyan was happy to see Grace's keen interest. She was going to be an important part of telling the story of how God delivered an entire people group.

"Grace, I have outlived all of those I knew from the island. What I found were the children, grandchildren and some of their extended family—a miracle in itself. Grace, I have a dream, a desire to tell this story of redemption. I want you to write this story."

Grace was completely instep and agreeable before he asked. "O.K.... stenographer, now I get it. Uncle Paiyan, I would be honored to write your story." Grace was now beginning to feel a real sense of purpose and belonging as a team member.

Paiyan continued, "Grace, we will be mostly separated from the other members of the advance team. You and I will be the 'advanced' advance team. We'll be going to some of the most primitive places found on earth. To us, most of the accommodations will be very crude even though the village leaders and their people will be giving us their best. From their perspective we will be treated like kings so we must be very gracious and strong."

The average young lady would have been squirming and eager to back pedal, but not Grace. She was leaning in and internally rising to the challenge being presented to her by her Uncle Paiyan. Paiyan could see by Grace's body language that she was not deterred. He concluded, "Grace, along the way, I'll be telling you the story of my family. Are you sure you can handle the rough and rigorous conditions?"

Grace took his comments and question seriously because they were not frivolous. Overseas travel, especially under these conditions, can be life threatening. She also identified with Paiyan's vision for documenting his important and remarkable testimony of God's grace upon his life. Grace reaffirmed her desire to be included on this important venture with such great and notable men of God.

Chapter Nineteen

Yes, Lord, Send Me

Grace stopped by St. Matthew's offices to check for any mail that may have come that wasn't forwarded. In a symphony of high pitched squeals, Andrea and Grace embraced like long lost friends. "Andrea, you've lost so much weight... you're gorgeous! How did you do it?"

What followed was a rapid exchange of quips, intertwined with terms of endearment, which only the female gender can master. "Oh honey, I'm just wearing more black these days."

"Seriously, you look great, who's doing your hair? ..."

Andrea got back to business when she remembered her new boss was due back any minute. Just at that moment, Father

Geyer stepped through the door to Andrea's office. "Andrea, do I have any messages that can't wait a few minutes while I run upstairs."

"No sir, you're clear. Father Geyer, I would like you to meet Grace Wheaton, a former intern here at St. Matthew's."

Father Geyer graciously responded, "It's my pleasure to meet you." After a brief pause, he asked, "Is that *the* Grace Wheaton? You know, young lady, you turned this entire diocese upside down. But, I think it's for the better so be at peace. Ladies, I have to run upstairs. Goodbye Ms. Wheaton."

Andrea was a little shocked. That's not what she had been led to believe. At one point she heard rumors of wanting to 'burn someone at the stake'—at least in effigy. A little embarrassed at her runaway thoughts, she chose to keep quiet and just say, "Gracie, you need to continue to pray for St. Matthew's; there's a lot in the balance here. I think you know what I mean. Oh by the way, you have some mail."

Grace missed several days of mail as she transitioned to her dad's mailing address. "Andrea, I was hoping you would have something for me."

Andrea responded with grimace. "I know I shouldn't have looked but Father Isaac wrote to you. From the thickness of the envelope, it's a very long letter."

Grace was relieved to hear that Frank had finally

written to her. "Oh good; it's about time. Frank must have taken a very long road home."

> *As Grace read the letter, her emotions were carried along with an ebb and flow orchestrated by an invisible conductor.*

Back at her dad's house Grace excitedly opened Frank's letter; an apparent treasure trove of information and journaling. It was indeed a very long letter, apparently written over a period of time. The pages showed wear and the marks of time like coffee rings, different colors of ink and one page had been wadded up and then unfolded. You could tell there had been a lot of emotions expended over the course of completing the letter—even the appearance of tear stains.

Sure enough there was a scrunched-up paragraph atop the first page that had been penned-in last. The appended paragraph explained how the letter had evolved over several weeks. As Grace read the letter, her emotions were carried along with an ebb and flow orchestrated by an invisible conductor. She rode the same emotional rollercoaster left in ink by a good friend. Grace added her own tear stains to Frank's—some of joy and some of sadness.

It was the last two pages that left Grace captivated and

speechless. Frank had explained in minute detail how God had given him a burden for New Guinea. He went on to explain that as he prayed and sought the Lord, the burden had only grown deeper. Frank knew that New Guinea was in his future but wasn't sure how to respond to the call that was certainly from God.

As Grace finished reading the last sentence she dropped her hands to her waist; still clutching the messy pages of Frank's letter. Her mouth was gaping in awe and wonderment. "So it's Frank who's going." Grace's first thought was to show her dad this incredible letter.

Grace was standing in the breakfast room next to the oversized bay window as she finished the letter from Frank. The light from the window and the view of the backyard created a sense of wellbeing—her senses were enriched, adding to the moment. Grace called out, "Dad, you've got to see this.… Dad, come here. You'll want to look at this letter from Frank." Grace turned to go find her dad, only to meet him coming from the den.

"Grace, are you O.K.? I could hear you but I didn't know what you were saying. What's up?"

Grace was still filled with wonderment from the contents of Frank's letter. "Dad, have you found anyone to fill the liaison position for our trip to New Guinea?" Sensing the electricity in Grace's queries, John explained there were no potential candidates.

As John read the letter, he knew God had finished putting together the M.I.M.G. advance team. "Well that completes the team. We need to contact Frank Isaac A.S.A.P. He's got a lot of catching-up to do. Grace, can you try to phone Frank? You may have to call directory assistance for his new phone number."

Grace was way ahead of her dad. Frank had written his new phone number, as an afterthought, in the appended paragraph that began his long letter. Grace headed back to the kitchen and began dialing Frank's number—there was no time to waste.

Frank's phone continued to ring beyond the normal four rings… then six… now eight. Grace was putting the receiver down when she heard a voice on the other end. She quickly pulled the phone to her ear when she heard Frank's voice. *"Please leave a message after the beep."* Trying not to be too anxious, Grace quickly explained the major details of her call. Then she couldn't help it; her pent up emotions escaped her. "Frank, this is so amazing how God has put this together. Please call as soon as you can."

Frank picked up the phone just as Grace was finishing her sentence. "Gracie, how are you? I was coming in from the backyard when I heard you on the recorder. You sounded pretty excited about something. What's going on?"

"Frank, you won't believe it. I got your letter and when I read how God gave you a burden for New Guinea, I just stood in the kitchen in amazement. Frank, my dad and five others are leaving in two weeks to setup a major evangelistic push in New Guinea. We need a key man to represent the ministry and to help coordinate the events and conferences that will follow in about twelve months. Frank, we need you for the advance team."

Frank was becoming a little emotional himself. "Grace, when you called, I was just in the backyard watering the plants and talking to God about New Guinea. How quickly things can change. What day will we be leaving and what would be my duties on the team?"

"Frank, I am going to let my dad fill you in on all the details; just know that God is in this. Here's my dad."

John was listening to the conversation as Grace broached the subject of being a team member. He was ready when Grace handed him the phone. "Hey Frank, John here. You're an answer to prayer, my brother. But this is very short notice, is this doable for you? Gracie didn't ask about your availability for this advance trip."

By the time John asked him, Frank had already digested

the impact of the phone call from Grace. He *was* ready. He *had been* ready. It was just a matter of getting a call. God had generously provided *way in advance*, the money, the available time and the personal experience to make this trip. "John, I've never been more ready for anything. When Grace called I was in the garden reciting a scripture I memorized out of Isaiah 6:8, *"...I heard the voice of the Lord, saying: "Whom shall I send, and who will go for Us?" Then I said, "Here am I! Send me."* John, I found this verse and memorized it the day after God called-out to me at Carey Lynn's graveside. So, I'm ready to go, let's do this! Just tell me when to be there and what to bring."

John was satisfied that Frank was the person for the job and God's will for New Guinea. "Frank can you be here by the end of this week? I would like to put you in charge of some last minute details. Grace told me you're gifted at handling details."

Frank agreed that he enjoyed putting the finishing touches on a project. He received a deep sense of satisfaction from being part of a job well done. "John, I'll be on a plane in 72 hours. I'll call you with the flight number and arrival time just before I leave here."

New Guinea   Huon Gulf

Chapter Twenty

The Persecuted Church

First Sidebar—Paiyan's Story The following three chapters explain how God began this monumental effort to reach deep into New Guinea with the Good News of Christ. The story will then resume with the Seattle departure.

THREE MONTHS PRIOR TO THE SEATTLE DEPARTURE:

It is here that Paiyan's story must be told. Paiyan was the central figure of the advance team for a reason. Twelve weeks ago, Paiyan made a personal journey to the northeastern shores of New Guinea. What he found there began his desire to reach the island nation with the Gospel. His amazing saga explains how this monumental missionary trip had its beginning. Here is his story.

Over the many years of traveling throughout the South Pacific, Paiyan had heard various stories about an island escape—possibly the same escape he had made. Putting all the bits of information together, he began to believe that some of his former neighbors and relatives had escaped their island home shortly after he did.

He then met a village pastor who provided details that Paiyan knew to be accurate from having been there himself. Apparently, these families miraculously made the long and dangerous journey by sea to the northeastern shores of New Guinea. This new and crucial information would change Paiyan's life forever. Paiyan decided to travel to New Guinea and search for the truth about these accounts.

Paiyan arrived in the general area described by the village pastor; only described as the northern shores of the Huon Gulf. After nearly two weeks of chasing dead end leads, Paiyan was taking a break at a modest nondescript sidewalk café. As he contemplated the many people he had talked to and the places he had searched, his eyes caught the image of a cross.

Directly across the narrow lane, he noticed a small storefront church that seemed inviting to him—a place of rest and refuge. Drawn, Paiyan crossed the narrow, dusty and somewhat congested street to explore his discovery. He left his native coffee concoction outside and walked through the makeshift archway adorned with a cross. There was a sense of peace and holy presence that enveloped him as he entered the small church. He immediately felt an overwhelming urgency to pray and ask God to lead him to the families of his past.

Just inside the door, Paiyan found a place to sit and pray. After praying for several minutes, with his head still bowed, a man approached him. "You must be Paiyan? We have been waiting for you to come. May I sit with you?"

Paiyan was perplexed to say the least. What an interesting question to hear after days and weeks of chasing shadows. "How were you expecting me?"

The apparent host spoke genteelly yet with a source of inner strength. "My name is Pastor Wanlee Michaels. I have known about you all of my life—since I was a child. Your reputation precedes you, my brother. For many years the stories of your missionary journeys would come back to encourage us. Just as we were about to give up we would hear of a great harvest of souls or the spiritual awakening of a village."

Paiyan was sitting and listening in rapt attention. Tears were forming as the words penetrated his heart. Paiyan was speechless as Wanlee continued, "We have known you were here on the island for many days. Word gets around quickly in our community. Our little church building is only a place for the authorities to *think* they have control over God's church.

The real church is 'underground' where thousands meet in small groups. All communication is by word of mouth with direct paths to key leaders. Yes, we have known every stop you have made."

Paiyan's mind was reeling. He had expected a rather non eventful pursuit of distant relatives, a happy reunion and then a sad departure—his curiosity satisfied. He was not expecting this clandestine twist to his efforts to find past friends and relatives. "Explain to me what happened to bring about this dual identity for your church."

> *Even today, every church must decide if it will succumb to some type of pressure to compromise God's Word.*

Wanlee passionately responded, "Make no mistake, there is no duality." Taking a long reverent pause, Wanlee continued, "Paiyan, throughout the history of God's church, His people have had to go underground at times. Even today, *every* church must decide if it will succumb to some type of pressure to compromise God's Word. For some churches, the compromise is to renounce Christ or walk into the face of death—it has always been this way. Right now, today, we are that church."

Paiyan had witnessed varying degrees of persecution

during his many years evangelizing the South Pacific. As a Christian brother, a godly compassion rose up in him. He needed more information—questions were coming to his mind rapid fire.

Pastor Wanlee implored, "Paiyan, for any more answers we must meet at a later time—you are being watched by the authorities as well. Your visit here today cannot look suspicious. Meet me at the arched bridge where you talked to the street vendor earlier today. Is four o'clock O.K?" After receiving a nod mixed with a look of astonishment, Wanlee continued, "Paiyan, please hear me carefully. Do not stand around as if you are waiting for someone. When I walk by, follow me by no less than thirty paces. Until then, put on a different color shirt and wear a hat and your boots."

Paiyan's head was spinning—this was too much. He decided to go back to his room and calm down. This would also be an opportunity to collect his thoughts and spend some time in prayer.

Chapter Twenty-One

Cloud of Witnesses

It was by complete accident that Paiyan recognized Pastor Wanlee as he went by. He looked as if he was trying to pass so Paiyan *wouldn't* see him. Wanlee had changed clothes and was mingling in a tightly packed crowd of people who *appeared* to be sightseers. Paiyan followed on the opposite side of the street about forty meters back. It was clear that Pastor Michaels had done this before. He was an expert at avoiding detection.

At the edge of the village, Pastor Wanlee began a steep ascent up a foliage covered trail that was almost indistinguishable. Just as Paiyan made an ever so casual turn to follow Wanlee, three men appeared out of nowhere and corralled Paiyan into an alleyway between buildings. Despite Paiyan large muscular appearance, he could only feign resistance. One of the men spoke rapidly under his breath, assuring Paiyan that he was safe—he would be taken to the meeting by another route.

For everyone's safety, Paiyan was blindfolded to avoid disclosing the location of the obscure highland village. After two hours of rough and rigorous hiking, Paiyan and the three men arrived without incident. When his blindfold was removed, a small grass hut village lay before him that was extremely primitive by anyone's standards.

Paiyan had been to countless villages across the Pacific but he saw a glaring difference. It was obvious that measures had been taken to reduce the 'footprint' created by several hundred people living as a community. He also noticed that there was no clearing or central gathering place which was so common and necessary for a village. Living in strategically dispersed huts, the villagers lived as outcasts. They had chosen to sacrifice the few modern conveniences that were available to them. These persecuted Christians had made the choice to live undetected and as freely as possible among themselves.

A few moments after Paiyan's arrival at the remote and hidden enclave, Pastor Wanlee appeared from the opposite perimeter. Walking toward Paiyan, Wanlee stopped and without a word motioned the four men to follow him. The group of men disappeared back into the jungle following yet a different trail.

After trekking several hundred meters along winding paths, the men slipped through a narrow opening in a vine covered escarpment. To a casual observer, it would have appeared that the men vanished without a trace. The confined passageway, created over eons of time, concealed the entrance to a large cavern. The hidden cavern measured thirty meters in all directions creating a pristine sanctuary.

Inside, twenty or so individuals were present and

waiting for Paiyan's arrival. All of those present were gathered around in holy reverence, in a sacred place. Pastor Wanlee spoke in a hushed tone. "We are gathered here on holy ground. God's Word tells us that where two or more are gathered in His name, He will be in their midst. Friends, God is with us in this place. Let us worship Him in His holiness and awesome power."

The people began to worship God freely in a majestic display of singing; voicing words of adoration to the Lord. Abandonment to the presence of God is an awesome experience for the true believer. Spontaneous prayers began to waft up as incense to a loving and Holy God.

After an extended time of worship before the Lord, Pastor Wanlee spoke to the group. "As you know, we have been praying for this day for a long time. Paiyan you are an answer to our prayers. Come speak to us and encourage us." Paiyan was feeling humbled by the honor being bestowed upon him. He was just coming to realize that his purpose in coming to New Guinea was not at all what he imagined.

It was now crystal clear. Everything that had transpired over the last forty years was preparing him for a divine purpose. Paiyan's trip here was to witness a blessing reserved for a faithful people. "I don't know what to say, I'm overwhelmed. This gathering today comes right from the pages of the Book of Acts. I have stepped into our Lord's desire for His Bride, a separate and holy people dependent on Him. I am humbled in your presence."

Pastor Wanlee asked everyone to sit and draw close. "Paiyan, could you please stand beside me, I want to introduce some dear friends of yours. These people gathered here are all descendants of the families that escaped from your home island so many years ago. Paiyan, you are the only one of your generation to be alive from those fateful days. You may have known some of these gathered here as small children or infants but none here would know you personally. You are revered because of the stories handed down from their parents as well as the reports that have come back to us from the various islands of the Pacific." As Pastor Wanlee was speaking, he became tearful as he mentioned the remarkable accounts that meant so much to him.

Gathering his emotions he continued, "Paiyan, you must realize that in our minds and hearts you are the reigning king of our people—you are of royal linage. You were the island prince when our peoples were dispersed years ago." Paiyan had all but forgotten the truth of that statement. His dad was European, but yes, his mother was a princess—the oldest daughter of the king. Paiyan's father, who had been knighted by the Queen of England, evangelized his home island.

When Paiyan was twelve years old, his father, Sir John Francis Taylor died in his arms. In his moment of death, one of the greatest evangelists of that era was simply his dad. In the poignancy of the moment, God gave John Taylor and his son a gift of immense eternal significance. Before he died, John was able to pray for Paiyan. The great evangelist, *and dad*, asked God to supernaturally pass on his mantle and anointing for evangelism. The remembrance of that day flooded over Paiyan and invigorated his spirit.

Pastor Wanlee continued. "Paiyan, you asked me earlier today about the cause for our hidden church. For now, I will share a brief chronicle of His people on this island. Before I begin, please know that God has specifically forbidden me from giving you certain details. Paiyan, please forgive me but I must be obedient." Paiyan had rarely seen such faithfulness and absolute trust in God.

With Paiyan's acceptance and affirmation, Pastor Wanlee began. "When our parents arrived, they knew it was a miracle—they should not have made this journey alive. The five refugee families were welcomed by the villagers along the northern coast of the Huon Gulf. It was later discovered that if they had landed on the opposite shoreline, none of us would be here. They would have been massacred on the spot—so God was with them."

After a brief pause Wanlee continued, "Paiyan as you know, our parents brought with them the Truth of Jeshua (*ye-shew-a* —the islanders know Jesus as Jeshua). His Words were received with gladness and many people believed in Jeshua. Over time, some villages received Him and others didn't; just as His Word tells us to expect. The Word of our families' testimony spread throughout much of the north island. One day, a little over two years ago, a group of fifteen missionaries from our church went into the interior. They were going to the valley region between the central mountain ranges. They never returned. A week later, their disfigured bodies were found hanging on the trees lining the main roadway between the coastal villages."

Tearfully, Wanlee continued, "During those times, fear turned many of the villagers away from the church. To God's glory, there were equally as many who came to faith and trusted God for His protection and grace. Our church began to grow mightily with *true* believers who chose to lean not on their own understanding but trust in the truth of God's Word. These are the ones who have become fearless in His anointing. Revelation 12:11 became our strength as we live each day since that tragic loss. *'And they overcame him by the blood of the Lamb and by the word of their testimony, and they did not love their lives to the death.'"* (NKJ)

Paiyan recognized he was literally living the realities of the first century church. He felt as if he had stepped through the portals of time right into the gardens of Nero. He was broken before the Lord. Paiyan had lived through many trials and tribulations over his years of ministry but these deaths were heart rending. It was at that very moment of anguish, that Paiyan knew he would come back to these beautiful and faithful people. His heart was eternally knitted to theirs.

Pastor Wanlee was not allowed to reveal to Paiyan the following important portion of this story. The complete story is that there were only fourteen bodies found along the roadway. The missing fifteenth person was thought to be Paiyan's nephew, Konii. The bodies were in very bad condition so no one could say for sure. Konii was the leader in charge of the missionary excursion into the valley. (Konii means: man of grace. This was also the name Paiyan gave to his second born son.)

The questions about Konii's condition and whereabouts weighed heavy on the entire church. Was Paiyan's nephew, Konii, in captivity—was he being tortured for information— was he still alive? Pastor Wanlee knew in his heart that the silence required by God was for a purpose. God was in control and that any human intervention would defeat His plans.

Chapter Twenty-Two

Momentary Absence

Pastor Wanlee concluded by saying that since the murders the church had grown stronger and more unified. The severity of the test brought a sense of fearlessness to the underground church members. The absence of fear allowed them to live each day with a new boldness and courage. In fact, ministry to the neediest, the widow and orphan was enhanced and not diminished. The knitting of hearts, under these extraordinary conditions, had been a blessing no one could have imagined or would be willing to give up.

Paiyan spoke up, "Dear brothers and sisters in Christ, my heart has been pricked by your sufferings as well as your devotion and courage. God has put on my heart to come back and join-in with your mission here in New Guinea." Pastor

Wanlee was grateful for Paiyan's sincere and gracious offer.

To honor Paiyan's heartfelt desire to return, Pastor Wanlee wanted to assemble his key pastors as well as the local small group leaders. Wanlee felt he needed the evening and night to hear from the Lord so he suggested a meeting the following day. This would give him time to pray about who should attend. "Paiyan, tomorrow we will have an assembly on the north beach for a family gathering. We will roast a pig and rejoice at your desire to come back."

The festivities were an awesome display of friendship and familial love—true early church *koinonia*. Paiyan was at peace. He had found the sense of family belonging for which he yearned. In some ways, he had been set adrift emotionally, when he and his young family escaped the island many years ago. Of course, he had dear friends and he had his own marvelous and loving family but when his ancestral roots were severed, he lost part of who he was. Now, today, Paiyan was being honored in his ancestral role as a prince and heir apparent to the throne of their fathers. The tribute was not an idolatrous affair but a desire to honor Paiyan as a leader placed by God, to bring governance to their

> *The festivities were an awesome display of friendship and familial love—true early church koinonia.*

peoples.

Since the night's gathering of families had a dual purpose, Pastor Wanlee covertly gathered the key leaders off to the side as the festivities continued. "Paiyan, I have prayed about your desire to return and join us. Please listen carefully to what you are about to hear. The Lord has a strategy for your return trip. *When you come back, the underground church is not to be your focus because in the eyes of many, we do not exist. Come as if we don't exist. Go to the tribal chiefs, the mayors, the official religious leaders as well as the governmental agencies and dignitaries. God will direct you and show you what He wants done and how to accomplish it."*

Pastor Wanlee finished with a long prayerful pause before continuing. "You may be surprised by these words—they were not what you expected to hear. Paiyan, there is a larger purpose that goes beyond our understanding. There is a private plane waiting for you down the beach. Go in peace my brother."

Once again, Paiyan was completely caught off guard. He had not had a chance to consider his departure, much less when or how he would leave. Paiyan had been fully engrossed with the last two days of covert travel, secret meetings and life or death suspense. He hadn't had a spare minute to think of anything else except what was unfolding before him. Was all of this scripted? Then it occurred to him. The meetings, the twists and turns of the last few days were organized, possibly rehearsed, for a long time. At that moment of remembrance, Pastor Wanlee's first words came back to him; "...*we've been expecting you....*"

As Paiyan walked down the beach toward the waiting pontoon plane, he felt as if he was walking through a veil from one existence into another. Paiyan was an old man by anyone's estimation. He had been to more places, had seen and experienced more, than most people would in two lifetimes. He was acutely familiar with all kinds of manifestations including the natural, the unnatural and the supernatural. He thought he had seen and experienced it all, until this week.

Safely back in Manila, Paiyan was eager to report on his trip to John Wheaton; his ministry partner. What started out as a personal trip expanded into a major effort to reach New Guinea, possibly the largest outreach of his ministry. John was a 'go' from the start and immediately began planning an advance trip.

Chapter Twenty-Three

Happy are the Feet of Them

Back to the Seattle Departure

The handshakes were passionate as the complete team came together in their first assembly with Bruce Phillips present. It was also the final meeting before the group departed early in the a.m. Assembled in John's home office, Grace and the others circled their folding chairs to face each other. Similar to a huddle before the big game winning play, the sense of expectancy was tangible.

Everyone present was already eager to go before the Lord as John opened the meeting with a call to pray. Each person prayed the burdens, concerns and promptings that God had put on their hearts. As one person finished praying, another would begin—each standing in agreement and adding to the prayers of the others. There would be moments of complete silence as each listened to the Holy Spirit with a desire to pray Spirit led prayers. John closed with a final prayer that reemphasized the common thread woven through the last hour of petitions before the Lord. "Lord, go before us and prepare the way. Give us favor with those we meet. Let this endeavor be for Your Glory."

The rendezvous' and the flight connections went like

clockwork. The Seattle team arrived safely at the Jackson's International Airport near the capitol city of Port Moresby, New Guinea. All six team members (Paul was already at the hotel), and a fair amount of gear, were gathered on the tarmac.

An open air tram, of sorts, came shooting and weaving diagonally across the concrete apron in a 'third world' fashion—one wheel was spinning with a nauseating wobble. In unison, Frank and Dr. Hamas whispered under their breath, "Lord, help us all." Somehow, six people with a sizeable amount of luggage and supplies were loaded onto the oversized golf cart.

The untraveled and inexperienced among the team were in awestruck terror as the undersized and overloaded tram bolted onto the busy streets of Port Moresby. Taken from the script of a Charlie Chaplin silent movie, the six team members were bounced around in what seemed to be a cruel comedy skit. Needless to say, the arrival at the historic Blauvelt Hotel was a much welcomed affair.

The local church pastors had taken care of everything down to the last detail. In two hours, the M.I.M.G advance team's itinerary would begin with a ballroom function within the hotel. The mayor, chief of police, chairman of the Chamber of Commerce as well as a representative of Full Gospel Businessmen's International were invited. The session opening speaker would be local evangelist, Bill Seichrist. Of course, the guests of honor were John Wheaton Jr. and Paiyan W. Taylor.

Since John was the keynote speaker for the M.I.M.G., he closed the evening with a short but rousing call to missions that was well received and applauded. Many well-wishers, volunteers as well as financial donors approached the team afterward to join in the missionary effort.

The local religious community had done a marvelous job of putting together a successful social event to kick off the campaign. Now the real work would begin—harnessing the momentum and enthusiasm created with the conference attendees. As the word spread outward into the outlying villages and townships, the invitations poured in. Within seventy-two hours a full agenda had developed for all three M.I.M.G. teams.

The seven member advance team was paired into three groups of two with Grace, Paiyan and Frank forming the odd pair. Bruce Phillips, in charge of the relief efforts, would be working side by side with Dr. Richard Hamas because their mission purposes were interrelated. Lastly, John Jr. and his son Paul, while attending to their own itinerary, would alternate between the other teams as requested, especially when a speech or sermon was needed. Now, each group would follow-up on contacts made during and after the gala event.

Two Weeks Later: After fulfilling two full weeks of engagements, meetings, roundtable discussions, fundraising efforts and prayer sessions, it was time to begin piecing together information and requests for ministry opportunities for the return trip. Each team member was exhausted, the schedule had been demanding. Yet, everyone was full of hope and vision for the upcoming missionary drive.

The advance team members were gathered for a final debriefing at the hotel restaurant. After completing the business at hand, John made a surprise announcement that was unanimously applauded. As a contingency move, he had scheduled-in an extra two days just in case things hadn't gone smoothly. He and Frank made that decision early on as a safety valve maneuver to prevent a chaotic ending to the trip. Everyone was encouraged to use the two extra days to stay and relax. Due to business and other scheduling issues, Dr. Hamas and Bruce Phillips opted to go ahead and return to Seattle.

By now, each of the remaining team members knew the area well enough to get around. However, John insisted that no one should go out alone. John rode with Dr. Hamas and Bruce Phillips to the airport to see them off that evening. Ironically, the outrageous driving no longer bothered the men after two weeks of traveling in the midst of sheer mayhem.

Chapter Twenty-Four

An Open Heaven

Paiyan knew immediately where he would spend his time utilizing the two remaining days. Eagerly, Paiyan extended an invitation with gusto. "Frank, Grace, I want you to come with me. I want to introduce you to the hidden church that brought us here." Paiyan had been almost nonstop in recounting his experiences to his friends. Grace and Frank were reenergized when Paiyan asked them go along to meet these authentic New Testament Saints.

Paiyan had been true to Pastor Wanlee's word given to him from the Lord. He had not sought out or focused on making contact with the underground church. Pastor Wanlee had told him to: *"...Come as if we don't exist...."* Now that the meetings were over and this was personal time, Paiyan wanted to see his 'new' old friend and bring him encouraging news.

While the trio made their way to the northern shore, it occurred to Paiyan that this entire area had escaped efforts to be reached by the advance team. He began to feel a little strange about that thought. All three teams met with every leader who came forward and indicated a need. How did this whole geographical area get left out—what was going on?

Paiyan and the others retraced his steps to the coastal

village of Cincittia, the place where he had previously met Pastor Wanlee. The three 'tourists' were walking shoulder to shoulder toward the area of town where, three months earlier, Paiyan had taken a break to have some coffee. He remembered the small sidewalk café well—the epicenter of where all this began.

As they approached the café, *Paiyan felt as if he was walking through a veil from one existence into another.* It was the same experience he felt when he walked down the beach to the pontoon plane. He now understood that he was stepping into a supernatural dimension—the alternate reality that always exists but few experience.

It now made sense. The 'early church' experiences of his last trip were just that—Spirit led encounters in the midst of spiritual warfare. It was now crystal clear. Pastor Wanlee was led along in the power of the Spirit as he walked in the Spirit—darkness was held at bay. This time the encounter was more perceptible, more recognizable—this time darkness was pushing back.

Grace and Frank had experienced the same perceivable feeling of transition. Both looked at Paiyan at the same time but it was Grace who spoke up. "What was that... what just happened?" Paiyan knew he had some explaining to do. They chose a table under the tattered green striped awning of the now infamous café to collect their thoughts. Paiyan spent a full hour 'connecting the dots' while rehashing the entire last three months along with his latest revelation. The awareness of 'penetrating the veil' allowed the three seasoned warriors to prepare for the impending clash in the heavenlies.

Paiyan, Grace and Frank each felt that a spiritual battle was eminent. But who or what were they up against? Even with that question unanswered, Paiyan felt everyone was prepared for what could be in store for them.

> *There was one thing that was needed, and that was a prayer covering.*

All three had stood victorious in the face of evil so undue fear was not an issue.

Paiyan felt there was one thing needed, and that was a prayer covering. Still gathered at the sidewalk café, each began to pray as they were led by the Holy Spirit. Petitions were passionately expressed asking for protection, wisdom, discernment, courage, spiritual covering, for favor and guidance. The spiritual heaviness seemed to lift but not dissipate.

After their time of prayer, Paiyan was now able to refocus on his original intentions of rejoining the church family he had grown to love. Regaining his sense of direction, he turned to point to the little storefront church where he met

Pastor Wanlee Michaels. To his utter amazement it was not there. His mouth was gaping open when Grace finally had to ask, "Paiyan are you O.K.?" Without speaking, Paiyan rose and started walking across the narrow street.

"China Tea Trading Company... it's not here... the church is not here. This is where the church was located. There's no hand carved archway, no cross... what is going on here?" Still standing outside, Paiyan considered the possibilities. Of course, any number of things could have transpired in the three months since he had been here. "Let's go inside and find out what happened to the church."

Not realizing what he was doing, Paiyan was about to reveal that he was privy to information that he wasn't supposed to know. Then, as if spoken audibly, he heard: *"in the eyes of many, we do not exist."* At that very moment, Paiyan's jaws locked shut leaving him unable to speak.

Entering the curio shop, unaware of Paiyan's dilemma, the trio stood in an awkward silence as the shopkeeper, Dysong, looked curiously at three 'shoppers.' As if reading from a script, Grace began a very touristy conversation with the storeowner. "I noticed a beautiful carved ivory pendant in the window, may I see it please... do you ship?" Chit-chatting with Dysong, Grace finally got around to asking the question. "How long has your family been in this location?" Dysong explained, in his broken English, that his family had been in the same storefront for three generations. Still speechless, Paiyan's facial expression went from dismay to exasperation.

When Dysong handed Grace her wrapped pendant he slipped a note into her hand. He looked right into her eyes and they remained locked in a mutual stare until she realized that he was trying tell her something. In a very nonchalant manner, Grace positioned herself so that she could read the note without bringing attention to herself. *"For your own safety, you must leave quickly. Please eat this note now!"* Ever so casually, Grace slipped the note into her mouth as if she was going to chew a stick of gum—it was raspberry flavored.

Grace said nothing to the others. She simply nodded (almost a bow) to Dysong and began to leave the shop immediately. Grace had been so successful in reading the note, without detection, that the men weren't aware what had just transpired. Frank and Paiyan had no choice but to follow.

Grace didn't slow down but went from shop to shop like a tourist might do if looking for a last minute gift. The men were willing to go along with Grace because she seemed to be on a special assignment and they were clueless anyway. She slowed her pace as the three reached a small historic looking park where a group of children were playing. This seemed like a safe place to catch their breath.

Grace, Frank and Paiyan found an ancient, cast iron park bench and sat for a few moments before anyone dared to speak. Grace broke the silence. "O.K., I think I have something here. Dysong handed me a note telling us to leave quickly, *that's why we left so quickly.*" The last half of her statement was made in a humorous singsong fashion. The combination of travel weariness, adrenaline and suspense was having an effect on the group—kind of like a punch-drunk boxer. Rational behavior seemed to be escaping them as their sensibilities were being challenged.

With Paiyan's speech returned to him, they took a few minutes to discuss the surreal encounter at the gift emporium and then decided to head back to their rooms. It wasn't long before Paiyan stopped walking. Annoyed with himself he spoke up in a troubled tone. "What are we doing? This is not making sense. Our brothers and sisters in Christ are in need, possibly in danger, and we're walking back to the lodge? We've got to go back to follow this thing through. We are in the middle of a spiritual battle and we can't just walk away as if defeated."

Simultaneously, the three agreed they must not be cajoled into walking away from a fight that has already been won by the shed blood of Jesus. Grace sensed they should return to the park and pick up where they left off.

Grace, Paiyan and Frank turned to reenter the small park. They were led to the center where a decorative cobblestone piazza created a focal point for the surrounding area. On the outer edges of the cobblestone clearing, walkways radiated outward like spokes in all directions. On the courtyard's edge, between each walkway, were placed a pair of park benches that were back-to-back facing in opposing directions. This arrangement allowed for different views of the park—wooded, serene vistas in one direction and people watching entertainment when viewing the piazza.

Frank was reminded of his life changing encounter with the forces of extreme evil in his parish office two months ago. He recalled how God had supernaturally given him words of praise and thanksgiving in the critical moments of the deadly satanic attack. Frank believed that if God had not intervened he would have succumbed to demonic oppression—surrendering in defeat. Instead, by cooperating with God, Frank had since enjoyed the fruits of the overwhelming victory won that momentous day.

"Paiyan, Grace, we need to sing praises and express thanksgiving to God—we need to lift up His name in the midst of this spiritual battle—*the battle is the Lord's.*" Both Grace and Paiyan knew from personal experience the biblical principle of praise and worship, how exalting God brings deliverance.

The three valiant warriors began boldly singing hymns and praise songs that glorified God. Their praise offerings were lifted up in unison, intensifying the angelic struggle being waged in the unseen principalities above Cincittia and the surrounding geographical area. A war was being fought for the control of the heavenly realm over this part of northeastern New Guinea—an open heaven was in the balance.

The intensity of the spiritual warfare was attracting a mixed reaction among the park inhabitants. Very few could remain neutral in their perception of what was transpiring before them. Many chose to scurry away to avoid the confrontation in their own hearts—to close their spiritual eyes and remain in their darkness. However, as some receded outward, others were making their way toward the center of the park. Hungry hearts slowly gravitated toward the sounds of heavenly singing and worship. The appeal was compelling those seeking goodness, mercy and righteousness—to enter in to this heavenly adulation.

Before long, there were dozens of people worshipping and crying out with praises and thanksgiving. Just as the acclaim reached a crescendo, the intensity slowly decreased to a reverent silence. Many of the worshippers remained in a prayerful posture; some kneeling, some sitting, others with lifted hands. This was a time of changed hearts as well as victory over darkness and death.

Paiyan knew that things had changed around him, the enemy was routed and in retreat. He felt a leading to go and find the hidden village where he was taken on his first trip. This was the next logical step in their quest to find Pastor Wanlee as well as the fate of His faithful and obedient people. "We must find the highland village with the secret sanctuary. If we can locate the hidden village, then we can find Pastor Wanlee and the underground church. I'm sure I can get us to the edge of town where the paths lead up to the village. We'll just have trust the Lord from there."

Paiyan, Grace and Frank made their way down a series of lanes retracing the turns that Pastor Wanlee had taken Paiyan months earlier. "O.K., this is the trail that Pastor Wanlee began his hike up into the jungle. And, I believe this is the path that I was taken blindfolded. I don't know where either path leads but we can choose."

Just as Paiyan finished his sentence, a six hooded brutes descended on the trio from all directions. The assailants seemed to be carrying out a prepared plan as they pulled large burlap sacks over their prey. Paiyan was being treated especially rough with elbows and knees to the abdomen. Frank and Grace were tied up and thrown into the bed of a waiting pickup truck. It was now apparent that Paiyan was being singled out to receive a beating and hideous ridicule. The taunting and slapping were meant to demoralize.

Grace sensed that she and Frank were unguarded so she managed to get up on her knees. Peeking through a tear in her gunnysack, she could see that the bullies had removed their hoods. They were making sport as they laughed and randomly kicked Paiyan—joking about his powerlessness. It was reminiscent of a childish taunt teasing a powerful beast behind the glass at the Seattle Zoo.

Growing tired of their impish folly, the gang of misfits dragged Paiyan to the truck and heaved him in with ignorant disdain. Incredibly, Paiyan seemed unfazed by the whole affair. Speaking through his sack, as if this was an ordinary occurrence, he sought to reassure his companions. "I'm fine… this is nothing… happens to me all the time." His unseen smile did not go unnoticed by his bound companions.

The driver of the pickup was a hapless backwoods buffoon. He mercilessly ground the gears as he ran over every hole and rock for sheer enjoyment. For over two hours, the three gunny sacked captives looked like live fish flip flopping on a Seattle pier.

Suddenly, the truck stopped but the pain continued—the bruises were countless and deep. Paiyan, Grace and Frank arrived alive but would their injuries be fatal? Would they be executed like the last missionaries who dared to go to the valley region? Their agonizing arrival held an air of dire uncertainty.

The truck had been seen coming—its arrival was expected. The seditious kidnappers were now the target for wilderness justice. The awaiting village tribesmen surrounded the truck to view the ill-gotten catch—the target of the morning hunt.

Chapter Twenty-Five
Out of the Darkness

Second Sidebar—Konii's Story; the surviving missionary leader.

TWO YEARS, SIX MONTHS PRIOR

Reprise: *…Pastor Wanlee was not allowed to reveal to Paiyan the complete story—there were only fourteen bodies desecrated along the roadway. The identity of the fifteenth person was thought to be Paiyan's nephew, Konii. The bodies were in very bad condition so no one could say for sure. Konii was the leader in charge of the missionary excursion into the valley.*

The questions about Konii's condition and whereabouts weighed heavy on the entire church. Was Paiyan's nephew, Konii, in captivity—was he being tortured for information—

was he still alive? Pastor Wanlee knew, in his heart, that the silence required by God was for a purpose. God was in control and that any human intervention would defeat His plans.

The cruelty dealt to the ambushed missionaries was barbaric. Konii was made to watch as his beloved brothers and sisters in Christ were tortured and murdered before his eyes. The bodies were piled like cordwood and left on the side of the path to rot. (The bodies were collected by government scouts who covertly witnessed the bloodshed. The missionaries were then hung on display to discourage the underground church). Konii was bound and then dragged behind an old Chevrolet pickup to the valley encampment of his belligerent captors. He was left for dead, still tied to the bumper, as the marauders simply left him and went on about the day having accomplished their mission.

> *Barely alive and semiconscious, Konii began moaning as he was being rolled to the edge of the water.*

The next morning Konii was untied so he could be discarded—thrown into the river; to be taken downstream. Barely alive and semiconscious, Konii began moaning as he was being rolled to the edge of the water. The two young boys, who had been given the mundane task of dumping Konii's body, were terrified when he began to moan and whimper. In horror, they hastily backed up and then began to run, falling over themselves as they made their retreat. Fearing for their own lives they didn't say anything to anyone about their failed assignment.

Later in the morning, a group of the tribal chief's indentured handmaidens were gathering water near the lifeless body. When Konii made a plea for help, several of the women screamed in fright, spoiling the familiar tranquility of the morning. The unexpected screams startled the three tribesmen who were assigned to protect the women during their routine trips to the river.

The often bored entourage, being caught off guard, stumbled down the embankment to the sight of the commotion. Interestingly, none of those present were privy to the previous day's massacre; to them Konii was an unknown entity. As the men were assuaged of the danger, one guard was sent back to the village encampment to report the helpless intruder. Meanwhile, the women's maternal instincts prevailed for the moment, as they began to render aid to the badly bruised and beaten Konii.

Melanio was the guard chosen to inform the tribal chief of Konii's presence. Chief Wasonga (Wä sông gă) was an irritable and lethargic long lived tribal chief. Since his abrupt ascent to village leader as an adolescent, Chief Wasonga's troubled rule covered a thirty kilometer stretch of the valley. His father was assassinated by a rival tribe when Wasonga was just fifteen years old. His mother, Luana, co-led the village with her young son until her death. The courageous Luana was shrewd and very smart. She deftly orchestrated the complete annihilation of the rival tribe that had killed her husband. Then seven years later, on the very day of the young Wasonga's coronation, as sole ruler of the village, she gave her life to once again save the village and ensure her son's reign as chief.

Melanio was brought before the ageing and bellicose chief to report his discovery. The chief was instantly bored with the whole affair and waved off Melanio before he could complete his first sentence. Melanio, risking insubordination, spoke anyway. The gruff uninterested response was typical of the chief in recent years. "Do with him as you want. It's of no concern to me."

The chief had been unaware of the raid perpetrated on the fifteen missionaries. It was Jarten, the eldest son of the chief, who had ordered the horrible bloodbath. Jarten was bitter for having to live in his father's shadow—thinking he was more than ready to take over his father's reign. In the last few years, Jarten had stealthily assembled a band of loyal followers within the ranks of the tribal warriors. Several key members within the tribal council were under his sway as well. Jarten planned to use subversion to overthrow his father.

Jarten, in a drunken stupor, ordered the raid to satisfy a dare from his disenfranchised men. In a rowdy confrontation, the men were spitefully questioning his resolve to standup to his father and take actions of his own. Chief Wasonga had become lazy and careless with his power by not paying attention to his son's plotting.

Melanio, the diligent guard who found Konii, was still loyal to the reigning chief. After his brief meeting with the chief, Melanio returned to rejoin his guarding party. When he returned to his post, Konii was gone and so were the women. His two fellow guards would not disclose what happened to the 'prisoner.' Melanio was not responsible, by the chief's own words, so he let it go.

Over the ensuing weeks, the women were able to keep Konii hidden long enough to bring him to a minimum level of health. The chief's inattentiveness and poor leadership would allow Konii ample opportunity to escape. The chance to make a run-for-it came but his freedom would elude him.

Ironically, even now, no one in the camp knew who Konii was or that he even existed. The only men who could identify him were a few members of the raiding party and they thought he was long gone, thus completely out of their memory. Even Jarten, the rebellious chief's son was not aware of Konii or any of the circumstances that surrounded him. Jarten was completely detached from the events of the massacre because he didn't even remember ordering it.

Konii never had a chance when he made his poorly planned attempt to escape. He was discovered and taken to the chief as an interloper. Chief Wasonga was not to be bothered. He was preoccupied with the musings of a castrated adulterer turned court jester. The improvised court jester's ability to amuse the chief was the only thing that kept him alive—he had become quite good at it. The chief's flippant attitude caused his men, who were still loyal to him, to question his leadership even further. Konii and his captors were told to wait outside the chief's chambers while the charades continued inside.

Knowing that sure death was only moments away, Konii began to pray silently, thanking God for His goodness and mercy and the life he had with Him. Suddenly, Chief Wasonga began shouting orders to have the captive brought before him. With Konii's hands tied behind his back, he was dropped on his knees before the chief. The chief sat emotionless as Konii's circumstances were described to him by the lead guard. For some reason the chief sat up straight in his oversized chair and leaned toward his prisoner. He proceeded to ask Konii a rather penetrating and sincere question, uncharacteristic of the latter reign of this apathetic leader. "What are you here for?"

Konii lifted his head and looked straight into the eyes of the chief. Like the account of Stephen, in the book of Acts, the glory of the Lord was shining out from Konii's countenance. In that moment, the chief was drawn toward the unquenchable flame of God's irresistible Love. This kind of love reminded him of a brief glimmer from his distant past. Rather than feeling threatened by Konii, the chief was drawn to him— Konii had the chiefs' favor, at least for the moment.

Konii was ready to speak. "Sir, I am here to bring you Good News—I am here to serve you."

These were the oddest words ever uttered to the chief, so much so he didn't understand what Konii meant by them. "What could you possibly mean by that? I have the power of life or death in my hands to do with you as I wish—you have no other choice but to serve me."

Konii replied in a calm assurance, "Sir, I do have a choice. To die is a minor thing compared to obeying my God and answering His call to love you and bring His freedom to you."

The chief was enraged with the apparent challenge to his authority. "Off with the prisoner, get him out of my sight."

The show of strength and decisiveness was

emboldening to chief's attendants. "What shall we do with him, sir?"

"Put him in the hole until I call for him." Immediately the chief began having a conversation with himself. "What could that possibly mean…, why would I say that." The chief did not know why he had uttered the words: *"until I call for him."* Konii's words would not leave the chief's mind. He couldn't escape the power behind them.

Chief Wasonga was unable to sleep that night. There was a war raging in the heavenlies for his soul. His physical body was being buffeted as he tossed and turned. Unknowingly, he was wrestling for his place in eternity.

The next morning the chief awoke and immediately called for Konii to be brought to him. "Explain to me, what is going on here? I perceive you have answers to questions that have plagued me since I was a young man."

For the next two years, Konii gained ever increasing favor with the chief. As Konii spent time with the chief, he taught him about God's Word which brought about a renewing of Wasonga's mind. The chief began to rule with renewed vigor and sensibilities. Chief Wasonga had regained his stature as a leader and won over most of the tribal men who had strayed, solidifying his rightful place with the tribal counsel.

Chief Wasonga's increased stature only served to

intensify his rebellious son's resentment. Fortunately, Jarten's loyal mutinous followers had dwindled to a dozen or so misfits that were nothing more than mindless goons. In a desperate attempt at a coup, the insanely covetous Jarten called his henchmen to a meeting.

Over the course of the last two years since Konii arrived, Jarten had heard the name Paiyan repeated over and over again and was sick of hearing it. He repeatedly sent his men out into the villages trying to capture Paiyan the first time he came to the island. Despite multiple opportunities, every attempt was foiled—as if he was untouchable. However, this time was different; he could sense Paiyan's vulnerability. Sure enough, when the time came Paiyan practically fell into his hands. His men even mocked at Paiyan's weakness and cowardice.

Back to the trio's terrifying arrival at their unknown destination.

Reprise: *The driver of the pick-up was a hapless backwoods buffoon. He mercilessly ground-the-gears and ran over every hole and rock for sheer enjoyment. For over two hours, the three gunny sacked captives looked like live fish flip flopping on a Seattle pier. Suddenly, the truck stopped but the pain continued—the bruises were countless and deep. Paiyan, Grace and Frank arrived alive but would their injuries be fatal? Would they be executed like the last missionaries who dared to go to the valley region? Their agonizing arrival held an air of dire uncertainty.*

The truck had been seen coming—its arrival was expected. The seditious kidnappers were now the target for wilderness justice. The awaiting village tribesmen surrounded the truck to view the ill-gotten catch—the target of their morning hunt.

The pickup arrived late in the afternoon to an unexpected reception. The ridiculous, ill-conceived coup had been revealed and the perpetrators were facing the wrath of Chief Wasonga. The mutinous men were seized and corralled by the chief's men. The chief however, did not constrain the deceitful Jarten because he had convinced his father that the mutiny was conceived among the men. He told his father that the seditious actions were their own. The kidnapping would somehow gain them an advantage.

Chief Wasonga didn't know the scope of this misguided abduction as he ordered the hostages removed from the truck bed. "Get those people over here, now!" His men jumped to it and untied the brutalized victims. The three captives were freed from their restraints and helped to their feet—none of which could remain standing.

The beating received in the rough trip was vicious

leaving Frank, Grace and Paiyan bloody and swollen. What was not bruised and bleeding was rubbed raw from the gunny sack—leaving Frank unrecognizable. Physically, Frank was the strongest and stood again to his feet as the chief approached them. In a somewhat humbled yet anxious tone the chief asked, "Are you the great Paiyan?" Frank was unable to speak so he gestured toward Paiyan, who was still on his knees yet slumped—caught midway in his attempt to stand erect.

In a gracious gesture, the chief reached down to Paiyan and offered him a helping hand. When the chief bent over, an unfolding drama was revealed to Frank's line-of-sight. The chief's heartfelt gesture towards Paiyan enraged the insanely jealous Jarten. He was going to lunge a spear at the two men hoping to kill one or both of them. Frank bolted, pushing Chief Wasonga to the ground and in the process falling over Paiyan—effectively shielding him from the spear. The spear found its mark piercing Frank's upper abdomen. The spear entered his chest cavity from the side penetrating his heart, killing him instantly.

In the ensuing chaos Grace began screaming in terror at the sight of Frank's murder. In absolute hysteria, Grace hopelessly tried to undo the damage. The already traumatized and exhausted Grace was overcome and went into shock. Paiyan was not much better. He was effectively buried under

Grace and Frank. Not aware of Frank's fate, Paiyan was helpless.

Ten of the chief's men ruthlessly tackled Jarten and in the process broke his neck accidently killing him. The tumultuous chaos that had erupted all around Chief Wasonga would not deter his attention from the travesty that lay before him. A hero of the faith that he had grown to love, now lay buried in a twisted heap of carnage. As soon as the unharmed chief was helped to his feet, he immediately fell forward to his knees weeping. The once hardened chief had never shed a tear in his adult life—God had been working on his heart.

Konii was across the village in a work detail tending to the large multi-acre garden he had initiated for the chief. Konii came running when he heard the screams and then saw the commotion. Not knowing what had transpired, Konii's first thought was that the chief had become ill. Grabbing the kneeling chief in a concerned embrace, Konii insisted "Chief, I'll go for help!"

Shaking his head, the heartbroken chief whispered to Konii, "No, don't leave me."

THE MAJOR SIDEBAR

Interlude of Darkness

This important interlude takes us to the origins of the persecuted church of New Guinea. This crucial storyline will bring this amazing story full circle. Please remember that the characters, places and circumstances, are completely fictional. Any perceived correlations are strictly by coincidence.

—44 YEARS EARLIER—

Circa 1945

Chapter Twenty-Six

The Escape of Evil

The white ash 'snowflakes' had been falling for over a week. When the mountain island started rumbling one month ago, many of the island people believed the gods were angry. As a young family man, Paiyan had rightly believed that the volcano would erupt any day.

When Paiyan was a youth, he was told many stories about the great mountain—how the occasional rumbling meant that the gods were angry. Paiyan's dad, Monteau (Mŏn tā ū), told him how the old tribal king and elders had once tried to appease the gods. Ignorant and desperate, the tribal elders attempted a ceremonial sacrifice involving the king's daughter—the island princess. Monteau explained to the young Paiyan that the gods of the underworld had nothing to do with the volcano's rumbling. Only Jeshua (*ye-shew-a*) had the power to move the earth.

Paiyan felt convinced that he and his family would need to leave the island very soon. Since the time he learned how to believe in Jeshua, Paiyan had a '*knowing*' about things that would bring harm to him. Once a large poisonous snake was ready to strike Paiyan and bring sure death. But Jeshua warned him just in time. He was able to turn away so the snake missed biting him.

Paiyan began building a pair of rafts almost two months ago even before he could feel the rumbles. A few weeks after Paiyan began building the rafts, his goats and pigs began acting strange; trying to runoff. He was forced to begin restraining them with ropes. Then a week later Paiyan began to feel the rumblings too.

Paiyan knew the evil tribal leaders must not discover his plans to leave the doomed island. He was convinced that if the king and his elders suspected Paiyan was trying to leave, they would kill him and his entire household. Fortunately, Paiyan and his family lived on a remote part of the island separated by a mountainous ridge that runs like a spine down the center of the island. Even so, he was always within reach if the evil king wanted to torment his family.

Paiyan's home was located on a protected horseshoe shaped cove on the windward side of the island. Beautiful and secluded as it was, living on the windward side of the island held a distinct disadvantage when choosing to exit with two cumbersome rafts. The tide, wind and currents would only throw him back upon the rock strewn beach unless he timed his escape perfectly. Paiyan was prepared to leave at a moment's notice as he watched and monitored the weather conditions. His concern for the other islanders was overridden by his inability to choose the timing of his escape. The other families were located with access to the leeward side of the island which meant they could leave as soon as they were ready.

Ironically, Paiyan did not know the evil King Moloch was making similar plans to leave the island. The king's escape was being organized in a heavily guarded lagoon protected inlet on the leeward side of the island. The evil king had dozens of men working around the clock to build, supply and launch three giant barge-like rafts. The cowardly and selfish king ordered any available resource or provision to be seized from the island people. Some of the islanders were even murdered to conceal his secret cruel escape.

> *Some of the islanders were even murdered to cover his secret cruel escape.*

The day of King Moloch's escape came and went. The remaining islanders were unaware that the king and thirty-eight men, women and children deserted in the middle of the night. The tyrant's watery flight was slow and methodical, drifting with the prevailing southerly winds and flowing ocean currents—it all seemed inequitable.

Meanwhile, early in the morning, the day after the king left unnoticed, fifty-four islanders (the future hidden church of New Guinea) congregated on northern tip of the island. A desolate place covered with massive windswept sand dunes. To the uninformed observer, this scene would have been seen as eerily bleak and depressing—a mass of desperate people seemingly trapped with no way to escape their impending doom.

Over the last two months, five families had joined together and stashed their longboats along with meager supplies on the leeward side of the northernmost tip of the island. Their oversized oceangoing canoes would hold eight to ten people along with provisions.

Five sentries were strategically placed along the ridges that encompassed the deserted beachhead. At the all clear signal, everyone quickly yet quietly began uncovering the longboats that were buried in the huge mountains of sand. If they had only known that the king was already gone, the fear and trepidation could have been avoided.

By ten o'clock, after hours of tension and toil, the canoes were in the water and loaded; ready to launch out to sea. Then, when the signal was given, the eight massive canoes were launched into the surf in four groups of two. Once out to sea, the eight outrigger longboats were lashed together in pairs, side by side; a practice meant to increase their stability on the open sea. The pairs of boats were then tethered together (three to five meters apart) end-to-end to form a long often serpentine caravan. The strong southbound ocean current was the same oceangoing highway that carried the evil king and his entourage.

Chapter Twenty-Seven

Murder on the High Seas

Two days into his corrupt and vicious island escape, King Moloch's flotilla approached the commercial shipping lanes. About one-hundred kilometers from their former island home, the malevolent king and his reluctant subjects were spotted by a Japanese patrol boat.

These relatively small but powerful gunboats typically patrolled the fringes of the shipping lanes. This particular sixty-foot patrol boat was scouting for enemy combatants attempting to ambush Japanese military ships. The patrol boat fell in line behind King Moloch's caravan and followed the train of barge like rafts for several minutes before closing in.

King Moloch knew immediately what he would do. He instructed the women and children to feign illness as the patrol boat approached their rafts. By acting ignorant and pleading for mercy, he caught the five Japanese sailors off guard as they boarded the lead raft. At just the right moment, King Moloch gave the signal and his men overpowered the boarding party. He ordered the captain tied up while the rest of the sailors were slain, stripped of their uniforms and dumped into the sea. King Moloch saved his clan by acting quickly. Capturing the patrol boat would prove invaluable; ensuring passage to a new home.

Drunk with conquest, King Moloch stood at the helm of his new boat. He triumphantly ordered his men to secure a tow rope to the lead raft. The king was fascinated with his new towboat but quickly realized he needed his detained sailor to operate the complex machine.

Wide-eyed with fear, Joonlee was ready to do anything to save his life.

Joonlee was the captured sailor who had just seen his comrade's throats cut and their bodies discarded. Wide-eyed with fear, Joonlee was ready to do anything to save his life. With his hands untied, but closely guarded, Joonlee began to slowly pull the giant rafts.

After only a few hours of towing, the lead raft began to slowly come apart. It was not able to withstand the forces of being pulled. Enraged, the quick tempered king began cutting at the ropes intending to abandon the rafts of men, women and children to perilously float on the high seas. Joonlee, the kidnapped sailor, eager to save his own life convinced the king to spare the others. Joonlee was quick to point out that in order to survive everyone was going to be needed.

The king calmed down as he listened to the common sense and wisdom of his new captive. Joonlee even pointed out the problem with the feeble raft. The tow ropes needed to be extended and tied to each of the barges. That way each barge would share the forces of being pulled. After a short delay of only four hours, Joonlee and a few men were able to rebuild and reinforce the lead raft. Once the tow ropes were reconfigured, the small convoy was once again underway.

The weeks before Joonlee's capture, persistent rumors of a Japanese surrender to the allied forces, brought fear and dread. His former crewmates had often discussed life after the war but their musings were framed in the context of a Japanese victory, not defeat. To a Japanese soldier, death and defeat are synonymous. Fearing he was doomed either way, Joonlee felt he had nothing to lose by cooperating with the Moloch. Nonetheless, cooperating with an enemy meant he was relinquishing any remaining vestiges of honor as a human being.

Over the course of the last few years of military duty, Joonlee had acquired a command of the island dialect enabling him to communicate with the king and foster his pretend alliance. Even knowing that he was being used, the prisoner-sailor proved his worth by stealing hundreds of gallons of diesel fuel on an overnight raid of his former patrol base. Joonlee's only hope was to prove himself to be invaluable; buying time to plan his escape.

As the motley crew traveled into the South Pacific, Joonlee realized that he would be doomed if Moloch sought another small remote island. Joonlee concluded that his only chance for freedom would be on a large populated landmass. He knew just the place. Two years ago, Joonlee participated in wartime maneuvers off the coast of New Guinea. He must now convince King Moloch to head for the port of call he visited during his training exercises.

With his plan thought out, Joonlee took the king to the patrol boat map room and laid out the charts of the region. He was sure he could convince the king to resettle in New Guinea. After considering Joonlee's ideas, the king was beginning to recognize how valuable Joonlee was becoming—the evil king liked Joonlee's plan.

By now, Joonlee estimated that they were seven-hundred kilometers from the northeastern tip of New Guinea. The ocean current was doing all the work as it carried the band of refugees toward New Guinea. Just by going with the flow,

Joonlee knew that navigating his way to New Guinea was going to be easy if he could avoid detection by enemy warships. He was able to guide the makeshift flotilla in and out of the shipping lanes as needed to avoid military warships of both flags.

As they floated and idled along in the natural flow, the ocean current came around the 'beak' of the bird head shaped island of New Guinea. Rounding the beak, the massive flowing current created an 'eddy affect' at the mouth of Huon Gulf. Under the right conditions, a floating object would tend to be released from the ocean current and 'cast' into the bay. The invisible clockwise swirling eddy effortlessly carried the patrol boat to its final destination.

The patrol boat and rafts made landfall just south of the mouth of the Markham River opposite the ocean side village of Lae. After diligently studying the various maps of New Guinea, King Moloch decided to resettle as far up into the interior as possible. His plan was to use the power of the patrol boat to navigate upriver going inland as far as possible. Unfortunately, the patrol boat had a seagoing hull so its draft was comparatively deep making river travel difficult as well as limited. Once the river became too shallow, the boat would have to be abandoned. The king's plan was to find a suitable uninhabited location as far upriver as possible to make a settlement.

King Moloch decided to send an advance landing party of five men to scout the river upstream for potential encampment sites. He chose Joonlee to lead the scouting party. He reasoned that his military experience would help insure the success of their inland incursion.

Joonlee was torn. Was this his chance to escape or should he go along, biding his time for a better opportunity? Reluctantly taking charge, Joonlee chose to utilize the Japanese military uniforms so the men could carry more supplies as well as weapons. Wearing the confiscated uniforms, Joonlee and the four tribesmen truly resembled a Japanese scouting party.

King Moloch instructed the five man troop to make note of sand bars and river depths of at least two meters. He told them to mark the furthest distance the boat could travel and then go an additional ten kilometers further up the river. The additional ten kilometers would create more isolation from anyone 'straying' inland from the coastal area. Once the five men reached their furthest point inland, they were instructed to study the terrain for a suitable permanent encampment. Defensibility from attacks and the potential for flooding were the two main criteria for choosing a settlement.

After spending the evening preparing and packing their gear, the scouting party was dropped off several kilometers upriver just before dawn. The patrol boat returned to a small inlet just south of the river delta to hide and wait.

The men were given four days to get in and out—to be retrieved at midnight of the fourth day. Once the men were retrieved, the flotilla would immediately begin traveling upriver under the cover of darkness. The impossible and illogical plan of night navigation was being driven by Moloch's paranoid and self-important persona.

Chapter Twenty-Eight

Snared

By the end of their first day of trekking inland, Joonlee and his men arrived at the 'dead end' spot for the patrol boat, about fifteen kilometers inland. This was the location that the river became too shallow for the boat to continue and would have to be abandoned. The scouting party had not seen any human activity all day so they were somewhat relaxed while pitching camp for the evening. The next day the team would make the last leg of the trek inland. Joonlee and the men were not aware that their every move was being watched. Unknown to them, they were only alive because they were being studied by the natives.

The next morning Joonlee found a 'message' letting him know they were not welcome. One of his four men was found hanging upside down pinned to a tree. His lifeless body was riddled with small spikes. Terror struck the group as they hastily broke camp and made their way to the river's edge.

A decision on how to proceed needed to be made quickly. Joonlee, hardened by four years of warlike conditions made the choice to continue with the mission. He instructed the men to be aware of their surroundings fully prepared to shoot-to-kill. Their progress was slowed considerably as they were forced to be on guard watching in all directions for a possible ambush.

Joonlee did not know there were two tribes in the area. One tribe was peaceful while the other clan was hostile and menacing. The two tribes clashed from time to time but presently held a fragile truce. The peaceable tribe was the larger clan but being peace loving didn't mean they were foolish or naive. The strong but friendly tribe had consistently maintained peace through strength by being diligently prepared to defend itself with overwhelming force, if needed.

The hostile tribe's Chief Kenwoo was formulating a plan to further deal with the Japanese scouting party. Kenwoo's watchmen brought back reports that the intruders were carrying weapons and appeared to be renegades. In a strategic move, Chief Kenwoo decided to let the scouting party pass for now. He saw an opportunity to become stronger through a pact with the armed scouting party. With an alliance, he could shift the balance of power with the larger rival clan.

Meanwhile, Joonlee and the remaining three men slowly and carefully tracked along the river's edge looking for any signs of an ambush. They eventually reached their estimated ten kilometer push noting several highland plateaus which appeared suitable for settling a village. One site in particular looked strategically defensible and was located on high ground. Joonlee felt he had accomplished his mission and could return with acceptable news. Except for the frightening execution the night before, the entire two days journey inland had been serenely peaceful. The motive behind the murdered comrade would continue to be a mystery.

Having reached the apex of their mission, the men

made a campsite and drew straws to determine who would take the first watch. Soon fear and dread began to take its toll on the two younger tribesman turned soldiers. During the night, the youngest 'soldier' was overcome with restlessness; tossing and turning in his sleep. He awoke abruptly shaking in fear and began to sob with an ebb and flow until dawn. With the unseasoned guard long asleep, the men were easy prey.

At first light, as the sun was coming up 'out of the river,' silhouettes were casting long shadows across the huddled unit of sleeping men. Joonlee was the first to witness the shocking sight of a fearsome war party. The native islanders encircled the men as if they were hunted quarry. The sight was enough to make a weak heart fail.

The natives stood motionless and intimidating, ready to snuff out the remaining trespassers in a swift few moments. Minutes passed… nothing. Then without moving another muscle, the most elaborately painted warrior made a sweeping gesture with his arm. He was clearly signaling Joonlee and his men to follow him. Without hesitation the men jumped to attention and left everything. Unarmed and vulnerable, the men fell into formation surrounded on all sides by painted warriors.

After about an hour's march in complete silence, the men arrived at a secluded village that seemed equally as quiet and eerie. Joonlee even thought that these people must be mute.

The captured men were taken to a hut and then escorted inside. Nothing was said or done for over six hours. At three o'clock a meal was brought in and left for the men. Nothing was spoken, only gestures to instruct the prisoners. As a natural reaction to the complete silence, the men felt compelled to whisper among themselves. No human sounds were heard all night.

The next morning the men were awakened early and escorted to a large triple hut with a thatch covered wooden extension that overhung a large platform porch. The covered entrance was decorated with symbolic and ceremonial motifs. The captured men were silently instructed to kneel and sit on their knees. Their hands were then tied behind their backs and their heads were forcibly pushed down to the ground. An hour passed before any motion was heard that would indicate that this ordeal would come to an explanation. The humiliation and degrading treatment was meant to heighten the fear and dread—serving a purpose.

Chief Kenwoo appeared from within the hut and stood over the men and studied them for a few minutes. He was especially intrigued with Joonlee and kicked him so as to turn him over onto his side. Now partially on his back, Joonlee was temporarily blinded by the brightness of looking up into the daylight. Unable to cover his eyes, he was forced to hopelessly squint to find his vision.

The chief asked Joonlee, in a perfect Japanese dialect, his name and rank. Joonlee could not process the question fast enough to please the chief so he was jerked up to his feet. Kenwoo slapped him across the face with a grass whip cutting his face with a dozen small excruciating cuts. Joonlee screamed and cried out his name in utter submission. The chief knew his strategy well; toying with his captives; conditioning them to be compliant. Fear of the unknown was tearing at the little remaining sanity the men possessed.

Just as suddenly as the terror began, it was over at least for the moment. The men were taken to a remote location and given a change of clothes with instructions to cleanup. The four men were then escorted to a very large circular hut that housed an open air meeting area where an elaborate meal was being prepared.

As the four captives were escorted into the gathering hut, Joonlee was able to see his cruel keeper for the first time. Chief Kenwoo was unmistakably a Japanese national dressed in elaborate chieftain garb. He addressed Joonlee in a curt military fashion decrying the reality that both men were nothing more than deserters. "Joonlee, come to attention."

The pretentious chief introduced himself as the Chief of the High Tribal Counsel. He then proceeded to list the scouting party's offenses beginning from the moment the five men started inland. Kenwoo mentioned, several times, that each of the singular infractions carried the death penalty. Joonlee's mind became numb from the lengthy verbal rant and quit processing information. The relentless chief knew he had to have the upper hand to get what wanted—an alliance where he was in total domination.

Chief Kenwoo presented the terms of his offer: parole that carried a death penalty for violating any given order. Unable to think clearly and seeing no other alternative, Joonlee relented. The moment he agreed to the death shrouded terms, everything changed. The feast began—Joonlee had sold his soul. The sham banquet began as a great celebration of the new alliance and friendship. But for Joonlee and his men, it was the beginning of a slave relationship and they knew it.

Chapter Twenty-Nine

The Assassination

Joonlee with his men and rifles meant that Chief Kenwoo could finally have a chance to gain the upper hand on his nemesis. Kenwoo had savored the moment when he could execute vengeance by killing the rival village's Chief Wasonga (Wä sông gă). The heart of Chief Kenwoo's plan was to assassinate the rival chief sending the leaderless village into confusion and bereavement. He could then overthrow the village in the midst of disarray—even during the memorial ceremony if necessary.

Having earlier interrogated his prisoners, Chief Kenwoo was intrigued to learn about King Moloch and the patrol boat. If it was possible to persuade Moloch to join the cause, Chief Kenwoo was certain he could finally rule the valley region. He understood the potential of involving King Moloch so he formulated a plan to bring Moloch into an alliance. Chief Kenwoo knew the real battle would emerge after the assassination. He needed help to defend against a possible retaliation from the larger more powerful tribe.

As soon as the assassination was accomplished, Joonlee and his men would be rushed back to King Moloch. Paddling with the current, the whole trip would only take a few hours reuniting them with the evil king and his waiting patrol boat. Here is where Moloch would be drawn into an ignoble alliance. The bait would be a promise, to King Moloch, for the right to inhabit the overthrown village as an elder or leader.

Approaching high noon, Chief Kenwoo gathered his five best warriors as well as the four reluctant sequestered recruits. Chief Kenwoo detailed his unfolding plan to the huddled troop of nine reluctant warriors. His vengeful scheme to murder the neighboring chief would be carried out immediately.

With Chief Kenwoo's plans and strategies conveyed to the assault team, he was ready to accomplish the assassination. The nine men slipped through the underbrush to stakeout the rival village long enough to locate Chief Wasonga's whereabouts. Joonlee was instructed to shoot the peaceful chief from a short distance so the rifle shot would be distinctly loud and heard by the villagers. A second and important part of the ruse was to propose a sham coalition to 'go after' the rogue 'white hunters.' Once the assault team was vacated from the scene, Chief Kenwoo could rush in and offer aid. This would allow Chief Kenwoo to lower their defenses so he could attack a few days later.

> *The hidden warrior was instructed to shoot his poison dart, only if the chief survived the rifle shot.*

Joonlee took aim only fifty meters from the entrance to the Chief Wasonga's home. In a failsafe maneuver, Chief Kenwoo's lead warrior was positioned ten meters away in a thick growth of underbrush. The hidden warrior was instructed to shoot his poison dart, only if the chief survived the rifle shot. Joonlee would only get one chance with his rifle. The remaining seven invaders were to create a diversion with a strategy for an easy escape. The mass confusion would allow the death squad to flee.

The plan worked flawlessly except that Joonlee completely missed his target requiring the poison dart to kill the friendly Chief Wasonga. The assassination was complete but not as planned so the raiders were fearful of Kenwoo's reaction. The presence of a poison dart meant that Chief Wasonga's death could not be blamed on an outsider.

As is the case with many criminals, the evil chief had not made viable contingency plans. The first obvious result of the failed assassination was that the scheme for a sham coalition was not going to work. A massive retaliation was now looming and Chief Kenwoo would unquestionably be the prime suspect. In a matter of moments the chief went from a pompous puppet-miester to an anxious and unnerved despot.

Even with the botched assassination, Chief Kenwoo decided he must continue with his original plan and rush the men back to King Moloch. It could still mean a win-win conclusion to a bad plan gone wrong. His plan to recruit King Moloch was now more crucial than ever—*it had to happen.*

Just as the men were preparing to leave, Kenwoo began to panic. At the last minute, Chief Kenwoo decided that *he must go* with the men and present his proposal for an alliance. The hastily arranged meeting between King Moloch and the Chief Kenwoo was over before it started. Immediately, King Moloch knew he was dealing with a loser, a poser, a pompous halfwit. King Moloch was a master strategist able to read people and situations instantly. Chief Kenwoo was no match for King Moloch.

King Moloch knew what he needed to do. He would go along with the chief until just the ideal moment. King Moloch recognized that Chief Kenwoo represented the far inferior clan in the fragile valley truce so an alliance with him would be foolhardy. King Moloch was no fool. He would not be a martyr for a pretender. He felt insulted to be in an alliance with this cowardly deserter posing as someone with authority. The only unknown for King Moloch was how to align with the winning side—always make sure you go with the winner.

Thinking he had gotten what he came for, Chief Kenwoo concluded the short lived meeting with Moloch. Kenwoo then ordered his best guide to stay behind to help navigate the patrol boat up the river. With the two four-man canoes stowed and camouflaged in a pile of logs, Kenwoo immediately left on a land based route to visit another village chief. Kenwoo believed he could persuade another tribe to join his debauched cause.

With the change of events, King Moloch no longer thought it necessary to travel by the cover of night. He immediately gave the order to begin navigating upriver. The entire group of refugees started a very slow passage upriver towing the three giant rafts. Kenwoo's guide knew the river so well that the caravan of weary travelers was able to travel much further than Joonlee had earlier predicted. So much so, the first night on the river was spent making a semi-permanent campsite. An eventual move to a final location could come much later.

It would seem, to the casual observer, that King Moloch was disinterested in the outcome of the looming confrontation. The truth is, King Moloch began plotting during the first few minutes of Chief Kenwoo's bidding. King Moloch was an expert schemer and knew he was in a good position to leverage the existing rivalry to his advantage. If he could achieve that goal, he would simply take advantage of the situation and make his move when it best suited him.

Having been given its location by Chief Kenwoo, King Moloch's first impression was to arrange an impromptu meeting with the leaderless clan. By inserting himself in the middle, he could obtain an advantage by learning the strengths and weaknesses of either side. If such a meeting were to take place it would need to be immediate. He would only have a limited amount of time before Chief Kenwoo arrived back in the area. King Moloch decided to seize the moment and avail himself to the leaderless community with an eye on the prize— a power grab.

The next morning, King Moloch staged a chance meeting by gathering a group of twenty, of what appeared to be, needy families members seeking refuge. Like before, the king chose to use the women and children to plead for mercy, setting up his victim. Imbedded in the group, he would reveal himself if the right opportunity was presented. If not, then the group could move on or retreat. In either case King Moloch would gain valuable information that would help him in his plotting.

Appearances were important. The group was instructed to look and act needy but worthy of help—humble and defenseless yet strong and able-bodied. The coached actors approach the traumatized village slowly; wearily pretending destitution.

A party of warriors approached the group in an overtly hostile fashion and tried to runoff the intruders. The aggressiveness of the security patrol was by command intended to fend off any detractors during a time of mourning. The women and children began to beg for mercy and plead for only the smallest amount of help; promising to quickly be on their way. One of the guards was ready to give in but a decision was made to have one of the men go and report.

Chief Wasonga's widow (Luana) had rightly assumed command of the fractured village and she was proving to be quite capable and clear minded. The assassinated chief had long made efforts to ensure his people would survive, even thrive, if he were removed. Chieftess Luana had been highly involved in the leadership and decision making—a true co-leader. Additionally, she was the shrewd one. Chieftess Luana agreed to allow the vagrants to enter the village. To King Moloch's credit, any other ploy would not have succeeded. His plan was working perfectly so far.

Chieftess Luana knew that her village was subject to another attack. She also knew that the needful mourning, as well as her husband's memorial, would have to wait. Luana risked losing more of her people if she wasn't diligent and prepared. She was forced to place the village on high alert with every person taking their assigned duties and responsibilities for defending the village. This successful tribe had earned a reputation of strength and honor. The high esteem gained through preparedness and diligence had paid many dividends allowing the people a greater degree of peace and prosperity. The expected yet unwarranted attack would be met with an overwhelming response.

What he didn't count on was the high level of sophistication at which this community operated. These diligent people were well prepared to take on any contingency. Moloch's visit was of no surprise and his predictable scheme was seen as childish. King Moloch didn't realize that he had been living in a 'fishbowl' since his arrival. He had no secrets. The slain chief's widow even knew of his hasty alliance with the Chief Kenwoo.

Witnessing the powerful village's adeptness under duress should have been an ominous sign to Moloch. It was quickly becoming clear that he and his group of twenty were at the complete mercy of this powerful clan. The crafty king was losing hope of achieving an upper hand much less a power grab. The pretend beggars were escorted to a large hut and given food to eat. Then, one by one, each adult was taken to be interrogated by the head elder as well as the appointed judge of the village. The chieftess would interview the key players as they were ferreted out by the judge.

Intuitively, Luana knew her answer, to the upcoming confrontation, was being brought to her. She felt a certainty that these interrogations were going to prove crucial for what lay ahead. Whether the imminent clash was to be defensive or offensive would be discovered here today.

Providentially, important information was now at Luana's fingertips as King Moloch was brought to her. The judge had skillfully identified Moloch as the only knowledgeable member of the ragtag group. Even though the chieftess was aware of his ruse, she did not let-on to King

Moloch. She intended on allowing him to expose himself, giving her the information she needed.

King Moloch was quite adept at reading people and knew he was up against a brilliant opponent. In an uncharacteristic yet calculated move, he decided to tell it just as it was—the complete truth. Without sparing any details, Moloch told the chieftess his reason for being there, how he got to her village as well as his plans. He even confessed to his quick tempered and ruthless slaying of the Japanese patrol boat crew.

Having sized up King Moloch, the chieftess knew that he was the answer to the nightmarish dilemma that had been thrust upon her tribe. She believed this hardened tyrant was brought to her to do a necessary but unpleasant task. It would be King Moloch who would completely annihilate Chief Kenwoo from the valley; eradicating an ongoing and contemptuous threat to her people. The chieftess would provide some tactical support but King Moloch would do the dirty work. Over the next hour, the adversarial strategists skillfully positioned and maneuvered as would any two chess masters going for checkmate.

King Moloch discovered he was in no position to negotiate but it didn't matter. He still wanted to get what he came for so he gave one last desperate try. "There is one matter of which you may not be aware. Chief Kenwoo left to visit another tribe—he spoke of forming an alliance."

Affirming what she already knew, Chieftess nodded her head. With his last moved made, Luana was ready to close the deal. "King Moloch, I have

> *With his last moved made, Luana was ready to close the deal. "King Moloch, I have but one offer for you..."*

but one offer for you. What I propose to you is very generous but potentially costly for you. If you want to settle in this valley you will have to pay a price to belong. Do what I say and I believe we can all live together peacefully."

King Moloch was interested in the terms of Luana's arrangement. He felt drawn in yet wanted to play hard-to-get. "How do you have the authority to offer me anything?"

Chieftess Luana smiled as if putting King Moloch in checkmate. "Except for Chief Kenwoo, every tribal village in this valley and along the northern coast is in a strategic alliance with me and the people of this village. In a shameful act of violence, Chief Kenwoo usurped control of a very weak village; a people we were trying to help. Chief Kenwoo has been a mindless marauder ever since; destroying the peace and tranquility of our valley. It is time for him to go, and you King

Moloch will rid our valley of his evil presence."

Chieftess Luana went on to explain how she would never allow the valley to live in turmoil again. She very forthrightly told King Moloch that he and his clan would be on probation with no tolerance. Then the Chieftess assured King Moloch that he would be removed from the valley quickly and forcefully if he disrupted the peace and tranquility that every person deserves.

King Moloch didn't like being dictated to in this manner. After all, he had ruled over an entire island with an iron fist without being questioned. Could he manage to coexist with neighbors or should he go and find another island to continue his immutable rule? At least for the moment, King Moloch cursorily agreed to take the offer extended to him—he really had no choice.

Chapter Thirty

Double Jeopardy

King Moloch and his cadre of actors were released by Luana. Moloch didn't see himself as retreating in defeat. He just needed to put his spin on the turn of events; making this deal with Chieftess Luana work for him. His strategy to be completely honest with the chieftess seemed to be the correct tactical move at the time, but was it?

Walking back to the temporary encampment, the king came to realize that Luana's deal was actually a win for him—he was getting what he came for. However, Moloch was not used to getting his way without cheating, lying or killing someone. It was just not King Moloch's nature to get along so easily—it didn't feel comfortable. He was in this life for the hunt; the thrill of conquest. He needed to be living on the edge—the brinkmanship and danger allowed him to breath.

Debauchery was his drink of choice. To King Moloch, safety and compliance was the same as death.

By the time his 'theatrical' troop made it back to their temporary quarters, King Moloch was disgusted with himself. He wanted to be in command of this conflict even if meant losing everything—*it was going to be all or nothing.* Counting the costs, King Moloch realized that both sides believed him to be their ally—this was a plus. How could he pull off a coup? Could he take Chieftess Luana's village and eliminate Chief Kenwoo in one-fell-swoop?

Joining with Chief Kenwoo was the only way to stage an attack against Chieftess Luana. He would have to make sure that Kenwoo took the lead so he would risk the heaviest casualties. As soon as the besieged leadership was taken out, King Moloch would give a signal for his men to

> *Grandiose plans built on pride leave gaping holes for deception to flood in.*

turn on their comrade allies, killing Chief Kenwoo first. This would leave King Moloch in charge of two fractured tribes. He could once again rule with absolute power.

Grandiose plans built on pride leave gaping holes for deception to flood in. And so it was with King Moloch. Blinded by pride, he failed to remember that he was up against a powerful, well informed and shrewd opponent who so far had out played him. Further, Chief Kenwoo, a supposed ally, was not only unreliable and unpredictable but he was as loathsome and despicable as King Moloch.

Incredibly, and as fate would have it, Chief Kenwoo had made identical plans to turn on King Moloch. The exception was that Chief Kenwoo had secured an alliance with a coastal tribe. Once the attack against Chieftess Luana proved successful, Kenwoo's devious plan was to surround King Moloch's men. His new northern ally would strike Moloch from the flank. King Moloch would be sandwiched with no way to escape. Seeing himself with the upper hand, Chief Kenwoo was drunk with grand illusions as the prevailing leader. He felt destined to rule the devastated tribe becoming the supreme chief of the valley.

The next morning, King Moloch was preparing to set out on the short jaunt to Chief Kenwoo's settlement. He wanted to present his plan for laying siege of Chieftess Luana's village. The time was ripe to strike the village while mourning would weaken their defenses. However, a contingent of men led by Chief Kenwoo was seen approaching Moloch's temporary encampment.

King Moloch, who was only minutes from leaving the camp, dismissed his awaiting entourage. With the few minutes he had before Kenwoo arrived, Moloch sent word out to his men. "Hide any preparations for battle—we need to feign weakness." The improvised encampment needed to appear normal, even vulnerable. And lastly, for his own deceitful plan to work, King Moloch needed to be welcoming and friendly to his 'most valuable' comrade and ally.

The pompous Chief Kenwoo, dressed in his gaudy chieftain attire, sauntered into the camp in a childish royal procession. As King Moloch looked on, he just shook his head in disbelief and uttered under his breath, "This is going to be easy." As if already supreme ruler of the valley, Chief Kenwoo had his nose-in-the-air displaying contemptuous disrespect for King Moloch.

With every intention of playing on the chief's already inflated ego, King Moloch took the submissive role. "Welcome, great chief, good to see you again so soon."

Ignoring the gracious yet insincere gesture, Chief Kenwoo authoritatively proclaimed, "I have the final plans on how to deal with the annoying harasser's widow. I think you will agree to what I propose."

Keeping with his ploy to disarm the arrogant pretender, King Moloch went along with status quo. "I'm sure you have a great strategy to defeat the weaken tribe. Let's see what you propose."

Chief Kenwoo entered the makeshift three-sided hut with arrogant disdain. Because of the massive plumage adorning his headdress, he was forced to bow down to enter the small meeting space. Thinking himself well above the mere immigrants, he waited for all eyes to be focused on him. "I have been given guidance by the gods—destroy this tribe that has kept me from my true destiny. Before I share my divine guidance you must swear allegiance to me and the god of Morphania."

King Moloch was about to lose it. This whole charade was already more than he could take. He couldn't wait to run a sword through this sniveling weasel. "With all due respects to your gods, let's just get to your plan of attack. And yes, I'm more than willing to help you into your destiny." King Moloch was pleased at his hidden wit about sending Kenwoo to his destiny. His inner smile allowed him to endure this halfwit's rambling until he could actually do the dirty deed.

Chief Kenwoo hesitated for a few moments and then preceded to layout his plan of attack on the peaceful village. In those few moments, his demeanor shifted from whimsical to an unemotional and eerily callous—his speech was suddenly mechanical and monotone. King Moloch could feel an evil presence enshroud their meeting place. He felt subjected to the malevolent force unable to fend off thoughts and impressions of unbridled hatred and wickedness. King Moloch was in this over his head and walking lockstep with the devil himself. Not sure what was happening, he found himself agreeing to the chief's plan of assault.

Oddly, King Moloch could only recall one thing from all of the offensive maneuvers given to him. He and his men were to follow behind Kenwoo's men as they struck at the leadership of their enemy. King Moloch seemed compelled to blindly obey the orders given to him. The meeting concluded when the leaders, including their respective top warriors, made a pact of allegiance.

Joonlee was not included in the meeting but was waiting nearby with a group of men. Exiting the hut, King Moloch motioned Joonlee to come to him. "Joonlee, get the six rifles and ammunition from the gun boat and bring them to Chief Kenwoo." Joonlee was not privy to any of the detailed plans but this order did not sound like something King Moloch would do under any circumstances. Joonlee stared in disbelief. He looked deeply into the eyes and facial expression of King Moloch, searching for more understanding. King Moloch's countenance was lifeless and his eyes had lost their fire. The dramatic change in King Moloch was disturbing to Joonlee causing him to become fearful.

When Joonlee reached the patrol boat, two of Chief

Kenwoo's men were waiting for him as if guarding the beached craft. Without speaking, the warriors allowed Joonlee to enter the boat. While retrieving the rifles, Joonlee noticed his ceremonial sword that had been stowed near the rifle locker. He carefully covered the sword with a blanket; hoping he wasn't being watched. Joonlee then loaded the guns and ammo into a duffle bag and hoisted the heavy gear onto the bow of the boat.

With every intention of delivering the guns to Chief Kenwoo, Joonlee was struck from behind just above the knees. A heavy wooden shaft was used to hit him with massive force. He fell hard burying his face in the coarse gravel of the sand bar. The searing pain was enough to cause Joonlee to momentarily blackout.

When Joonlee came to, his blurry vision only allowed him to see the blood soaked gravel where his face had smashed into the beach. As expected, the duffle bag full of weapons was gone from his side where he dropped it. Trying to stand, the ripped flesh of his bruised and damaged thighs kept him from standing erect. Dazed and half-bent-over, Joonlee hobbled back toward camp.

King Moloch caught sight of Joonlee entering the camp and approached him wanting to know where he had been. Moloch seemed oblivious to the beating as the hobbled Joonlee

listened with a bloody gravel pocked face. The confused
Joonlee was unable to make sense of what was happening.
There was a surreal feeling about the camp and especially with
King Moloch. In a gruff and unapologetic tone Moloch barked,
"We're taking Luana's village in the morning so we need to get
ready. Go get cleaned up and meet me at my hut."

Chapter Thirty-One
Death at Every Hand

By nightfall Joonlee was deathly ill and could not leave his
bed. Open to infection, the welts on his legs were swollen and
red. A raging fever began choking the life from Joonlee. Even
without the fever, he would be useless to King Moloch as his
knees were stiff and locked into a bent position.

Before waking his men, King Moloch searched for and
found the Samurai sword he had longed to wear since the day
he saw it stashed in the Japanese patrol boat. Then Moloch
assembled his nineteen men at four a.m. sharp—leaving
Joonlee for dead. It was obvious that King Moloch was not
acting on his own accord. He would never follow anyone's
orders much less carry them out so carefully. Minus Joonlee,
the reluctant warriors started the one hour march toward the
agreed staging area. Their arrival would be just before daylight

precisely as planned.

While still under the cover of darkness, the men were walking single file through an area near the river bank where large boulders were heaped eight meters high. King Moloch was last in the meandering line of men stretched out over fifty meters. Without warning, Moloch was tripped from behind causing him to fall forward. His uncontrollable fall caused him to hit his head against a small boulder. The commotion and moan was heard by the man directly in front of Moloch. Still shrouded in darkness, the alerted warrior doubled back to see what had taken place. King Moloch grumbled, "I just tripped on a rock, go on I'll catch up."

King Moloch managed to stand up long enough to discover his sword was missing from its scabbard. At the sound of 'swoosh,' King Moloch instinctively raised his right arm only to have it lopped off below his shoulder. The force of the blow caused him to fall backwards against a huge boulder and slide down sideways into a dying heap.

Unaware that King Moloch was missing, his remaining men assembled at the agreed staging area, as instructed. Within minutes, King Moloch's men took their final combat positions and were ready for the signal to be given by Chief Kenwoo. Their only weapons were whittled spears made the day before. Chief Kenwoo placed his six riflemen with direct aim at

Chieftess Luana's quarters. The porch where her husband had been assassinated was once again in the sites of gunmen.

As daylight began to illuminate the village grounds, there appeared to be a gathering at the hut of Chieftess Luana. Chief Kenwoo was ecstatic. How could he be so lucky to have a dozen standing targets to takeout? Everything was in place. As soon as the first rounds were fired, the attackers were to rush the hut. In the ensuing confusion, the elders and leaders would be sought out and killed

The moment came for Chief Kenwoo to order the sixty-man war party with riflemen to standup, find their targets and attack. The unexpected noise was deafening. The moment the attackers were fully erect, hundreds of arrows were unleashed from every direction. In less than thirty seconds, every attacker was riddled with multiple arrows. The beautifully decorated headdress, with its elaborate plumage, was still affixed to Chief Kenwoo's detached head—his chosen destiny achieved. There was no sound of victory only the smothering stench of death and loss.

Joonlee realized he must have been left behind because when he awoke, it was daylight and perfectly quiet. Now he lay at death's door in a mostly deserted camp. Unable to move without excruciating pain, hopelessness began to set in. The twenty women and children who had remained in the camp would soon be captives of Chieftess Luana.

Only an indigenous native would know the tribal custom when a village is conquered in battle. Chieftess Luana knew that the women of Chief Kenwoo's tribe would kill themselves with self-inflicted wounds upon hearing the news of defeat. Wisely, she prepared in advance to capture the women to save them from killing their children and then cutting their own throats. The youngest children of Chief Kenwoo's vanquished tribe would be adopted and raised as children of Luana's village. The defeated warrior's widows would serve a life sentence as indentured workers—captives in a battle lost.

Chapter Thirty-Two
Glimmer of Light

Joonlee opened his eyes for the first time in two weeks. Taking in the dreamlike experience, Joonlee slowly turned his head looking for clues in this unfamiliar place. Next to him, King Moloch was laying on a military issue canvas cot retrieved from the Japanese gun boat. Still in a coma brought about by a severe blow to his head, the one armed despot looked to be near death.

A young, eight-year-old, 'nurse' was attending one of

the captured women. She had partially cut her throat before being stopped by Luana's rescue squad. Joonlee watched and wondered about this place and the serenity that he felt. The young 'daughter of the tribe' was preparing to leave the infirmary hut when Joonlee called out to her. The supposed language barrier reduced their conversation to nods and hand gestures. Having reached an impasse, the young girl quickly turned and hurried out.

Moments later Chieftess Luana entered the hut and walked over to Joonlee. "Good morning. Did you have something you wanted to ask?" Joonlee had many questions but the most troubling were the questions of 'why.' "Why did you save my life? Why did you spare King Moloch? Why do you care about the ones who tried to destroy you and your people? Why didn't the little girl speak?"

A rapt smile revealed Luana's heart. "Oh that's Tania. She is the most wonderful child who came from Chief Kenwoo's tribe. She has been adopted by a family here in our village." Luana paused before proceeding with tempered sadness. "When Chief Kenwoo usurped the once friendly but struggling tribe, he cut out their tongues. There is good news. Tania's tongue was only partially removed so she can speak fairly well. She is just very shy with strangers about her slurred speech."

Joonlee recoiled at the cruel words—shocked at the viciousness. He closed his eyes tight displaying a pained look as he envisioned the young Tania enduring the brutality. Joonlee remembered the complete silence the day he and the scouting party were captured. There were no spoken words—it all made sense now.

Chieftess Luana continued, "Before I tell you the reason that we are a peace loving people, I want to make something perfectly clear. We are a tribe that believes in justice. Yes, you and Moloch were spared but you both are considered indentured workers on strict probation. You will be retained in servitude as laborers. Even so, you will be treated fairly. Eventually, it is hoped that you will become a contributing part of this community. Even today, there will be no chains or shackles other than an appeal to your humanity. You will be expected to restore what you have taken and find peace as you do."

Chieftess Luana continued, "You asked about the undeserved kindness we have shown you. There is much to be told but I will tell this for now. Many years ago my grandfather was the leader of this tribe, in this very place. We were not always a peace loving people. Then one day, a dignitary entered our village and spent several months teaching my ancestors about a God called Jeshua. The man was kind and his face glowed with the glory of Jeshua. His name was Monteau (Mŏn tā ū). A name given to him by the Pacific islanders which means 'messenger of the Great God.' Monteau was from the great continent of Europe—his actual name was Sir John Francis Taylor."

Joonlee wanted to know more. His life was wrecked and wasted and he longed for peace and purpose. "I want to know more about this God you call Jeshua. When can you tell me more?"

Chieftess Luana began weeping. "I want to know more about Jeshua too. I do not know Him like my father or my grandfather. I know all the stories and witnessed many miracles but I was too young and stubborn to heed my father's guidance. I remember my father telling me many times that someday Jeshua will come to earth and gather His people together and build a great Kingdom. My father told me that unless I know Jeshua personally, I would not be gathered into His family. Now that I'm older, I have wept many nights longing about how to know Jeshua as my God."

Taking a moment to recover from her poignant remembrance, Luana continued, "Our ways are slowly changing and I fear that someday our people will forget about Jeshua. I hope that my own son can someday know the one true God the way our fathers knew Him. Someday my son will be the chief of this tribe and I want his life to be restful and happy. I want our village to continue to be peace loving as he reigns.

Luana was only able to offer a glimmer of Light to Joonlee. Even so, a spiritual seed was planted in Joonlee's yearning heart. There would be no harvest today.

Soon, King Moloch came out of his coma and began to gain strength. Unfortunately, his head injury deepened his anger and violent temper rendering him unable to enjoy any aspect of life. His speech was slurred and his gait was a disjointed shuffle. King Moloch was a lost man desperately taking and grabbing at any kindness offered him—willing to bring anyone down to his meager and lifeless existence.

The day eventually came when a physically healthier King Moloch played on Joonlee's growing humanity. Moloch relentlessly tried to convince Joonlee they needed to leave the village and strike out own their own. In a convoluted diatribe, King Moloch twisted the basis of their relationship. He somehow 'proved' that Joonlee was indebted to him and owed his existence to him. After weeks of harassment, Joonlee relented. In the middle of the night the two rescued ingrates turned their backs on hope and goodness to return to a life of vagrancy and lack.

Chapter Thirty-Three

A Dog Returns to its Vomit

'All or nothing' he chanted as he shook his fist at the generous offer made by Chieftess Luana just months ago. King Moloch was leaving the valley just as he prophesied—with nothing. He made his gamble and lost. Now living the results of his wager, he was limping, scowling and barking orders at the subservient Joonlee. Any normal person would see this as running away from a good thing. For Joonlee, missing his chance to find a measure of peace produced overwhelming shame and regret. But not for King Moloch whose deceived mind was given over to pride and rebellion.

The gun boat was still tied up and beached just as it was the day they arrived over four months ago. Unable to climb into the boat, the one armed Moloch callously demanded Joonlee's assistance at every turn—a pitiful scene to endure. After an exhausting struggle, Joonlee managed to launch the beached craft to head downstream to a fate unknown.

"The north shores… take us to the north shores," demanded Moloch, "The tribe that made the alliance with Chief Kenwoo was from the north shore. Sounds like my kind of people. I want to go there and settle in… make my mark before I die." It was almost laughable that Moloch wasn't aware the supposed alliance with Chief Kenwoo was not an alliance at all. The northern coastal tribe was merely upholding their original tried-and-true coalition made with Chieftess Luana and her husband. Participating in the defense of Luana's village, the coastal tribe held the flank when the brief one-sided skirmish took place—simply retreating and returning home after the needless and pointless massacre.

Cruising along on his extended offshore passage, the errant Moloch passed within a few miles of the newly settled families of his former island. The Christian refugees, who escaped the doomed volcanic island, miraculously made the oceangoing voyage to the north shores of the Huon Gulf. The unfortunate irony is that these two forces would meet to perpetuate the timeless struggle of good against evil—darkness and light colliding in an effort to lay claim to precious human souls.

Moloch and Joonlee steadily cruised northward along the outer banks of the north shore. Misguided in his search for the evil ally, King Moloch intended to stop at each coastal village that was visible and accessible by boat. Moloch's imagined integration into the north shore village community would have to be handled in a discreet manner. If he continued to be a hateful bully, his remaining days will be short lived.

As if protected by divine providence, access to the first

two villages was thwarted. The first village could only be reached if the secrets of navigating the reef were known. Two narrow openings were available for those who knew how to find them. The second village was located on a coastal plateau overlooking the beach. Its access was impossible for the pair of feeble and exhausted runaways.

Just before reaching the third coastal village, the boat ran out of diesel. For a brief instant a light shone on Joonlee's sickened heart. A glimpse of freedom loomed before him as a fleeting thought that teased his shackled mind. The adrenaline rushed as Joonlee saw this as his chance to escape from Moloch's grip. Still a half-kilometer out to sea, he knew the crippled Moloch would be unable to swim to safety.

> *A glimpse of freedom loomed before him as a fleeting thought that teased his shackled mind.*

In a rash and clumsy attempt to grab the inflatable life raft, Joonlee exposed his disloyalty. The stowed raft was hopelessly entangled in coils of ropes. Moloch was aware of his own physical limitations and wisely decided to not make an issue of Joonlee's intentions to abandon him.

It shouldn't ever be this way but Joonlee's glimmer of hope for freedom was quickly snuffed out. The browbeaten and subservient Joonlee was guilt ridden making him easily manipulated by King Moloch. Back in Moloch's maniacal grip, the decision was made to row ashore. Joonlee secured the raft from its lair and pulled the cord inflating the undersized four man craft.

In a snap decision, Moloch decided to abandon the patrol boat and sink it—scripting an unconscious metaphor. He ordered Joonlee to open the ballast and turnoff the bilge pumps. It would be slow to sink but there would be no notice of the camouflaged vessel silently slipping into the deep.

No sooner had the men pulled away from the sinking patrol boat, the raft showed signs of deflating. Joonlee began to row with every ounce of muscle he possessed. He was in a race for his life. With the shore in sight, the little remaining use the raft held was ripped away by the reef, leaving the men in yet another fight for their lives. A large wave picked them up and tossed the rumpled mass into the outer edges of the tranquil lagoon. In the process of being saved from the sharp coral, Moloch and Joonlee were raked across the reef transforming their exposed flesh into raw meat.

A lone fisherman, who was out for his daily catch of fish, noticed the cascade of bodies roil over into the lagoon. Darting across the pristine waters in his one man outrigger, the native islander secured the semiconscious survivors and began to tow them to shore. The men were bleeding and on the verge of shock as the fisherman drug them up the beach to the tree line. He wanted to protect them from the sun while he went for help.

The fisherman didn't need to run far, the whole village was on its way to assist in the rescue. A crowd of natives engulfed the men hoisting each one onto a 'bed of hands.' They were then carried away with amazing speed. The primitive yet effective transit was rough but Moloch and Joonlee were being cared for within minutes of being pulled ashore.

If it weren't for these attentive and caring natives, the waterlogged men would have surely died in the surf. Their wounds would have become infected within hours if the barracudas hadn't eaten them alive or simply drowned or died of exposure. There seemed to be no justifiable reason Moloch had been spared death so many times in the past few months. Surely there must be a purpose for this wretched man to go on living; cheating death against all odds.

Chapter Thirty-Four

Giants in the Land

The Moomba tribe was perhaps one of the most unique of all the tribes along the northern coast of New Guinea. Although small in stature this clan was very intelligent, contemplative and introspective; a meek people. The arrival of Joonlee and Moloch could not have been more intriguing to this unusual and amiable tribe.

Oddly, and converse to reality, the chance appearance of the two fugitives was perceived as an omen that must be heeded. The Moombas saw themselves accepting their fate believing the gods were intervening in their behalf. The consensus of opinion among the Moombas' leaders was to respond to these imposing 'guests' in a subservient manner. Their erroneous perception was unintentional but secretly orchestrated by unseen forces.

The interlopers made for an intimidating duo. Joonlee towered over his hosts with his height of just under two-hundred centimeters (six feet tall). The daunting Moloch, with his coarse and mean spirited demeanor, intimidated the meek tribe. The crippled Moloch had always commanded allegiance by brutalizing others into submission if necessary. Fortunately, his most recent near death experience, as well as his bodily injuries, was leaving him a subdued and mellowed man. The possibility of a fresh start also motivated Moloch to present a more reasonable persona to the Moomba tribe.

Moloch was brilliant in his ability to read people. He could quickly assess and then produce a plan to gain control of an immediate situation. Moloch had been able to survive where others would have succumbed. However, the Moombas were a different kind of challenge to Moloch. They operated on a different level, not on a base or primeval consciousness. The combination of meekness and intelligence disarmed Moloch's ingrained defiance; drawing him into a 'higher existence.' Over the months, this way of thinking began to appeal to Moloch which brought a measure of refinement to his life.

The more poised Moombas were not taken seriously by many of the neighboring tribal leaders. Heeding the arrival of Moloch and Joonlee as an omen, the prevailing opinion among the Moomba's elders was to allow the more roughhewn Moloch to represent their interests. Without knowing the reason or why, Moloch found himself being groomed as figurehead leader—the monarch he always claimed to be but never deserved. Would this be his chance to finish his incorrigible life with a glimmer of redeeming hope?

Astonishingly, Moloch adapted to his new role and managed to win the hearts and minds of many tribal councils in the immediate region. As the Moombas continued to groom

Moloch, he learned a new and better approach to leadership; becoming quite the diplomat. He was able to form a regional political power base that moved beyond the simple tribal alliances of times past. Intertribal commerce grew as a direct result of the more sophisticated network of governance.

Over the next five years Moloch became the most powerful man in northern New Guinea. As would be expected, Moloch also produced his share of detractors. Many times he faced a tribe that would have nothing to do with him. When he was rejected, Moloch would have difficulty controlling his rage often vowing to extract vengeance upon the village leaders who refused to deal with him. Early on and through no small coincidence, Joonlee discovered that there was a common theme among the villages rejecting Moloch. Each of these villages were receiving and adhering to the teachings of a certain group of missionaries.

Moloch felt subverted and began a search for the perpetrators responsible for the rising threat to his dominance. He assembled five pairs of undercover spies to infiltrate several of the villages which were defying his regional governance. Moloch wanted to trace the origin of this irritating and contemptuous persuasion. If he could locate the missionary leaders, he vowed to end their influence.

Chapter Thirty-Five

The Battle Line is Drawn

Over the next week the spy teams began to bring back reports to Moloch. The teams had quickly discovered there was no need for spies. There were no secrets or hidden agendas. Moloch himself could have readily walked right into the missionary headquarters. The various church leaders as well as the location of the missionary's home village was readily known by everyone.

Unknown to Moloch, these missionaries were the very same families who were once under his dominating control. The refugee Christians were on a collision course with their former evil king.

In the early years of Moloch's rise to power, most of the villages eagerly accepted the Good News brought by the wonderful and giving missionaries. That was until Moloch understood the reason he was losing his influence among many of the villages. Moloch was obsessed with his monarchial reign and was not going to see his stature diminished by the religious fanatics. He began to slip back into his old ways of brutality and dominating control at any cost.

Moloch decided to visit every village and demand allegiance and utter loyalty or face his fury. He made it clear that he was not going to allow the visible presence of any church or the gathering of Christians in any village in northern New Guinea. Over the ensuing months, fear enveloped the countryside as he encouraged those loyal to him to seek out and report anyone violating his directives. Those who would not join him were put on notice of pending retribution. Eventually, a cold dread enveloped the countless tribes and villages of northern New Guinea. The new and besieged church of New Guinea was forced to go underground.

Joonlee had been put in charge of spearheading Moloch's efforts to suppress the growing Christian church. Being the face of evil, Joonlee witnessed over and over again the same generous loving spirit that Luana had shown him when he was near death. Many of the confrontations with the village leaders involved facing down a genuinely peaceful people with spiteful malice.

It was not long before Joonlee began to wrestle with the undeserved injustices and hardship he was inflicting week after week. Eventually, the inner conflict brought him to a place where he sought out members of the underground church; not to bring dread but in search of inner peace. In the secret place of Joonlee's heart, the seed planted by Chieftess Luana began to germinate.

Soon, Joonlee began living a double life—one life of

seeking peace and another of destroying peace. The inner turmoil was ripping at the fabric of his soul. Joonlee had become the target of his own torment. If he hadn't been shown the Light by Chieftess Luana, he would not know anything other than the empty hopelessness he had always known.

Joonlee's life had been tumultuous as far back as he could remember. However, since he had known Moloch, his influence of unbridled wantonness was destroying any vestige of humanity that Joonlee possessed. The raging battle within him had to find resolution or he would suffer the fate of unending torment. In the midst of this raging conflict, Joonlee was

> *The raging battle within him must find resolution or he would suffer the fate of unending torment.*

being drawn and wooed toward the Light and the inner peace He offered.

Joonlee came to a place where his physical life no longer mattered. If he could only grab hold and obtain the fullness that Jeshua was giving to the people of His church. Every day the contrast became more obvious as he saw the hollow wretchedness of his past in one hand and the tranquility and peace he longed for in the other.

The day came when the desire for Jeshua overcame his

waning resistance to give his whole life to serve the God who was drawing him. Joonlee arranged a meeting with Mateo, an elder in the now hidden church. Joonlee could no longer live without Jeshua in his life. In true brokenness, grieved and shameful, Joonlee wept uncontrollable in Mateo's arms. Pleading for Jeshua to forgive him and pledging to be faithful, Joonlee became a believer.

The relief and tranquility came in waves. The crushing burdens of guilt and shame were lifted as the reality of God's goodness flooded in. Joonlee was translated from the realm of darkness and thrust into the Kingdom of Light. No longer a slave to iniquity, Joonlee was freed to walk where he could not go before—to be the person he was always intended to be. The fear of death no longer had a hold on Joonlee. He was finally resting in the peace he had so desperately longed for.

Unfortunately, Joonlee's new found faith would put him and many others in jeopardy. If Moloch were to find out Joonlee was secretly meeting with the leaders of the Christian underground, he would be killed if for no other reason than to be made an example. Anyone found to be associated with Joonlee would be in grave danger as well.

Joonlee's clandestine meetings with the missionaries did not go unnoticed. Not that he was seen coming or going or even talking to a leader of the underground church. Moloch noticed a change in Joonlee that could not be explained in any other way. He was becoming a new person before Moloch's eyes. In a surreal confrontation that was beyond the natural realm, the Light within Joonlee was openly confronted by a dark accusing spirit within Moloch. Joonlee's life was now in peril for his blatant display of disloyalty to Moloch.

It wasn't long before Moloch had undeniable proof that Joonlee had defected to become part of the Christian church. Moloch took Joonlee's betrayal as an opportunity to deal a cruel blow to the hidden church. He was going to allow Joonlee to lead him to a prized catch—maybe several key leaders that could be captured and interrogated.

Moloch gathered a gang of ten of his strongest henchmen to do his dirty work. He charged them to follow Joonlee to his next meeting with the church leaders. Moloch's instructions were straightforward, "Severely beat Joonlee and anyone who meets with him. Leave them alive so they can tell the others to give up their ridiculous and worthless God. But bring Joonlee back to me."

Barely two weeks after Joonlee surrendered his life, to Jeshua, he would be laying at death's door. Joonlee had been less careful in how he evaded detection since he became a believer. Was he being careless or had he become fearless since settling his eternal destination?

Joonlee requested to meet in a park like area adjacent to the village square—not a usual or safe place. The park and the square were separated by a huge open air market—a hubbub of frenzied activity. Joonlee often went through the market for no other reason than to 'disappear' if he thought he was being followed. The clamor of the crowded bazaar was often a cover for a secret meeting in an off-street doorway. Other times he might use it to slip undetected into the home of a church member to be ushered out the back alleyway an hour later. Today, he planned on using the bazaar to make his way unnoticed into the park.

Intent on catching anyone who dared to meet with Joonlee, the ten thugs spread out creating a dragnet to prevent any escape by their defenseless prey. Unknown to his pursuers, Joonlee had been tipped off concerning the ambush. He avoided the meeting to prevent exposing the underground network. He knew the muggers had no knowledge of his intended location so he led them in endless circles.

Eventually the hunters grew weary of the chase and closed-in on Joonlee. They ruthlessly dragged him to a remote and hidden alleyway and beat him senseless leaving him for dead. The moment Moloch's henchmen left the bloody scene, Joonlee was scooped up and carried away to a place of safety.

Early on, several church members had been assigned to

help Joonlee as he tried to negotiate his double identity. These brave believers were not bodyguards but more like guardian angels sent to avert harm, if possible. In this case his deflectors were helpless to intervene; knowing that their battle was not against flesh and blood.

When the troop of thugs reported back to Moloch he was furious. "I told you to bring him to me!"

"But Moloch… he's dead."

Their dismal and muted response only infuriated Moloch to scream out in a ghastly shriek. "Bring him to me now!" The hellions scurried out like scolded dogs to retrieve their toyed kill. Joonlee had been left as a crumpled lifeless heap discarded in a desolate alleyway. Their return to the killing field would yield no body—Joonlee had vanished. Out of a fear for their lives, the cowardly bullies scattered and did not return to Moloch with the unwanted news.

> *The hellions scurried out like scolded dogs to retrieve their toyed kill.*

Chapter Thirty-Six
Dwelling in the Secret Place

Joonlee was taken to a high mountain village with a secret hidden sanctuary. The concealed meeting place was hewn out of a massive escarpment—created by the hands of nature.

Joonlee was holding on to the precious new life that Jeshua had given to him only weeks before. For many days Joonlee would slip in and out of consciousness. He tenaciously clung to the promise of a redeemed and restored life—that hope kept him alive.

There was constant prayer and attention given to Joonlee; forming a day and night vigil. The spirit led prayers had a common theme: *"His inner wounds would be healed along with his bodily wounds."* The result of this prophetic revelation produced focused prayer that eventually brought about a completely healed and transformed Joonlee whose past had no hold on him.

FIVE YEARS LATER —Circa 1952
Seven years after Joonlee arrived in New Guinea

Looking back, it was apparent that the beating, as horrible as it was, *provided the only way Joonlee could have been severed from Moloch.* Miraculously, Joonlee was 'dead' to Moloch. He was also dead to the horrors of his past—healed of the pain and shame. Joonlee was released to walk in freedom and grace.

Since coming to the highland village, Joonlee was free to abide in the presence of the God who saved him. Cloistered *in the secret place,* of the hidden highland village, Joonlee *grew in the full stature of Jeshua.* He was enjoying the greatest treasure this side of heaven; communing with God. Joonlee studied the scriptures *abiding under the shadow of the Almighty.* (The refugee families of the hidden church brought five Bibles with them when they escaped—Bibles given to them by Monteau over forty-eight years ago.)

Joonlee became a prominent leader of the hidden church. He was charged with keeping everyone as safe as possible—to thrive in a hostile environment. He oversaw the highly developed system of communication connecting thousands of believers across northern New Guinea. The dedicated group of believers comprised a network for undercover intelligence including sentries, watchmen, diversion actors, decoys, moles, runners and couriers. Their missions were to deliver information, derail impending danger if possible, distract a stalker or even lay down their own lives if necessary. The effectiveness of this elite group required absolute trust, a surrendered life and flawless execution of duties. A mistake or miscue could mean the death of a beloved brother or sister of faith.

As a church leader, Joonlee spent hours each day in prayer and study of the Bible. One day, Joonlee's attention was drawn to a scripture he had read many times before. Yet this time the verse brought tears to his eyes. The verse read: *"A bruised reed He will not break, and smoking flax He will not quench...."* He was reminded of one of the most important days of his life.

Joonlee's heart was flooded with emotion as he was reminded of Chieftess Luana the day she told him what she knew about Jeshua. He recalled how she wept, longing to know the God of her fathers. Luana explained how her own father had encouraged her to seek after Jeshua and surrender to Him. Luana wept tears of regret for not listening to her wise and loving father's advice. Today, Joonlee understood that *Luana was the smoking flax that Jeshua would not quench.*

Joonlee knew that Luana was the reason he began his journey with Jeshua. Even though she was only faintly reflecting the Light, she still was able to give Joonlee a ray of hope to his darkened heart. Slowly the yearning for peace and happiness began to grow until he too longed for a life with Jeshua. Because of a chance meeting with a flickering flame, Joonlee was living a blessed life free from the horrors of his younger years.

Over the next few days, Joonlee developed a burning desire to go and see Chieftess Luana. Joonlee knew he had to make his way back to Luana's village and teach her about Jeshua. If he could reach her village, he could bring the joys of his faith full circle.

Joonlee began to see this trip to see Luana as an important assignment—being strongly drawn. Joonlee felt a sense of urgency about the eternal importance of this trip. *Yes, he would do it.* He would bring her the Good News of Jeshua that she longed for. He knew in his spirit that there was a great deal in the balance—possibly the fate of the entire valley region or even more.

The journey to Chieftess Luana's village would be very dangerous. Oddly enough, the valley was once a place of serenity where one could travel without fear. Peace, harmony and goodwill flourished after Chief Kenwoo was removed. It wasn't until Moloch *and the old Joonlee* began their reign of terror did intertribal relations became hostile and divided. The irony, of course, was that Joonlee was now facing the consequences of his own making.

The next day Joonlee called a meeting of his top men to draft plans for the overland journey to Chieftess Luana's village. Because of the dangers, Joonlee's advisors suggested sending a small team ahead to prepare the way—sending word back when all contacts were made. The idea was to secure the route as well as setup the meeting with Chieftess Luana.

As a church leader traveling covertly, Joonlee would have a contact person in each village awaiting his arrival. He would then be escorted to the next village. Joonlee was eager to leave immediately but his advisors insisted he wait the necessary five days for the runners to accomplish their mission and return with the all-go.

Early the next day the appointed team left the highland village with instructions for Manuel, the team leader, to remain in the valley village as Joonlee's personal assistant. Manuel would then escort him on the return trip back to the highland village.

Joonlee's concern for the safety of the underground church was obvious to his team. Well aware of grave danger, he questioned what would happen to His church if he was killed on this trip?

Waiting on the advance team to return would give Joonlee time with Pastor Wan, Joonlee's second-in-command. He was like a father to Wan, a young family man who would one day take over Joonlee's position of keeping the church safe. Their relationship was so close that Wan even named his new infant son, Wanlee.

Joonlee painstakingly reviewed his duties with Pastor

Wan—not that Wan was lacking in any area. The truth was that Wan was very capable and was already carrying much of Joonlee's load. So much so that Joonlee was able to devote ample time to study and prayer. Dwelling in the secret place allowed Joonlee to receive divine direction and wisdom for directing the underground church.

Chapter Thirty-Seven
The Valley of the Shadow of Death

The expertise and competence of Joonlee's men proved priceless as he navigated the highland trails leading to Luana's village. Each friendly hamlet on the route had provided an escort to execute the exact maneuvers needed to get Joonlee to the next leg of his trek. The only real danger he had faced was a small troop of Moloch's 'enforcers.' The confrontation was narrowly avoided by scaling down a small ridge and waiting for the danger to pass.

It was early morning when Joonlee paused at the final highland plateau—a small clearing that offered a panoramic view of much of the valley. Joonlee and his guide, Hino, decided to rest before making the steep and winding descent to the valley floor.

A lush garden of ferns, flowers, fruit bearing trees and

vines offered a breathtaking setting for their brief respite. It quickly became obvious to Joonlee that the garden was set in stark contrast to its surroundings. Curious, he stood to draw close to the inviting garden setting. As he took his first step, *he felt as if he was walking through a veil from one existence into another.* Immediately, two angelic beings made their presence known—standing on either side of a small shimmering pool of water.

The majesty of the moment was breathtaking as Joonlee realized that he was now alone with the heavenly beings. Intuitively, he understood that he was experiencing a very important and holy moment meant to prepare him, in some way, for what lay ahead. The slightly larger male angel gave their names as Merci and Adoni. Merci spoke to Joonlee, "You have found favor in the sight of God. We were sent to give you a special message of encouragement. His words to you are: *"My son, after today, this valley will no longer be held captive by the power of death. I have brought you here today. Know that the Spirit of the Lord is upon you. I have anointed you to bring Good News to this valley and to proclaim to captive hearts – 'be released in the name of Jeshua.'"*

After a long silence meant for meditating on the Word of the Lord, Adoni spoke to Joonlee. "Fear not for we will accompany you into the valley *and we are many*—the Spirit of the Lord says, '*Come.*'"

Suddenly, a small fountain of bubbling water began to overfill the small crystalline pool. The overflowing water began to make its way down the steep incline winding its way toward the valley village. At that very moment a sheer gust of cool wind, that was almost imperceptible to the human senses, blew upon the men. Joonlee knew in his heart that the spirit realm had shifted once again.

Joonlee and Hino made the long and arduous descent in only a few moments of time. The Spirit led warriors, along with their unseen escorts, entered the desolate village.

The forward guide, Manuel, who had been instructed to remain in the village, was nowhere to be found. Apparently, no arrangement for Joonlee's arrival had been made. There was no contact and no introduction—only foreboding—the face of evil was everywhere.

By now the bubbling spring had created a small streamlet that meandered and wound its way through the center of the village dividing it in half. The heaviness of encamped darkness began swirling and coalescing drawing back from the Life giving stream. Indeed the Glory of the Lord was going before them. Unnatural wailing could be heard as evil spirits were being rebuked and forced to leave the village, not able to remain in the glory of God's presence.

As the stream of Living Water wound its way to the entrance of Chieftess Luana's home, it created a wide pathway free of darkness and death. Knowing that an open heaven was in the balance, Joonlee took heart in the words of the Jeshua. He knew the battle was the Lord's.

Joonlee approached the same building into which he had fired a bullet seven years ago. Joonlee's heart was pricked as he took a moment to consider the difference the Lord had made in his life in the last few years. Back then,

> *Joonlee approached the same building into which he had fired a bullet seven years ago.*

he was being used as an instrument of death—now he was here as an emissary to bring Life.

Joonlee entered the large dimly lit room. A gathering room intended to be both a receiving room for guests as well as a place to conduct official business. Hino, his faithful guide, remained on the oversized covered porch to guard the entrance and to watch for intruders.

While Joonlee was slowly surveying the uninhabited meeting room, he noticed his long lost ceremonial Samurai sword. It was mounted on a beautiful tapestry that hung from the interior wall. The wonderment of seeing his sword captured his complete attention as he considered how it could have gotten here. His thoughts were coming rapid fire as he thought about its significance—displayed here in this epicenter of spiritual battle. The large sword represented his old life and who he used to be—how it once held his dreams and aspirations.

Joonlee slowly approached the sword with his back to the entire room. Still caught in rapt contemplation, Chieftess Luana interrupted his intense gaze with a faint and strange raspy voice. "That sword is significant to the people of this village. It represents the day we defended ourselves from a vile and evil attack on our village."

Without turning around, Joonlee could sense that Luana was feeble and weak. Her soft spoken and slow speech did not prepare him for what he saw when he turned to greet her—his reason for being here. With an uncharacteristic gasp and a look of shock, Joonlee was presented with a contradiction. The mental picture of the Luana he remembered was betrayed. Joonlee expected to see the same gentle and gracious woman of his past. Sullen and lifeless, Luana looked like a skeleton with heavy makeup applied like war-paint. As ridiculous as it might seem, she was wearing Chief Kenwoo's elaborate headdress that she kept as a trophy of war.

Joonlee, at that moment, would have fled from the sight of Luana if it wasn't for a supernatural anointing of God's grace. In His grace, compassion poured over Joonlee giving him the ability to see Luana through God's eyes. His heart was broken for this desperate and lost soul. Joonlee began to walk toward Luana as he spoke. "Luana, I have Good News... I have met the God of your fathers. I came so that you can know Him too."

Just as Joonlee was close enough to reach out to Luana, a loud gruff voice came from Luana. "I don't want you here—go and leave this valley!" The voice trailed off as it maintained a low animal like growl. Amazingly, Joonlee was not startled or put off by this strange occurrence. He had dealt with demonic possession many times over the last few years and had diligently studied the scriptures for revelation about demons and demonic possession.

Speaking to the demon who addressed him, Joonlee demanded, "In Jeshua's name I command you to tell me your name."

At the sound of Jeshua's name being spoken, Luana began flailing her arms and retreating backwards in an uncontrollable fashion. Fearful that she would fall and injure herself, Joonlee demanded the demon to stop and answer his question. "I am Devon." In a commanding voice Joonlee asked if there were other demons possessing Luana. "Infirmity is with me."

Joonlee knew that the demons had to respond to the name of Jeshua. They had no power to resist the commands given in His name. Joonlee needed to know by what means the demons had permission to possess Luana. "Devon... Infirmity... by whose assignment and by whose authority have you taken possession of Luana? Answer me quickly and completely in Jeshua's name."

"Our assignment was given to us by Morphania—Luana gave us permission to enter-in."

Now it was only a matter of Joonlee commanding the demons to leave. However, Luana must, by her own free will and volition, renounce her motives and actions that opened her soul to demonic possession.

After Joonlee commanded the demons to leave, Luana was no longer animated by the power of the evil spirits. Too weak to stand, Luana began slumping as if to collapse. Joonlee was able to catch her but both were off balance and went crashing to the floor. A cloud of dust erupted around the disheveled bodies.

As the dust settled, Joonlee was still lying on his back with Luana next to him. He could sense the supernatural realm was shifting in transition as the spiritual darkness was lifting and dissipating. Even the natural realm was responding to the absence of evil—the room was more illuminated than before.

Joonlee began blinking his eyes, trying and focus, as he took notice of something troubling. To his utter amazement, Joonlee saw that the Samurai sword was missing from its mount on the wall of tapestry.

Joonlee picked up the malnourished Luana who was semiconscious but seemed to be breathing normally. Carrying Luana, Joonlee quickly discovered that the adjoining rooms were the Chieftess' living quarters built onto the more public meeting room. He located Luana's bedroom and gently laid her across the bed. Anxious to find help, he stepped out the backdoor to an alleyway—a few paces off the village square. As Joonlee entered the public common area, he was encouraged to see people milling about.

Chapter Thirty-Eight
The River of Life

The River of Life was a supernatural manifestation of God's Living Water flowing from His throne room. The results of His presence were manifested by Light and Life returning to the people of the village.

To Joonlee's delight, Tania came running across the central clearing. In her adorable slurred speech, she squealed with sheer joy. "We knew you would come and save us from the horrible darkness that overtook our village." Stopping to catch her breath Tania continued, "Your emissary, Manuel, stayed with us and explained all the wonderful and miraculous things that have happened to you since you left. We couldn't wait to see you in person so you could tell us everything there is to know about Jeshua."

Tania was now fifteen and an adult in the eyes of her village. If there was anyone Joonlee longed to see besides Luana, it was Tania. "Tania, it is good to see you but I need your help with Luana. She is resting in her home. Can you come with me to check on her?"

Tania drew back a little expressing a fearful look. "Luana hasn't been herself lately—she is really unpredictable—she can be downright evil at times."

Joonlee assured her that everything was going to be different. Luana just needed to be loved and nurtured back to health. "Tania, can you arrange for around the clock care for Luana?"

Tania was bright and bubbly again and quickly replied, "If you say so, I can get plenty of help."

Joonlee and Tania reentered the backdoor of Luana's home to find her awake but very groggy. Joonlee spoke to her in a soft and reassuring voice, "Luana, everything is going to be just fine. You'll be well in a few days and we can finally talk about your lifelong dream." Joonlee turned to Tania with a request. "Will you remove the war-paint and clean her face as soon as you can, please? Also, please let me know if she begins to talk—and Tania, *this is very important. Don't allow her to call on any spirits or gods or recite any incantations*—cover her mouth if you have to and send someone to find me." Tania's eyes widened a little as Joonlee briefly explained the demonic confrontation that transpired earlier.

The next order of business was to check on Hino who was guarding the front porch. As Joonlee made his way to the front of the building, he retrieved Kenwoo's headdress that had fallen off Luana's head when she fell. He was concerned that the headdress held a direct connection to the demonic realm. He needed to destroy any association to evil spirits that could be used as a point of contact.

Hino was still standing guard when Joonlee stepped back onto the porch. "This may seem like a peculiar question but did you allow anyone enter the front room about an hour ago?"

Hino timidly answered, "No sir but I have to tell you—I don't think I've been here the whole time."

Joonlee looked puzzled at such a confession. "What do mean you weren't here?"

Hino continued, "I'm not sure. I remember that it was

dark and foreboding as I stood here. The next thing I noticed was the darkness lifting. People started to come out of their houses but I don't remember anything in between. I can't explain it, sir." Joonlee knew that unexplainable occurrences were not uncommon during up close spiritual warfare, especially during demonic deliverance.

Joonlee's next concern for Manuel who was supposed to be in the village to greet him. Joonlee knew from talking to Tania that Manuel had arrived and stayed for a while. Where was he now? Joonlee was confident that his best guide would never leave his duty post unless there was a justifiable reason.

Joonlee also wanted to find Luana's son, Wasonga. The young Wasonga was only fifteen when his father, the village chief, was assassinated by Chief Kenwoo's men. The pressure to fill the void left by his father was immense for Wasonga, a mere adolescent. He had grown up too fast attempting to walk in the shadow of a greatly respected and beloved leader. Wasonga carried the weight and burden of a once noble but now declining village.

Now twenty-two years of age, Wasonga was shirking his responsibilities to co-lead the village—he had become self-absorbed and restless. Many times he had wished he could just runaway and never look back. He wanted to escape his responsibilities and live a normal life.

The village's slow decline began seven years ago shortly after Chieftess Luana achieved retribution against Chief Kenwoo's clan. Once the threats to peace were removed, Luana began a grieving process that never seemed to end. Unfortunately, Luana was very unstable over the ensuing months and prone to making unwise decisions.

More recently, Luana unwittingly opened the door to evil influence when she became enamored with Chief Kenwoo's headdress and a talisman-idol that he had worn. As a result, Luana slowly became more hardened and tyrannical as she was drawn-in by seductions, dreams and vain imaginations offered to her by the deceiving spirits connected to Kenwoo's charms.

Then, eight days before Joonlee arrived at the Luana's village, the status quo was disrupted. Joonlee's decision to obey God's prompting to visit Luana brought about an all-out demonic assault on the village. The overwhelming spiritual darkness, that had overtaken the village, was brought about by a cadre of demons on assignment to destroy Wasonga and Luana.

The very day that Joonlee announced his intentions to go to see Luana, Morphania (demonic prince over the valley principality) sent the spirit of suicide, the spirit of infirmity and the spirit of depression to try and thwart Jeshua's plan of redemption. The trio, of assigned demonic spirits, was sent with the intention to kill Wasonga and Luana so their Salvation would be impossible.

Seven years ago, Luana's plea set in motion a divine plan to orchestrate a *kairos moment* for her and her son. All of the tribulation that Joonlee endured over the last seven years could now be seen as a divine answer to Luana's petition. In a glorious and merciful way, Joonlee had been uniquely prepared and preserved, to be used for this purpose.

Hino was no longer needed as a guard so Joonlee reassigned him to search for the two missing men. "Hino, ask around and see if you can discover what may have happened to Manuel or Wasonga. Report back to me in two hours; I'll be with Luana."

Leaving the front porch, Joonlee reentered the village headquarters to check on Luana. Tania had been very busy. She had removed the awful masklike makeup, shampooed Luana's hair and applied a locally prepared emollient to moisturize her abused and neglected complexion.

Joonlee decided to stand back out of view and watch as Tania continued to care for the sickly chieftess. Tania was especially careful and gentle with Luana as she repositioned her and then began combing her still damp hair. Only hours earlier, Luana epitomized the face of death. Now life was flowing back to her.

Tania caught a glimpse of Joonlee standing across the room and smiled. In a beckoning hand motion she signaled Joonlee to come to Luana's bedside. Tania whispered a quick update on Luana's condition. "She is much stronger than she looks. Can you watch after her while I go and get some broth? Also, while I'm gone I'll let everyone know we need volunteers."

Joonlee took a chair and moved it close so he could watch and pray while holding Luana's hand. With his head bowed, Joonlee began a heartfelt petition for Luana's recovery—both physical and spiritual. He continued to pray for the safety and wellbeing of Wasonga and Manuel as well.

Unknown to Joonlee, Luana was not asleep but resting with her eyes closed. The moment he took her hand, she opened her eyes to witness Joonlee's fervent prayers. Moved to tears, she remembered a similar setting that occurred seven years ago when Joonlee was gravely ill.

Speaking softly, Luana offered appreciation. "Jeshua sent you to save our village—I knew He would not forsake our people." Joonlee breathed a sigh of relief. Luana was going to be O.K.

Within the span of an hour, Hino spoke to several

people who had seen Wasonga leaving the village. He was described as being ushered or pushed along as the evil presence retreated from the village. No one could say *who* or *what* was driving Wasonga to the edge of the village; disappearing into the wilderness. Was Wasonga a casualty of the tumultuous and turbulent rout of spiritual darkness?

Hino was tempted to go after Wasonga but had been ordered to report back to Joonlee. He decided to go ahead and report early, hoping to be released to search for Wasonga. He had a feeling that Wasonga could be in real danger so the sooner he could go, the better.

Hino also longed to find his friend, Manuel, but was unable to find anyone who knew his whereabouts. The only helpful comment was that it had been days since the much loved emissary had been seen. Manuel was the more experienced scout and Hino knew that with his help, Wasonga could be found quickly.

Joonlee had fastened the front public entrance to Chieftess Luana's home so Hino had to make his way around to the back. The rear door to Luana's living quarters was standing open so the sights and sounds were audible to anyone nearby. Hino could hear Joonlee and Luana discussing Wasonga. He didn't want to interrupt but felt he must. Hino called out to Joonlee from outside the backdoor. "Joonlee, I must talk to you about Wasonga."

The timing couldn't have been better. "Hino, come in. What did you find out about Wasonga?"

An air of anticipation was quickly mounting as Hino made his way to Luana's bedside. Hino spoke first. "Wasonga was seen this morning leaving the village under 'supposed' duress. No one could say for sure who or what was escorting him onto the highland trail."

Luana quickly interjected, "The highland trail is controlled by Moloch's allies—he must have been kidnapped."

With a look of dismay, Hino turned to Joonlee. "Sir, I need Manuel to go with me but he hasn't been seen for several days. I know he could find Wasonga; Manuel's the best scout there is."

Chapter Thirty-Nine
The Ultimate Sacrifice

The day Manuel arrived in the village, two of Moloch's bounty hunters were tipped-off by a disloyal villager named Cabot who lived near the entrance to the highland trail. The mercenaries were leery of trying to enter the village; still known to deal fiercely with interlopers, even in its fallen state. Early that afternoon, Manuel felt the shift immediately—the spiritual realm was in turmoil. The natural senses were quick to betray the realities of the spirit realm—only faintly able to perceive the upheaval taking place in the heavenlies. A massive battle was just beginning to rage in the unseen but very real principalities above the valley village. The Spirit within Manuel, was the only restraining force preventing an immediate assault by the demonic forces assigned to defeat Joonlee's mission.

Three Days Later: Cabot persuaded Manuel that the village was being threatened; sending him into the trap. Actually, Manuel knew better than to allow himself to be drawn away from his assigned post but the deception was tailor-made for him. Appealing to a suppressed prideful streak, Manuel *was given* the idea that he was the only one who could save the village—*he believed the lie and was snared*. Blinded by pride, he was easily led to the outskirts of the village. In a strangely careless manner Manuel took the trail leading to the highlands. Of no surprise to the otherworldly observers, he was taken captive by the waiting henchmen.

At that moment, the wayward Wasonga was hiding out in an obscure cave that had become his escape from reality. He often spent entire days moping in his unseemly home away from home that was located just off the highland trail. To the casual observer, Wasonga appeared to be an easy target for the assigned demonic attack—he seemed weak in mind and spirit.

However, the demonic realm is often blithely dimwitted. For deep within the human spirit is the embedded desire to know

> *For deep within the human spirit is the embedded desire to know the Creator.*

the Creator. Luana fed that desire in Wasonga, at every opportunity.

Wasonga was sitting just inside the entrance of his cave when he heard a commotion coming up the trail. He quickly stepped back inside and waited to assess the threat. To his horror, he witnessed a bound and gagged Manuel being pushed and dragged up the trail. Wasonga was struck with fear and dread causing him to be overwhelmed with a sense of powerlessness. At the precise moment that Wasonga saw Manuel being manhandled, Joonlee was praying—preparing to leave the highland sanctuary. Because of Joonlee's intercessory petitions, Wasonga snapped out of his feelings of helplessness. Within a few moments he knew he had to attempt the rescue of his close friend.

From the moment Manuel arrived at the valley village, he and Wasonga developed a mutual bond. Very close in age, Manuel was the brother that Wasonga had always longed for. The more mature Manuel had empathy for Wasonga's struggles. Manuel understood the trials and pressures that came with enormous responsibility. He too was forced to grow up quickly.

From a very early age Wasonga had been trained to take over the village defenses from his father. Military training was drilled into him. Wasonga made his father proud by exceling in every aspect of defensive combat. Despite his recent wayward years, Wasonga was still a very capable warrior. Fortunately, he knew the highland trail as he had hunted and scouted the area countless times before Moloch overtook the highland region.

Wasonga left his cave and tracked up the highland trail following behind Manuel and his kidnappers. It was late in the afternoon when they stopped for the night at an often used encampment. The rugged campsite was used as a surveillance hub for the region by several groups of Moloch's conspirators. After a few minutes of watching from a distance, Wasonga quickly decided to make a hasty retreat; retracing his steps to get help. His strategy was to bring back several men who could help him overthrow the campsite and rescue Manuel.

It was not going to be that easy. Wasonga was unaware that a third bounty hunter fell-in behind him as he ascended the trail following Manuel. Wasonga's pursuer allowed him to make the climb with plans to ambush him at just the right moment. Just as Wasonga made his decision to retreat, the lone bounty hunter made his move to capture Wasonga. The bounty hunter made the grave mistake of underestimating Wasonga when he tried to wrestle him to the ground. Within a few moments Wasonga had mortally wounded his assailant.

The deadly confrontation occurred less than fifty meters from the kidnapper's campsite. Faint noises of the scuffle attracted the attention of one of the men. Wasonga frantically dragged the body to a ravine just off the steep pathway. He quickly covered the body with brush and disappeared down the trail. Both of Manuel's two kidnappers walked down the path a short distance to investigate the noise but shrugged off the interruption.

Quickly descending the highland trail, Wasonga was unaware that he was not in danger. Worried, he decided slip into his hidden cave and spend the night just in case he was being followed. He would then make a break for the village in the morning. It took a while before Wasonga's adrenaline ebbed allowing him to sit still and think rationally. As Wasonga sat in his cave, he knew he had to come up with a plan to rescue Manuel. Thinking deeply, he considered how he had alienated nearly every warrior in the village. His waning loyalty and erratic behavior was apparent to everyone—he would have to do this alone.

The morning Joonlee entered the village
accompanied by the River of Life.

The next morning Wasonga left his cave and entered the outskirts of the village. He sensed a much different place than when he left just twenty-four hours earlier—a sensation of depression began overtaking him. As he neared the village square, he started to feel ill and his gait was becoming involuntary. By the time he reached the front porch of his home, his mind had become foggy and confused.

Entering the front room, thoughts of hopelessness and despair overwhelmed him. His thoughts were trying to kill him. *What am I doing here?... I can't go on living like this... I must escape this hateful place... it's not worth living for... I can't take this anymore.*

In a mechanical motion, Wasonga removed the Samurai sword from its mount on the tapestry covered wall. Without realizing the angelic intervention, Wasonga *'accidently'* broke the beaded necklace that secured the talisman to the hilt of the sword. Luana had tied the talisman-idol to the sword to display her treasured trophies of war and victory—to her near demise.

As Hino stood guard on the front porch, he did not see Wasonga enter and then leave his home. He was shrouded to natural sight which meant no help was coming. Wasonga had no way of knowing that his demonically inspired mission to secure the sword was meant for his own destruction.

Wasonga was returning to the highland trail, nearing the edge of town, when the retreating forces of demonic hordes buffeted him causing him to stumble headlong. Eventually, he misstepped and fell forward cutting his forehead; giving him a slight concussion. Lying in the middle of the roadway, Wasonga recovered after several long minutes of writhing and moaning. Groggy but freed from the demonic attacks on his mind, Wasonga slowly regained his sense of resolve to free his friend.

Bruised and sore, Wasonga slowly made his way up the highland trail. This time he made every effort to be careful and avoid detection. He decided to briefly stop at his cave to rest and get something to eat. Instead he found his hideaway was ransacked. Whoever had been here was angry with a vicious intent on finding and killing Wasonga.

Frozen with fear, Wasonga cowered against the back wall of his cave and began to weep. His best efforts were being thwarted and it was taking a toll on him. At that same moment, Joonlee began to pray at Luana's bedside. As a response, Wasonga's overwhelming feelings and fearful thoughts began to dissipate. Even in the absence of fear, he was emotionally disheveled—it had already been a horrific morning. As Joonlee continued to pray, a fresh resolve filled Wasonga. His physical body was being renewed and strengthened as well.

Wasonga drew his sword as he sensed someone's presence just outside the cave. As he moved closer to the cave entrance, he could hear audible voices engaged in an argument laced with cruel intentions of murder. "Dead or alive... that's what he told us. I'm takin'em in on the back of my mule... the monies' the same. Either you're with me or against me. You decide right now or I'll cut your throat before your next breath." There was a brief muffled tussle, a squeak, a moan and fading sounds of a body tumbling down the steep embankment just outside the cave.

Wasonga was sure he had the advantage of surprise so he stepped out of the cave with the sword ready to defend his life. With his back to Wasonga, the bounty hunter watched the body of his former cohort careen down the steep ravine. The marauder's prideful sneer turned to awestruck terror as he turned to face a wielded sword. Swoosh! Wasonga was afoot, moving uphill before the hired killer hit the ground. He had to reach Manuel—was he still alive?

Wasonga could not have known that the assassins who ransacked his cave were two freelance henchmen sent down from the base camp. The original kidnappers still held Manuel captive—only waiting for the freelancers to return.

Expecting only friendlies to approach, the camp was

not on guard. Wasonga stumbled—he had walked up too close to make such an error. Fortunately, he was able to recover from his reckless mistake before he was actually seen by the bounty hunters. However, having heard the noises of Wasonga's approach left them curious when he didn't continue into the camp. Meanwhile, Manuel had untied himself and had been waiting for a distraction to make a break and escape when he saw Wasonga approach the camp. His stumble came as if planned in advance.

Incredibly, Wasonga's blunder allowed him to setup an impromptu ambush for the alerted bounty hunters. Fraught with inexperience, Wasonga was lying in wait when caught from behind by the rough and tumble mercenary. With a ruthless choking grip on Wasonga's neck, the ambusher was ready to do him in. Wasonga's miscue appeared to be a stroke of genius because it allowed Manuel to shadow his captor as he circled around behind Wasonga. Picking up a hefty rock, Manuel struck Wasonga's would-be killer. All three were thrown off balance and went tumbling off the short mound of loose gravel.

Wasonga quickly jumped to his feet. He valiantly recovered his sword to fend off the remaining kidnapper but it was too late. The lone kidnapper already had Manuel by the throat with a dagger slowly cutting his jugular. Wasonga

> *Wasonga lunged with his sword only to miss and fall helplessly at Manuel's feet.*

lunged with his sword only to miss and fall helplessly at Manuel's feet. A gush of blood rained down on Wasonga as he desperately tried to right himself.

Played out in slow motion, Wasonga looked up only to see their entwined bodies cascading over the steepest ledge in the area. In an instant, Manuel and his attacker were gone out of sight. Manuel had used his last ounce of strength to push them both over the edge; saving Wasonga. He was in a state of shock—evil had run amuck with death at every turn. Tenuously holding onto his last thread of sanity, Wasonga drifted aimlessly down the highland trail, unable to care for his own safety.

Wasonga had just appeared from the base of the highland trail as Hino was approaching from the village. Hino drew near the blood covered Wasonga as he mindlessly ambled along the road leading toward the village. Wasonga fell into Hino's arms as he reached out to steady the weak and wounded warrior. Hino was a small man unable to carry Wasonga so he dragged him over to a familiar shaded clearing by the river's edge. Hino then ran for help yelling as he entered the village square.

Joonlee recognized Hino's calls for help so he abruptly left Luana as she lay sleeping. Hino did not have much information except that Wasonga was completely blood soaked with a gash on his forehead that appeared to be a mortal wound. Joonlee snapped into his military training mode and ordered Hino, "Run to the infirmary. Grab a blanket and a stretcher. Let them know that we'll be coming back with Wasonga. We'll wait for you at the clearing." Turning to a group of gathered men, Joonlee implored, "One of you go and find Tania to render first aid. The rest of you come with me."

Chapter Forty

Dream Fulfilled

Once in the infirmary, it was discovered that Wasonga was more bruised and broken in mind and emotion than in body. Even so, he wasn't doing well. (His turning point came a few days later when Luana was able to begin visiting her ailing son.) The moment Wasonga was brought to the infirmary and his condition assessed, Joonlee hurried back to Luana's bedside—she was still very vulnerable both physically and spiritually.

Joonlee knew it was time to lead Luana in prayer to receive Jeshua as her Savior and Lord—he didn't want any distractions. Even so, Tania insisted on coming with him even over his objections. It then occurred to him that Tania wanted *'to receive'* as well. Jeshua's redeeming power had been made so obvious to her that she was not leaving Joonlee's side until she got what he had.

Luana was wide awake appearing very lucid, almost cheerful. Joonlee took his chair and began telling Luana what had transpired over the last three days, beginning with his dramatic arrival. During the recounting of events, Luana went through a full range of emotions—from shame to anger to disgust and finally gratefulness—often weeping. Joonlee ended with a pause and smiled at the humbled Luana. "I'm here now. We can finally have the conversation about Jeshua that we both longed for seven years ago"

Luana was brought to tears. "Not for me… it's too late for me… I'm too dirty and spoiled for Jeshua. I'll be of no value to Him."

Joonlee began weeping as well but his tears were of joy not regret. "Luana, that's the beauty of Jeshua—He loves you just as you are. He tells us in His Word that even when we were in a horrible state of rebellion, He gave His life to save us—to rescue us from a life of death and destruction—just like He saved your village from overwhelming darkness and death."

Jeshua's Spirit was moving in the hearts of Luana and Tania; drawing them with His great love. Tania spoke first. Her eagerness could no longer be contained. "What must I do to be saved?"

Joonlee looked into Tania's yearning eyes with a sober sincerity reserved for such a holy moment. "Tania, the Bible tells us: *believe on the Lord Jesus Christ, and you will be saved... ask for forgiveness for your life of rebellion towards Him... turn from your sin*—and Romans 10:8-11 explains: *if you confess with your mouth that Jesus is Lord and believe in your heart that God raised him from the dead, you will be saved. For it is by believing in your heart that you are made right with God, and it is by confessing with your mouth that you are saved.*"

Joonlee continued, "Tania, in the Bible, when Salvation is explained, you will always find a statement something like this: *and they continued in the Word* or *they spoke the Word to them who believed.* It is important to continue in the Word, *it is the Bread of Life.*"

Tania was ready to make her confession of faith. With heartfelt brokenness and sincere statements she was ushered into Jeshua's Kingdom—translated from darkness to light. Overjoyed, Tania couldn't wait to tell her mother and friends about her glorious experience. "Joonlee, thank you so much.

May I be excused so I can tell my family about Jeshua?"

"Go Tania! Go tell everyone."

Luana was still struggling with her past but desperately wanted to believe. Joonlee sensed her remorse. "Luana, Jeshua knew you from your mother's womb—he has known everything about you from the beginning of time. That is why He died for you. If you didn't need a Savior, there would have been no need from Him to die for you. All the mistakes you've made *qualifies* you to need His mercy."

Luana stopped weeping as she came to a realization. "I think I see what you're saying. It's coming back to me. I remember my dad talking about Jeshua's mercy. I never really understood what he was telling me. Now I see Jeshua's mercy. I understand how He could still love me. I want His mercy!"

Luana's new found excitement was spilling over onto Joonlee as she began spontaneously thanking Jeshua for His Salvation and mercy. "Thank you Lord for seeing my need for a Savior and extending Your mercy to me. I take for myself Your gift of faith and receive You as my Lord and Savior. Forgive me for failing You in so many ways—please be with me and guide me every day for the rest of my life." Joonlee was overwhelmed with gratitude for Jeshua's amazing grace. Joonlee was blessed to witness Luana enter His Kingdom in such a glorious way.

Captivated with a sudden sense of urgency, Luana insisted, "I must see Wasonga as soon as possible—he must know Jeshua too."

Joonlee was agreeable. "As soon as you both are ready, I'll make it so." In all the excitement, Joonlee almost forgot about the headdress. "Luana, I must talk to you about a very important issue. Please listen carefully. I believe the darkness and dread, you have experienced personally, was brought about by your connection to Kenwoo's headdress. You may not understand this right now but you can align yourself with evil spirits by calling out to them and by making contact with them through various objects. Any object dedicated for the worship of a certain spirit or demonic entity can entrap you. I am certain you have given permission for association through Kenwoo's headdress. The spirit or demon gave you power but it was a destructive power meant to bring ruin in your life or to the lives of others."

Luana confessed, "I know exactly what you are saying and it is completely true. I can personally attest to what you say. I was innocent at first... I hate to admit it but I soon learned about the power then I knew what I was doing. After that, I couldn't quit; it was too late... I was a captive."

Pausing, Joonlee instructed Luana, "It is vitally important to renounce any connection that you once held. I recommend that you specifically ask forgiveness for your willing involvement. And lastly, you should ask for Jeshua's power to overcome any demonic spirits who may come to test your resolve. I can't tell you how important recanting is to your wellbeing. Even so, you must freely and willingly do this for yourself—I can't do it for you."

Luana, understood the gravity of what Joonlee was saying. "I will... I understand completely." The straight talk reminded Luana about the talisman. "Joonlee, you didn't mention finding the carved idol? The real power is in the Talisman."

Joonlee was a little stunned—it all made more sense. There was a sense of urgency rising in Joonlee's voice. "Where do you keep the idol?"

Feeling a little rebuked, Luana meekly replied, "The idol is tied to the sword that is in the front room—it's on display."

Joonlee was really concerned now because he knew the sword was missing. He hurried to the gathering room and approached the tapestry. Joonlee placed his hand where the sword had once hung and briefly wondered about the mysterious disappearance and its meaning. He was slowing realizing there was much more to this enigma than he first thought.

Reactively, he turned his head to look at the entry door as if being called. There was nothing there to beckon him but he turned anyway and began to walk towards the door. When he took his first step, his toe kicked the talisman, revealing its presence. Joonlee was relieved—there would not be another battle with evil today. Unceremoniously, he burned the headdress and idol.

Chapter Forty-One

The Journals

The village seemed more alive than at any time in recent memory. Last evening, several people followed Tania and Luana into a New Life with Jeshua—a glorious night of rejoicing. Now, the morning was filled with an air of expectancy among the villagers. Luana could sense the excitement and wanted to try to walk. Maybe she could make it to the infirmary to see her son, Wasonga.

The morning shift caretaker helped Luana get dressed and out into the village square. Luana quickly realized that she was too weak and unable to walk the one hundred meters to the infirmary. Instead, she sat down to breathe-in some fresh air and enjoy the sunshine.

Ironically, the sheer enjoyment of the moment

reminded her that she was gravely ill, beyond her current frailty. The ensuing poignant moments of inner reflection were not wasted on self-pity. Luana was at peace—with herself and with Jeshua—not much else mattered. She just wanted to enjoy the little time she thought she had left. She wondered about her son. He would soon become chief and would need to take a wife. Would she live long enough to witness Wasonga's coronation and his wedding ceremony?

Deep in thought, Luana had her head thrown back to take in the soothing warmth of the sun. Luana had another concern that had been weighing on her. It was Monteau's journals. Her eyes were closed to the brightness as she mused out loud in a quiet but audible tone. "Oh, the journals... what to do with Monteau's journals."

Joonlee had noticed Luana sitting in the square and decided to join her. Taking a seat next to her, Joonlee was captivated by her personal query. "What do you know about Monteau?"

Luana was not surprised by his question even though she was hoping for a heaven sent answer to her own musings. "Joonlee, we've got a lot of work to do. Help me back to the house." Joonlee was delighted to see Luana's growing energy and vitality.

Luana was out of breath by the time she was back in

bed. "Joonlee get your chair and listen very carefully—I have a very important story to tell you. You may not remember, but I briefly spoke of Monteau seven years ago, when you were very ill. Monteau was a missionary from England who had been knighted by the Queen of England. His given name was Sir John Francis Taylor. Before he came to our village, we were not always a peace loving people. Monteau spent many months talking to my grandfather and my father about Jeshua."

Years ago, when Joonlee first heard Luana mention the story of Monteau, he had been too ill to remember any details. Even so, he knew much about Monteau from the many stories kept alive by the hidden church. (Each person, who makes up the hidden church of New Guinea, could trace their spiritual roots back to Monteau.) Joonlee kept silent so he could learn all he could about Monteau's visit to New Guinea; carefully listening to every word that Luana spoke. Joonlee was very interested in the history of Monteau's connection to Luana's tribe. "You mention Monteau's journals. Why would he leave his journals?"

Luana had no answer. "No one knows but I have kept them safely stowed away. I believe they are very important and someday I hope his story will be told. Joonlee, if something happens to me can you make sure the journals are kept safe?"

Joonlee was unsettled. "Luana, I'm not sure I can make

a promise like that. I'm an outsider to your village and I'm not sure how long I will be here. The underground church is under constant threat so the journals may not be safe if I take them with me. I believe Wasonga will take good care of them—I'll talk to him about it."

Joonlee could see that Luana's concerns about the journals were not satisfied. "Luana, may I see the journals when you're feeling better?"

Luana lit up and insisted he stay and look through the journals. "I've got all day and there is nothing I would like better. In the front room, behind the tapestry is a beautiful hand carved trunk. Once you unbuckle the large leather straps, you'll see locks. The key is in the top drawer," pointing to a native handmade dresser. Luana continued, "There are twelve leather bound journals, a large Bible and a handsome wooden box containing personal letters."

Joonlee was speechless as he looked through the treasure trove of perfectly preserved antiquity. The seagoing chest was designed to protect its contents under the harshest environments so the journals were in pristine condition. In utmost reverence, he carefully perused the extraordinary documents. The journals were perfectly penned; the handwriting was flawless. Monteau, of course, wrote in formal 'King's English' so Joonlee struggled to understand what he

268

was reading. Somewhat easier to read was the exquisite carved leather bible; a typeset King James translation.

> "Luana, I've got to read these journals no matter how long it takes me.

Joonlee was beginning to grasp the historical significance of the journals as he began relating his own experiences of leading the hidden church. Joonlee's mind was racing. "Luana, I've got to read these journals no matter how long it takes me. May I use your desk in the front room to study the journals?"

Luana was delighted. "One of my greatest hopes has been that someday Monteau's journals would be made known. No one in the village can read the words… so yes, please shed some light for all to see."

Joonlee's personal priority was to find the portions written about the early families of the hidden church. Luana mentioned that Monteau's visit was fifty-five years ago so Joonlee concentrated on the journals which were written in the early eighteen-nineties. As quickly as he could, Joonlee searched for words or phrases that mentioned the Pacific islands. There it was, '*Philippines archipelago.*' Reading a little further he found the exact longitude and latitude for the volcanic island Monteau evangelized—the origin of the hidden church of New Guinea. Joonlee was fascinated with his discoveries.

Joonlee knew the Philippine islands well. His military training included memorizing all of the island chains of the entire pacific theater. With his maps (which had sunk with his patrol boat) he could have easily located the island. Joonlee's excitement was developing into an all-consuming passion.

Joonlee spent the rest of the afternoon going through the contents of Monteau's trunk. There emerged clues revealing a much larger and escalating mystery—he was being swept away with intrigue. Significant clues were leading to speculative answers. There were hints that Monteau intended to come back. There was also evidence pointing to an unexpected departure. And lastly, Monteau may have been in mortal danger when he left.

Joonlee couldn't wait to include Luana in on his findings hoping she could shed some light on his questions. He carefully repacked the trunk and placed it back behind the tapestry. When he quietly checked-in on Luana, she was sound asleep. He decided to take a break so he left through the front room. Knowing she needed her rest, he didn't want to disturb her.

The sun was in the western sky leaving the front porch shaded and serenely peaceful. The only distraction was two children playing chase in the distance—actually adding to the feel good ambiance. Slowly, Joonlee's excitement transitioned into sober contemplation. Monteau's remarkable journals were going to change his life. But how did Joonlee's destiny fit into the overall significance of Monteau's chronicles?

It suddenly occurred to him that he was indeed a part of the story being told by Monteau. With the help of Luana and Pastor Wan, Joonlee was in the unique position to seamlessly continue right where Monteau left off. Joonlee could record a detailed legacy of Monteau—bringing it forward at least half of a century. His elation was becoming borderline euphoric. He couldn't wait another minute—he would begin tonight.

Joonlee quickly returned to the trunk anxious to delve into the deepest mystery and greatest unfolding story. One of the major clues that Joonlee drew upon was an empty journal apparently intended to be used at a later date. While retrieving the blank journal, in his unbridled enthusiasm, Joonlee made enough noise to wake Luana from her nap. "Joonlee, is that you?"

Joonlee apologetically answered Luana, "I am sorry to be so noisy. I'm a little excited about what I've found. The journals have an amazing story to tell and we are all a part of it—I need your help, Luana."

Joonlee explained his ideas about what the contents of

the trunk contained. Luana had thought many times about Monteau's legacy from her perspective. However, when Joonlee showed her the journal entries that related to the escaped families of the Philippine islands, Monteau's legacy became much more incredible. Reveling in all the intricate connections, Joonlee went on to explain how God preserved him so he could in turn bring her the Salvation of Jeshua—how the story has come full circle.

"Luana, you must hear this... think back to when you saved my life seven years ago. At that time you explained how there was a remnant of God's goodness residing in you that prompted you to save my life. Because of Monteau, your tribe was blessed with goodness and mercy. You chose to extend that mercy to me when I was dying. Now, seven years later God divinely sent me to show you the same mercy and grace in your darkest hour." Luana was weeping tears of gratitude as she realized the truth Joonlee was sharing—she was in awe of God's faithfulness.

Eager to get started on the journal, Joonlee continued, "Luana, do I have your permission to use the blank journal to continue recording Monteau's legacy?" Still overwhelmed with emotions, Luana nodded 'yes' and then pointed to her small writing table in the corner of the room. Clearing her throat, she spoke softly, "There are quills and ink in the drawer of my desk... may I make a suggestion?"

Joonlee had not considered how he was going to write without pen and ink. "Of course, I want all of your ideas and comments. This writing must be a collaboration. What is your suggestion?"

Luana continued in a soft and humbled voice. "I have some stationary. Possibly you could write your drafts and make corrections on the stationary and then carefully transcribe the finished work into the journal." Joonlee was embarrassed at his impetuous plans to start writing.

Sitting next to Luana's bed, Joonlee bowed his head and spoke in a surprisingly sad tone considering the jubilance of the last hour. "Before we go any further, I must tell you about something else I found in the trunk. You may not understand until you hear everything I have to say." Luana nodded as he continued, "Monteau had started to translate the New Testament in a separate journal that was hidden in the false bottom of the trunk. There were many notes pertaining to his progress. One of his last notations indicated that he was being forced to leave under duress. Also, I found many hidden items that were personal as well as sentimental. Even though there are indications that his original plan was to return, something caused him to believe he was not going to survive. His journals stop abruptly as well."

Luana's eyes widened as she remembered an event when she was about eight years old. "I may have an answer for you. I remember a group of German soldiers coming to our village on several occasions during that time. I believe Monteau was here during one of those German inspections. I don't recall any trouble but I was too young to understand."

Joonlee was saddened further when he realized that Monteau may have paid with his life and couldn't return. "Luana, I would like to finish Monteau's work here in your village even if takes me the rest of my life. I've been thinking… if I can send Manuel or Hino back to Pastor Wan for his recounting of the hidden church, I could stay here and finish what Monteau started. I believe your village is important for reaching the valley region with the Good News of Jeshua."

Luana was delighted to be included in such a noble effort. "If there is anything you need please let me know and you will have it."

Joonlee nodded in appreciation and then made a gracious offer as he left the room. "Maybe tomorrow we can get you over to see Wasonga."

Luana smiled "I would like that."

Chapter Forty-Two

Manuel's Home Going Celebration

Joonlee was ready to start his writing endeavor but he first needed to prepare Hino or Manuel for the trip back to the sanctuary village. Then, when the chosen runner returned with Pastor Wan's account of the hidden church, Joonlee could combine their efforts and record them in the journal. Once he finished the journal entries, he could then start the long process of translating the New Testament into the native language of the valley.

Before tracking down Hino to discuss his new assignment, Joonlee wanted to check on Wasonga to see if he was any better. Providentially, Hino had volunteered to take the evening vigil and was glad to have Joonlee stop by. "Joonlee, I'm glad you're here. Wasonga has been saying some things as he comes and goes from his sleep. He mentioned Manuel several times—it doesn't sound good for Manuel."

Up until now Joonlee had not been overly concerned about Manuel. He was a very capable backwoodsman. Upon hearing Hino's remarks, Joonlee became anxious and tried to arouse Wasonga. Wasonga woke up and became somewhat alert from his sleep. "Wasonga, tell me what you know about Manuel."

With a pained and partially coherent response,

Wasonga moaned, "He's dead… I killed him."

Joonlee was provoked. "Where is he? What have you done with him?"

"He fell off the ledge… to save me… but it was my fault."

Joonlee was now conflicted but managed to calm down a little with the better explanation. "What ledge, Wasonga, where is he?" Wasonga couldn't answer; falling back into unconsciousness.

Joonlee was now convinced that Manuel was in trouble and a search effort was needed. Turning, he spoke to Hino, "I want you to organize a search party tonight—get ropes, a stretcher and anything else you think we may need. We know Wasonga came from the direction of the highland trail but I want to sweep the town and surrounding area first before we start up the highland trail. Let everyone know that we'll start searching early enough to be at the trailhead by 9:00 a.m. Go and make preparations for tomorrow—I'll stay here with Wasonga."

Unknown to Joonlee there was another search underway. Cabot was one of the villagers who had described Wasonga as being 'pushed along' toward the highland trail. He was also the informant who setup Manuel. By shamefully taking money from the bounty hunters, Cabot contributed to

Manuel's death. He would be considered a murderer in any culture. As bad as that was, it was only the small picture. Cabot set in motion a chain of events yet to unfold.

Cabot lived on the extreme western edge of the village, just ten meters off the village road. On the fateful morning of extreme darkness, Cabot noticed Wasonga as he walked by headed toward the village. An hour later he saw Wasonga return with the Samurai sword strapped to his side. In an odd sort of manner, Wasonga was seemingly being ushered along until he lost his footing and stumbled; falling headlong onto the roadway. After several minutes, as Cabot watched on, Wasonga recovered enough to make his way up the highland trail. But the curious spectacle was not done. The next morning Cabot looked on as Hino rescued the despondent Wasonga. As Cabot watched the unfolding drama, he noticed Wasonga did not have the celebrated village sword with him.

Cabot was a genuine scoundrel prone to greed and covetousness. He had kindled an unrighteous yearning for the sword which drove him to go after it. Aware of the pending search for Manuel, Cabot got up before dawn (the morning of the search for Manuel) and went up the trail to find the sword—he wanted it for himself. The unintended consequences of Cabot's betrayal were set to increase multifold. The multiple killings that took place as a result of his moral duplicity would have a deadly ripple effect.

By seven a.m. Cabot had reached the highland camp where the bloodbath had taken place. He had no idea what he was looking for other than the shiny sword. That's when he came across the place where Manuel had been murdered. There was dried blood all over the ground and the sword lay right where Wasonga

> *Standing in a killing field, Cabot was gripped with fear.*

had left it—only partially visible under a blood drenched bush.

Standing in a killing field, Cabot was gripped with fear. He grabbed the sword and started running down the path toward the valley. The sword was not sheathed. Despite falling several times he managed to get up and continue at a frantic pace. His moment came when he caught his toe on a root and went flying headlong… landing on the sword's edge. He was filleted—rendered helpless he bled to death. Even his death would not avert the future events he unwittingly set in motion.

Leading the search party, Joonlee was not looking uphill so he did not see Cabot until he almost stepped on him. Joonlee recoiled in horror at the bloody site. Instinctively, he waved off the search party by signaling a retreat. Not knowing what threat he was up against, Joonlee quickly stepped off the path to survey the situation. After studying the scene for a few minutes, he realized that Cabot must have been dead for at least an hour.

As the minutes passed it was becoming apparent that any danger had past. He signaled the others to stay back while he attended to Cabot. Joonlee carefully turned Cabot over to reveal the Samurai sword's edge still embedded in his chest bone. It now seemed obvious what had happened but why was he running and who was he running from? Not sure what lay ahead, Joonlee decided to take Cabot's body to the village and return with the rifles.

Joonlee thought he was finished with this kind of warfare. He decided not to issue rifles to anyone since he wasn't sure who could actually fire a rifle. There was more danger of someone getting shot by a novice so he just took one rifle for himself. He could not find anyone who could wield a sword so it was left behind as well.

Before returning to the highland trail, Joonlee queried the men about the location of a ledge as described by Wasonga. The men all agreed that there was only one place along the trail that could be described as having a ledge. There was a bluff near a camp where two highland paths cross.

In all, fifteen men made their way up the often steep and serpentine highland trail for a second attempt to find Manuel. Joonlee led the search party wielding the carbine in correct military fashion. Complete silence was ordered with a promise of stiff punishment for any infraction. Joonlee paused often to survey the troops as well as watch and listen for any clues of danger. After two long hours of uphill marching, the unit approached the crossroads basecamp where Manuel had lunged over the cliff entangled with his killer. Upon reaching the blood soaked bluff, it was apparent that Manuel would not be found alive.

Hoping to retrieve Manuel's body, Joonlee sent five men around to a more climbable location to descend the bluff. As is often the case, after several days in the untamed wilderness, there would not be much left to bring home. Nonetheless, an order was given to gather Manuel's remains and rejoin the group at a location further down the trail. Joonlee was not aware that there were five other bodies strewn along the highland trail. That fortunate lack of knowledge (about the other bodies) helped make the somber return trip as uneventful as it should have been.

No one knew the already notorious Cabot had deceived Manuel for a few coins. If the truth were known, his memorial would surely have been vastly different. Manuel was honored by everyone with heartfelt gratitude as a hero in every aspect. Cabot only received mention because he lay next to a model of human dignity.

Joonlee delivered an eloquent eulogy based on his lengthy friendship but more importantly Manuel's devotion to his Lord Jeshua. "Manuel is at home with Jeshua. What an exciting privilege to walk into the presence of Jeshua after this tour here on earth." Joonlee took the opportunity to extend an invitation for others to receive Jeshua as Lord and Savior. Several of the villagers responded because of the signs and wonders they had witnessed over the last week.

Maybe Joonlee should have taken the remainder of the day to reflect on the memorials, but he couldn't. Hino had to be briefed on his new assignment to reach Pastor Wan's highland village. Joonlee wrote a lengthy letter explaining many of the recent developments in the valley. He, of course, shared the good news about Luana as well as the remarkable discovery of Monteau's journals. His most earnest request was reserved for last—Pastor Wan's recounting of the establishment of the hidden church of New Guinea.

Chapter Forty-Three

The Final Showdown

If there was such a thing as a staunch supporter for the maniacal Moloch, even the most ardent admirer would not believe he could still be alive. He had cheated death so many times the odds would have to be stacked against him. Yet the one-armed Moloch lived a shamelessly opulent lifestyle leading a coalition of provinces, townships and trade groups. His firm grip on the regional commerce as well as governmental interactions gave him dictatorial control over the entire northern region of New Guinea especially the coastal hamlets and villages along the north shores.

Moloch had no direct connection to the five dead bounty hunters. However, he was always interested in the entrapment and capture of members of the hidden church.

Moloch had become the ultimate nemesis of everything good or righteous.

It would be several weeks before word finally reached Moloch regarding a body that was cut-in-two on one of the highland trails. Much of the outback areas were lawless so finding bodies in the wild was nothing new. Consequently, Moloch didn't show any interest. Then, about a week later, a startling thought came to him while he was having afternoon tea on his palatial mountaintop veranda. As he was taking in the magnificent panoramic view of the river delta, his eyes widened. He began choking on his tea and sputtering at mid gulp. Waving his sole remaining arm, unable to speak while choking, he coughed out an order to his valet, "Assemble my security team! Now!"

The five men quickly came running from all directions from within the huge mansion. Hastily coming to attention, the men were not sure what to expect. By now Moloch had cleared his throat but still had trouble speaking. "On what highland trail was the dead body found?"

Not sure which incident he was referring too, the wilderness captain cautiously responded, "Sir, I would be the one to know that answer—when was this body discovered?"

Moloch had a very short temper but realized his men were eager to help so he controlled himself as best he could. "I received a report a couple of weeks ago about a body that was cut-in-half on a highland trail. Where is that trail?"

The captain answered quickly. "That trail rises from the western end of the valley floor about twenty-five kilometers upriver from the delta. There has been little activity in that area for years. It's probably nothing sir."

Moloch was furious for the apparent insubordination. He began screaming right into the ear of the wilderness captain as he stood at full attention. "You let me decided if there is a problem. Don't you ever give me advice again... DO YOU UNDERSTAND!?" Fearing for his life, the captain acknowledged in the affirmative.

Moloch's mind was racing—who had the sword? It must have been found by someone in the valley. Speaking to his men, he attempted to explain his mystery and intrigue. "There is only one way a body could have been cut-in-two on this island—by a large Samurai sword—the same sword that took my arm... and I want that sword brought to me. Go back to the area and take enough men to search the entire region if needed. Find that sword and bring me the fool who used it. I want to know what's going on in the valley. Have your plans, provisions and men ready to go by midweek." After a brief pause the quick thinking Moloch came up with a brilliant idea. "Clear my schedule for Thursday. I'm going too."

Moloch's inspired plan was steeped in vengeance. He calculated how he could, once-and-for-all end his loathing for the valley village he had come to hate. Moloch had tried numerous times to bring the noble tribe under his control. Not only had he failed to subdue the village but his efforts cost him dearly on every attempt. Now was his chance to do away with his nemesis, Chieftess Luana. Moloch decided that he would go directly to her.

Moloch had been waiting months for delivery of his new nineteen-fifty-two Chevrolet pickup truck. It arrived the day before all the way from the United States. Moloch was already established as a man of means but now he owned a rarity for this part of the world. He would drive right into Luana's village square as if he owned the place. Along with his uniformed and heavily armed men, the intimidation alone should make her cower. He intended to produce enough chaos to allow his armed troops to eliminate her as well as her highest ranking leaders.

Moloch's day finally came. At seven a.m. the ten armed guardsmen piled-in his new truck with their lieutenant riding upfront with Moloch. In an unexpected scene, not meant for comic relief, the shiny new truck was squatting to the ground under a load it was never built to carry. To further the hilarity, Moloch ignored his obvious miscalculation, determined to carry out his brilliant plan.

The only wheeled access to Luana's valley village was a dirt road that followed the river inland from the delta. Under ideal conditions, the trip from Moloch's headquarters would have taken four hours or more. As the noon hour came and went, the one truck cavalcade was still bouncing along the river road with an hour to go. The guardsmen were being tossed in all directions even having to stop twice to retrieve a soldier who was thrown out.

Moloch did not know that Luana was fully aware of his pending arrival. Hino had successfully made the trek up to the hidden village only to be immediately sent back with the details of a looming confrontation. In a strategic move, Luana decided to thwart Moloch's intentions by planning Wasonga's coronation and wedding ceremonies to coincide with his arrival. Timing would be difficult so the height of pageantry would be reenacted if necessary.

The twin ceremonies would disguise a military defense. Everyone would be wearing ceremonial attire designed to create a joyful time of celebration. From this staged setting, Luana planned to use the same winning tactic from seven years earlier. There would be an overwhelming response to any show of intent—no prisoners and no mercy. Luana would not provoke Moloch. In fact, she wanted to give him every opportunity to back down and leave.

Fortunately, Wasonga's actual ceremonies were completed long before the wispy plume of dust was seen coming up the river road. Just as rehearsed, everyone took their places to reenact the ceremonies. Gaiety and celebration was in the air with laughter and frivolity on open display. The village square was occupied with groups of lavishly dressed people meandering around. Moloch's plan to take center stage was foiled. He couldn't make the ruckus he wanted. By Luana's orders, no one would pay him any attention—he was to be ignored.

Act One ended by a signal from Luana and *Act Two* began as planned. The gaiety and ceremony continued in full effect. The 'actors' were now instructed to casually reposition themselves taking their defensive and offensive positions. The casual observer would not have realized the change. The roaming groups of well-wishers concealed a deadly response ready at the slightest offensive gesture.

Hoping to salvage some of his original plan for intimidation, Moloch lined up his men directly in front of the public meeting room in a regal display of his power and authority. Luana walked by Moloch's assemblage and all but ignored him as she entered the public chambers. She wanted this confrontation on her terms and her official chamber was her turf. Once inside, she instructed her assistant to invite Moloch in for his meeting.

Luana queried the dust covered Moloch as she took a seat behind her desk "Are you here to see me?—have a seat." Moloch was so disenfranchised from his rhetoric that he actually removed his hat in a respectful gesture. Fatefully, this was the same room, the same desk and Moloch was sitting in the same chair that he occupied seven years earlier. The scene was an eerie rematch of his attempt to outwit Luana under similar circumstances.

In a brief moment of contemplation, Moloch looked up to see the Samurai sword hanging on the elegant tapestry. At first, his eyes brightened to see the prize he'd come for. Then he realized the sword and scabbard were mounted in such a way as to form a cross—the symbol of the underground church.

Moloch's indignation was palpable. Gritting his teeth he announced, "I'm here to retrieve my sword and the idiot who used it to kill one of my men. He'll stand trial for murder."

Very calmly, Luana replied as if Moloch was interested in a history lesson, "That sword is very important to every person in this village. It is part of our history—I'm sorry but I can't give it to you."

Moloch began to squint his eyes and furl his brow as he slowly stood up. "I didn't ask you to give me the sword. I said I was here to take it. You don't have any choice in the matter." As he spoke those last words, he pulled back his jacket to reveal his revolver.

Luana rose from behind her desk and lifted the sword from its mounting, leaving the scabbard hanging in its vertical position. She slowly and carefully walked around her desk to stand directly in front of the unflinching Moloch. "That's more like it. Now do what you have to do to get that coward in here so I can be on my way."

> *"You wouldn't shoot me would you?—I saved your life… remember?"*

Luana feigned a defeated look as she stared directly into Moloch's eyes. "You wouldn't shoot me would you?—I saved your life… remember?"

Moloch's steely countenance softened slightly for a moment. His resolve quickly returned with a gruesome confession. "I came here to kill you and as many others as I can. But now I'll let you live… to see them slaughtered."

A tear tickled down Luana's cheek as she lifted the sword to hand to Moloch. At the last instant she ran the sword through his middle with enough force to knock him down.

When he fell backwards, the sword stuck in the wood floor causing Moloch to ride the blade back out. With his last gasp he managed to free his revolver and fire off two shots, one of which struck Luana in the heart—killing her instantly.

Outside, the shots set off pandemonium. The soldiers were still standing at attention with their rifles shouldered. Just as happened seven years earlier, their first offensive action unleashed an overwhelming storm of fury upon them—the unaware soldiers were dead while standing.

Joonlee had been standing out of sight behind Luana just in case things went terribly wrong. *He was prepared for what happened—it was no surprise.* Joonlee was the only other person who knew of her terminal illness. Both knew that no matter the outcome, what happened today would be Luana's final act as chieftess. Only hours before her death, she told Joonlee of her secret plan to deal with Moloch in this final showdown. She convinced Joonlee that she was the only one who could persuade Moloch to do anything. Unfortunately, Joonlee couldn't be directly involved because of the fact that Joonlee was dead to Moloch precluding a controlled outcome. Luana had purposely lured Moloch into a position where she could either dissuade him from his plans of destruction or prevent him from carrying them out. She knew very well it might cost everything to save her people—she was prepared.

Chapter Forty-Four

Wasonga's Reign

Tania was good for Wasonga. As his new wife, she brought stability to his shattered life—stability that he would need to be a good chief and finally come out of his depression. With all threats to the village greatly diminished, Wasonga had few worries. He only needed to build on the accomplishments of his parent's former reign by fully restoring the noble reputation that was almost lost. Unfortunately, Wasonga possessed a character flaw of unknown origin. He could not and would not heed the call of Jeshua who was beckoning him.

Joonlee remained in the village, as planned, to finish his work of compiling his journal. Once the final drafts were completed Joonlee began to slowly and very carefully copy the results into the empty journal left by Monteau. Transcribing the finished work took an entire month to accomplish—trying to be as careful as Monteau. With the journal complete and carefully stowed away with Monteau's original twelve, Joonlee would be ready to begin the most important assignment of his life—translating the New Testament.

Fortunately, Monteau's unfinished translation work was begun in a Portuguese derivative common among the island dialects. Monteau's partially completed work revealed that he was not only a brilliant scholar but fluent in the Portuguese language. Joonlee was neither so his work was going to be slow and arduous. However, in a rather miraculous fashion, help was provided. Over the next few months two individuals came to the village. Both were literate and knowledgeable enough in the Portuguese language to speed Joonlee's work considerably.

Tania's pregnancy was celebrated by all—a high point in Wasonga's early reign. Fertility is a sign that affirms the anointing of leadership in many cultures—an heir would be born. Even so, tragedy would accompany the birth of Jarten. Tania struggled heroically to live and be the mother that her son would need. But after only a week with her newborn son, she lost her fight. The complications of giving birth took its toll and overwhelmed the young mother's body.

Tania's untimely death sent Wasonga back over the edge. He was driven headlong into despair and depression. Convinced that Jeshua was punishing him, he clenched his fist toward heaven and cursed God. Every person that had ever gotten close enough to love Wasonga, despite his diminished character, had been ruthlessly ripped from him—his dad, Manuel, his mother, and now Tania.

With vindictive anger, Wasonga struck out at the closest representation of Jeshua—he banished Joonlee from the village. Fortunately, there was a unanimous and collective outcry among the villagers pleading mercy for Joonlee. It was well understood that Joonlee was the only remaining influence left to bring stability to the insecure and wavering Wasonga. Wasonga relented but isolated Joonlee from his rule; no longer seeking his counsel. He was given Cabot's old hut on the western edge of the village allowing him to continue his work.

It took three long years of study and uninterrupted work for Joonlee to finish his translation. His imposed isolation from the village turned out to be a divine intervention. The inherent distractions of village life were removed helping Joonlee in speed and accuracy. In addition, the separation also allowed Wasonga to rise a few levels as chief because he was forced to mature without a ready hand to hold. Time and Wasonga's maturing process also brought with it a mood of reconciliation toward the blameless Joonlee.

Word of Joonlee's achievement spread among the villagers and quickly reached Wasonga. Seeing an opportunity to right a wrong, the remorseful Wasonga decided to make plans for a celebration dinner to honor Joonlee and his completed work.

Joonlee had sacrificed much in the effort to finish the translation. He had not taken care of himself so his health had deteriorated considerably. Joonlee had aged fifteen years by anyone's estimation. The multiple bodily injuries of his past were complicating his health further diminishing his physical stature and appearance. A much younger Wasonga was shocked at the site of Joonlee. Wasonga's punishment had cruelly taken its toll on the man who should have held his highest honor and respect. Wasonga was sickened and broken hearted for what he had done to Joonlee.

Seated around an elegantly prepared table, originally conceived to bring resolution and new beginnings, Wasonga pleaded for Joonlee's forgiveness. "Joonlee, I beg you to forgive me for what I have done to you... please allow me to make it up to you in some way."

Joonlee had already seen God's clear and steady hand using the unfortunate events of the past for the ultimate good. "All is well my friend. God knew what He was doing even when you didn't." Wasonga was completely mystified by the Joonlee's amiable response. Joonlee continued, "I do have two requests I think you'll find agreeable."

Out of an ever-deepening respect, Joonlee had Wasonga's complete if not raptured attention. "Anything you ask will be done... I vow to do it."

Joonlee continued, "I made a promise to your mother the day she died. I assured her that I would keep Monteau's journals safe as long as I lived. I considered this to be her dying wish. I also promised her that I would discuss with you her desire to preserve the journals. And secondly, I need your help in publishing the New Testament that I have translated. I want every villager in the valley to have God's Word—*Wasonga, I want you to have a copy."*

Wasonga was true to his word and diligently honored Joonlee's requests. As a display of his greatest honor and respect, Wasonga built the ailing Joonlee a beautiful home complete with every comfort. He also assigned caretakers to help Joonlee in any capacity. Joonlee lived another three and one half years.

This completes the *'Interlude of Darkness'*—the story of the origins of the persecuted church of New Guinea.

Chapter Forty-Five

Monteau's Legacy

Sir John Francis Taylor

We now return to the story where Paiyan, Frank and Grace are kidnapped and taken to Chief Wasonga's (the young Wasonga grown old) village as it had emerged thirty-five years later. We return to the main story just after Frank's tragic death.

—*35 YEARS LATER*—

Circa 1987

Reprise: Ten of the Chief Wasonga's men ruthlessly tackled Jarten and in the process broke his neck accidently killing him. The tumultuous chaos that had erupted all around Chief Wasonga would not deter his attention from the travesty that lay before him. A hero of the faith that he had grown to love, now lay buried in a twisted heap of carnage. As soon as the unharmed chief was helped to his feet, he immediately fell forward to his knees weeping. The once hardened chief had never shed a tear in his adult life—God had been working on his heart.

Konii was across the village in a work detail tending to the large multi-acre garden he had initiated for the chief. Konii came running when he heard the screams and then saw the commotion. Not knowing what had transpired, Konii's first thought was that the chief had become ill. Grabbing the kneeling chief in a concerned embrace, Konii insisted, "Chief, I'll go for help!"

Shaking his head, the heartbroken chief whispered to Konii, "No, don't leave me." Harkening back to his many losses of loved ones, Wasonga couldn't bear to think of losing Konii who had become like a son. "Send someone else but you must stay here with me."

Konii had in many respects become second-in-charge often carrying out direct orders that affected the whole village. He was comfortable with directives given to him by Wasonga. Konii had long ago seen his 'internment' as his calling or mission. *What was meant for harm was being used to bring about a victory for Jeshua's kingdom and eternal plan.*

Konii responded with a rapid fire list of orders. First, Paiyan, Grace as well as Frank's body were quickly taken to the infirmary. Konii then sent a pair of elders, using the truck, to the port city of Lae; the closest city with ambulance service. Lae was situated at the river delta so the trip would take about two hours along the rough river road. Lae had a small airport so once the ambulance was dispatched to the village, the elders were told to arrange for air flight to Port Moresby.

Unfortunately, the ambulance was not allowed to leave

Lae until the following morning. There were too many risks associated with a trip into the interior so late in the day. The next day the medics arrived at ten-fifteen a.m. and immediately began treating Paiyan and Grace.

Grace's bruises were determined to be deep with a potential for internal injuries. She had also endured a tremendous emotional shock. Paiyan's wounds and bruises were not as life threatening so he (awkwardly) felt an urgent need to stay behind. It would be impossible to follow his urging with Grace so badly injured and with Frank's body needing to be taken to the hospital morgue. Everyone was deeply heartbroken over Frank's premature death with Paiyan and Grace struggling through a deep sense of grief.

With Wasonga's emotional strain eased, Konii suggested that he accompany Grace and Paiyan along with Frank's body to Port Moresby. He would stay with Grace at the hospital making the necessary steps to locate her dad.

Konii was discussing the last minute details with Chief Wasonga, at Paiyan's bedside, when Grace began waking up from a deep sleep. Still slightly groggy, she listened for several minutes, to the ongoing conversation, that often included her name. "Hey guys, listen up."

The men turned to find the black and blue Grace sporting a slim smile through puffy lips. "Grace, you look…"

Grace interrupted Paiyan midsentence. "Frank told me on several occasions that if anything happened while he was here, he wanted to be buried in New Guinea. It had something to do with an epitaph he read while visiting his wife's gravesite. Don't take him away from here."

Paiyan wasn't convinced, "I don't think Frank's parents would appreciate a decision like that without their O.K."

Grace quickly replied, "He told them the same thing—I was there when he made the phone call." After a very long pause to hold back a flood of tears, Grace continued, "I'm not sure what day it is, *but I am sure* that dad is still in Port Moresby. I'm also quite sure he's looking for us and has alerted the authorities."

Paiyan thought that the emotionally spent Grace was finished so in a parental tone he suggested she get some rest. Grace protested, "Paiyan, I'm not through, just give me a minute. From what I've heard, you guys need all the help you can get. Paiyan you are not staying here. (Grace had heard him verbally struggling over his strong urge to stay). You're coming back to the States to get checked out."

> *"If I ran back to the States every time something like this happened, I would be on an airplane half the time."*

Grace's last statement was made as a loving gesture of deep concern but Paiyan couldn't help but smile. In a jovial tone meant to turn the mood of the conversation Paiyan replied, "If I ran back to the States every time something like this happened, I would be on an airplane half the time." In a more serious tone, Paiyan continued, "Grace, I don't think all of this has come about by accident. I have a feeling in my spirit there is a reason for us being here. I want to find out what is."

Chief Wasonga couldn't hold back. He had been waiting for the right moment. "Paiyan, *you are here* for a purpose. I want to show you what it is." Wasonga turned to Konii and whispered, "Go and get Volume One of the journals and Monteau's carved leather Bible."

While Konii was away getting the journal and Bible, Wasonga began telling Paiyan how Konii had taught him daily about Jeshua. He went on to explain the remarkable narratives centered on Paiyan. Konii's retelling of the stories had deepened Wasonga's respect for the man he had never met before today. Tearfully, he went on to describe the day Konii prayed with him to receive New Life with Jeshua—a fulfillment of his mother's plea made forty-four years earlier.

He could no longer hold his back the incredible story of Monteau's journals. In childlike excitement he told Paiyan how Konii had discovered, by reading Monteau's journals, that he was Konii's great uncle. Paiyan was brought to tears. His passion, to find lost friends or family, had finally been fulfilled. But to learn of the existence his dad's journals was too much to ask.

When Konii returned with the journal and Monteau's Bible it was a holy and sacred moment. Chief Wasonga tearfully spoke, "Paiyan, it is my honor to present you with your father's Bible and this first journal that records the beginnings of your families' godly heritage. Because of your father, every person standing here has a New Life in Jeshua."

Grace and Paiyan both realized that their destinies were intertwined with the divine preservation of the journals—the story of their joint heritage. What Paiyan had hoped for, in the telling of his story was expanded beyond his wildest dreams. Not only had he found a long lost nephew, he had found an astonishing and cherished link to his dad—Monteau's journals.

The '*His Story*' Chronicles will continue with

Volume Two '*The Tent Maker*'

*~ **His Story** ~*
As told by Grace Chloe Wheaton

Volume Two

'The Tent Maker'

'His Story' as told by *Grace Chloe Wheaton*

English Countryside

1865

Chapter One

The Fox and the Hound

"Great jump John," yelled Bradley as the two riders galloped past a too narrow stone gate. John was forced to jump the low stone wall as Bradley stole the center. John's demanding jump providentially placed him in a better position for a sharp turn demanded by the howling hounds—giving John the advantage.

Bradley heeled his steed lying low in the saddle trying to take John before their path turned toward the wood. Best friends and chief conspirators for fun and frivolity gave way to a more serious competition. The challenge at hand was mystically shifted to the defeat of a cohort's ego. Putting down the fox would have to wait.

Reaching the wood in a fiercely fought tie, the boughs were tearing at the reckless pair. Something would have to give or be thrown to the ground—giving the fox a momentary but unsure win. Bradley was taking the worst of the beatings but it was John who took flight. Flipping backwards, landing on his hands and knees, John collapsed to a chest pounding flop. Witnessing the spine-chilling episode, Bradley ruthlessly pulled back on his reigns risking injury to his horse. Revolting, the horse stood on its hind legs trying to meet Bradley's unexpected and callous command.

Still lying face down, John was trying to recover from his blinding retracement. Needing to catch his breath, the prone John struggled to push himself over onto his back to ease his labored breathing.

An accomplished rider, Bradley dismounted his saddle and rode-the-stirrup the last ten meters launching him at full stride toward his fallen friend. Bradley was surveying the damage as his best friend lay motionless with his eyes closed.

It was only the slightest of few moments before John smiled up at Bradley "I kept my face up old chap… see… not a scratch"—sportingly pointing to his prized possession. "You know the ladies wouldn't appreciate me mess'n up this handsome mug." Ignoring Bradley's offer to lend a hand, John jumped to his feet as further proof of his proud vanity.

Bradley, who was used to John's antics, wondered if the acrobatic dismount had been staged for comedic effect. Not yet certain, Bradley quipped his angst, "You could have been killed you bloody fool."

The ever jovial John was feeling pleased with his apparent recovery from inept horsemanship when he suddenly passed out. Bradley was completely caught off guard as he made a drastic attempt to catch his falling friend. John fell unhindered into a crumpled heap as Bradley's grab missed him completely. John's relapse jolted Bradley back to his former dread; ceding to momentary helplessness. This time John's often mused vanity would give way to sizable gashes on his chin and forehead.

> *This time John's often mused vanity would give way to sizable gashes on his chin and forehead.*

If John was flawlessly good looking then Bradley was ruggedly handsome—six-foot-tall, red wavy hair and a ruddy freckled complexion that sported a bold protruding chin line. These overgrown pampered boys, turned men, had rarely faced a trying moment. Nanny's, housekeepers, cooks and maids provided a shield of protection—spared the nasty necessity of having to grow up and face the more harsh realities of life.

Inherited privilege allowed them to act on any whim to embrace the pleasure of the moment—considered an entitlement for their ilk. The need to act decisively was something of a stretch for either of these coddled aristocrats in the offing.

The hounds could once again be heard. The ruckus was coming toward the stranded and injured duo. One thing Bradley did know was that he shouldn't move John from where he lay. Forced to take action, Bradley began to follow some heaven sent inclinations meant to guide him in easing John's silent suffering. With the ever approaching squawking dogs, Bradley quickly tied-up the horses and then removed his coat. He folded the red obligatory garment and placed it under John's head and then bolted toward the sound of advancing hoofs.

It is often a rider is involuntarily dismounted in the chase so Bradley's flailing arms would be routinely ignored. After all it was a competition and the unfortunate fate of a contender shouldn't betray the genuine needs of a worthy challenger. It must have been Bradley's screams of desperation that halted the lone wary rider who was straggling behind in the pursuit. Subconsciously, the 'Good Samaritan' (Peter Mann) had already contemplated giving up the hunt so Bradley's cries for help offered a chance to redeem himself. So as not to reveal his lost cause, Peter blasted, "What's your problem man?! Can't you see I'm in the hunt?"

Bradley was breathless and speechless as he grabbed Peter's bootstraps of the still mounted rescuer. Bradley was intent on retaining him until he could speak. Still gasping for air Bradley pleaded, "John Taylor is down… he needs help. Ride to the paddock and secure the surrey. Quick! Bring it man!" Before releasing Peter, Bradley pointed to a grove of trees where the horses could still be seen tied to the low hanging branches. "He's there... bring the carriage there... hurry... God's speed!"

—*To Be Continued*—

*~ **His Story** ~*
As told by *Grace Chloe Wheaton*

Taylor - Wheaton Heritage
1923 - 1965

Continued from front inside cover

1924	Chloe Wheaton born – Papa Wheaton's second born - daughter
1927	Charles Lindbergh flies "Spirit of St. Louis" – John Jr. decides he will be a pilot and fly aero planes.
1928	
1929	John Francis Wheaton dies – (John Jr.'s grandpa)
1932	The great harvest miracle brings renewal in Clearwater springs. Chloe goes to circus.
1933	The miracle at Christmas – The Angel and Anna Chloe dies from diphtheria
1940	John Wheaton Jr. marries Elizabeth
1941	John Wheaton Jr. enlist in air force, Elizabeth stays stateside in San Diego
1942	Papa Wheaton dies
1945	Paiyan's family escapes big island - 3 weeks later arrive at new home on deserted & uncharted island
1946	John Wheaton Jr. re-enlist becomes career pilot. Accidental tractor drop over pacific.
1947	John Wheaton Jr. decommissioned – wife leaves
1948	John Wheaton Jr. reassigned to Europe. Becomes interested in and uncovers his lineage
1950	John Jr.'s wife, Elizabeth, repents and becomes radically saved but does not seek out her husband.
1951	Elizabeth moves to Seattle from San Diego
1956	John Jr. contacted by Joey about uncharted island with cornfields. Request temporary reassignment to check out island.
1957	Discovers Paiyan to be great uncle.
1961	Resigns from military to become full time missionary to the islands near Paiyan's island
1962	John Jr. visits church in Seattle Washington to raise funds for missionary work. Meets Elizabeth and renews vows – She joins John on mission field.
1963	Grace Chloe Wheaton born
1965	Francis 'Paul' Wheaton born.

↓

1987	Grace & Paiyan discover Sir John's journals and begin writing the chronicles of *'His Story'*